LOVING MEG

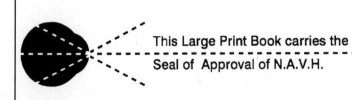

This Large Print Book carries the
Seal of Approval of N.A.V.H.

LOVING MEG

SKYE TAYLOR

THORNDIKE PRESS
A part of Gale, Cengage Learning

GALE
CENGAGE Learning·

Farmington Hills, Mich • San Francisco • New York • Waterville, Maine
Meriden, Conn • Mason, Ohio • Chicago

GALE
CENGAGE Learning

LIBRARY OF CONGRESS CATALOGING-IN-PUBLICATION DATA

Taylor, Skye.
    Loving Meg / by Skye Taylor.
      pages cm. — (The Camerons of Tide's Way ; book 2) —(Thorndike press large print clean reads)
    ISBN 978-1-4104-7805-4 (hardcover) — ISBN 1-4104-7805-X (hardcover)
    1. Women soldiers—Fiction. 2. Married people—Fiction. 3. Families of military personnel—Fiction. 4. Large type books. I. Title.
PS3620.A974L68 2015
813'.6—dc23   2014049814

Published in 2015 by arrangement with BelleBooks, Inc.

Printed in Mexico
1 2 3 4 5 6 7 19 18 17 16 15

This story is dedicated to all the warriors who believe in the American ideal and put their lives on the line to protect it. But especially to those who come home broken in body and spirit, and to the K-9s who help them come all the way home.

God bless the K-9s for Warriors program and other programs like them who are doing such a wonderful job of training these dogs, rescuing both dogs and soldiers.

TO MY READERS

Dogs have a long military history, beginning in ancient times. They have served as messengers, scouts, mascots, sentries, and trackers. In today's military, they often wear tactical vests, cameras, and microphones to send information back to the troops who follow them. They are trained to sniff out bombs and have saved countless soldiers' lives in the war against terrorism.

We are only just beginning to realize the enormous potential of dogs for saving the lives of soldiers *after* they return from war zones. Warriors with PTSD struggle to leave their war behind and find their way back to civilian life. They come home suffering both physical and psychological wounds, still reacting as they did in combat: hyper-vigilant and trusting no one, not even their family and friends. The VA's answer to date has been to prescribe expensive, highly addictive medications, and as the statistics show they do not work. Their pain and anguish far too often ends in suicide, devastating families, friends, and former comrades.

K-9s for Warriors, Located in Ponte Vedra, Florida, is just one of many organizations that have sprung up across the country for the express purpose of training dogs to work with returned soldiers, especially those suffering from PTSD. They obtain most of their dogs from rescue shelters, and their mission statement says, "We rescue the dogs, they rescue their warriors."

Meg Cameron doesn't suffer from PTSD, but she has her share of difficulty finding her way to fit in again as a wife and mother. Ben Cameron has seen the difference a service dog can make in the lives of veterans, and he is determined to expand his canine breeding and training facility to include just such a program. This country owes a huge debt to the men and women who sacrifice so much in the service of our country, and for my part, I plan to pay it back by sharing a portion of all proceeds from this book with the K-9s for Warriors program.

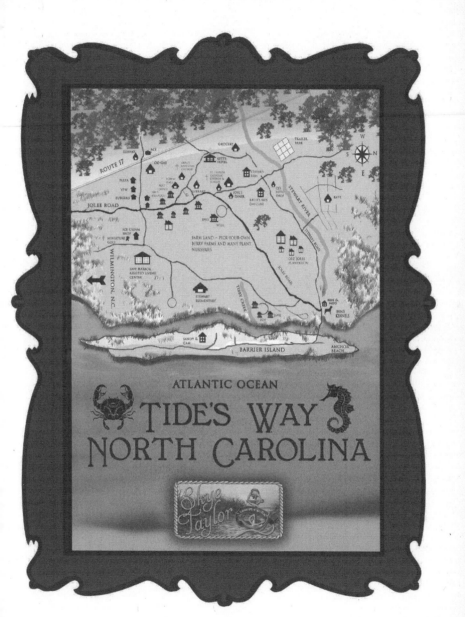

ATLANTIC OCEAN

TIDE'S WAY
NORTH CAROLINA

CHAPTER 1

Meg shrugged her backpack up higher on her shoulder as she joined the stream of passengers that had just come off the flight from Dulles to Wilmington, North Carolina, and were now filing past the empty chairs of the waiting area and toward the security exit. Her unaccustomed loafers felt stiff and made a hollow sound on the tile floor that seemed to echo the thudding of her heart. A man in a navy blue suit jostled past, then stopped and looked at her as if he thought he might know her. But then he shrugged, apologized, and moved on. She nodded at him absently. She had bigger things on her mind.

As she approached the hallway leading to the main lobby, she halted abruptly. Her heart thumped harder. Ben would be out there waiting for her. Maybe he'd brought Rick and Evan with him. It had been three hundred and fifty-eight days since she'd last seen her husband and her little boys. Three hundred and fifty-eight days that had changed her forever.

The crush of people flowed past her like water around a boulder in a riverbed. Her chest felt tight. It was difficult to breathe. It felt a lot like every time she'd moved out to accompany a convoy in Iraq.

All those days ago when she'd been walking the other way with tears brimming in her eyes, she'd been naïve. Committed, eager, and incredibly naïve. She wasn't the same woman who had said goodbye to Ben that day. She was no longer innocent. And her idealism had fled in the face of the things she had seen. And done.

Would Ben notice?

Would he see it in her eyes? Feel it in her touch? Surely he would hear it when she cried out in her nightmares. Would he still love her if he knew the whole of it? If he knew how far she had grown away from the girl he had fallen in love with?

Meg drew in a ragged breath, squared her shoulders, and stepped out. *Suck it up, Marine. Ben's waiting. Oorah.*

Ben Cameron hurried up to the security barrier, his gaze fixed on the stream of travelers making their way toward the lobby.

12

The TSA agent glared at him, but he ignored her. He was looking for just one person. One very special person. It had been so long.

There'd been an accident on the way, and he'd been late getting to the airport. Racing into the building, assuming she would beat him to baggage claim, he'd gone straight there. But her familiar diminutive figure wasn't anywhere in sight, nor had he seen a bulging green duffle bag among the jumble of luggage, boxes, golf clubs, and car seats moving past on the carousel.

The plane was on the ground. He'd checked the app on his phone while waiting impatiently to get past the logjam of police vehicles on Route 17 along the coast from Wilmington, along with a wrecker and an ambulance at the accident scene. She *had* made the connection. She'd called after she'd boarded the plane in DC to give him her airline and flight number and when it was due to land. Her voice had sounded matter-of-fact and unemotional. Very military. She was a Marine, after all. And she'd been in a war zone for almost a year. A place where emotions didn't belong. At least not those reserved for the husband left behind.

He glanced back the way he'd come in, then again down the hall guarded by the

13

vigilant TSA agent. Then he saw her.

Meg came around the corner and strode toward him.

Her hair was pulled back into a tight ponytail, the dark sheen of it glistening under the bright fluorescent lights. Head up, she looked straight ahead. Shoulders back. Very squared away. *His* Marine. *His* Meg.

At the sight of her, his heart leapt and shuddered into a staccato rhythm. Meg was back. Whole and unharmed. And as beautiful as his memory had promised. He couldn't wait to hold her again. He couldn't wait to kiss her and feel her arms circle tight around his neck. To feel her lips returning his hunger and longing.

Her stride was long and confident, but it still seemed to take forever for her to reach him.

"Meg," Ben whispered huskily as he finally swept her into his embrace. His life was whole again. "Oh, Meg." His eyes stung, and his heart hammered madly in his chest. "I've missed you so much."

CHAPTER 2

Crushed in Ben's exuberant embrace in the busy airport lobby, Meg felt lightheaded and breathless. His voice husky and tight with emotion, he kept murmuring disjointed phrases of love and welcome. She tipped her head back to reply, but before she could utter a word, his mouth claimed hers.

Vaguely aware of clapping in the background, Meg surrendered to the shelter of Ben's embrace. His kiss was hard, demanding, and fierce, but she welcomed the hungry passion and returned it with a need as great as his. When he stopped to catch his breath, she buried her face against his shirtfront, her arms locked tight around his neck. There was so much she couldn't face just yet, but in Ben's arms she felt safe. At last.

Ben set Meg back on her feet and released his possessive grip. His cheeks wet with tears, he grinned and wept openly at the

15

same time.

Her eyes were painfully dry.

Meg wanted to cry with him. She wanted to cling to him and tell him she had missed him as much as he had missed her. She stood mute. It felt like someone had packed her up in cotton wool so thick that the world couldn't get in.

Ben didn't appear to notice. He hugged her again, then swung her off her feet, twirling her in a celebratory circle before setting her down once more. He wrapped his arm about her shoulders and propelled her toward baggage claim to get her gear. She waited while Ben shouldered his way through the crowd to claim a desert-dusty duffle bag that appeared among the jumble of suitcases. "This it?" he asked, hoisting the bulky bag off the carousel.

She nodded, and he swung the bag over his shoulder as if it weighed nothing, then grabbed her hand and led her from the terminal.

His fingers were strong, his palm calloused and warm, just like she remembered. His strength, his confidence, his reliability — everything she'd always admired about him — seeped into her through their clasped hands as they zigzagged through the parking lot to his truck. She began to feel more like herself.

When they reached the truck, Ben dumped her duffle into the bed and turned toward her. He pulled her into his embrace, rocking her back and forth, as if trying to absorb the reality that she was actually, really, and truly home. This time, he was as wordless as she, just rocking and hugging as though he might never let her go. Ben had hugged her the same way all those years ago on the day she'd turned eighteen, and they'd kissed for the first time. He'd waited five years for her to grow up, and that day had marked the beginning of their commitment as lovers instead of just friends. Today was another turning point, but Ben didn't know it yet. She wasn't the same innocent girl she'd been then. War had changed her. It would be like falling in love all over again. But would he? Once he understood how different she was inside?

Meg felt, rather than heard the shuddering sob of relief and happiness that ran through her husband's big, strong body. She had thought she'd cry buckets once she was back in Ben's arms again after a year of hell, but still her tears didn't come. After several long minutes, Ben held her away and grinned.

"Damn, but it's good to have you back."

He kissed her again before digging into his pants pocket for his truck keys.

He opened her door for her like the gentleman he was and waited for her to climb in before loping around to the driver's side and hauling himself into his seat. He leaned across the seat to kiss her yet again before starting the engine.

On the drive home, Ben kept reaching across the gap between the seats to touch her: squeezing her hand, or her thigh, and once running the back of his fingers down her cheek before blowing her a kiss. He gabbed on about Rick and Evan and how they'd been counting down the days. How they'd cleaned their rooms until the fussiest drill sergeant would have been impressed. How they'd wanted to come with him to the airport but reluctantly agreed to let Dad go alone if they could help decorate for the party.

Meg groaned inwardly. She should have known there would be a welcoming party. Ben's family was big on parties, and they'd all be there along with numerous friends and neighbors. Uneasiness set in. How was she going to hold herself together and get through the next few hours?

By the time they pulled onto Jolee Road and drove through her hometown, Meg was so taut with apprehension her muscles ached. Homes and businesses so familiar and yet so alien lined the main street of Tide's Way and brought back a rush of memories. She watched the buildings glide by as snatches of long-ago events tugged at her mind.

The statue of General Jolee appeared, dominating Tide's Way's little common. She and a bunch of rowdy friends had festooned it with orange crepe paper one long-ago Halloween. Across from the park she'd gotten her first kiss in the shadows of the public library. Chris Wilson had been as inexperienced as she. They'd both been nervous and excited. And there was Joel's Diner where she'd called Ben from to come and rescue her the night she'd run away from home because her big brother wouldn't let her go camping on the beach with a questionable bunch of boys from the trailer park. It was hard to remember being so young or so innocent. Tide's Way never changed, but she surely had.

As they got closer to the beach, Meg rolled down the window and sniffed the salty scent of the ocean. So different from the desert she'd spent the last year in. This was home. This was coastal North Carolina where she'd spent all but two years of her life: the beach, the ocean, the small town, everyone-knows-everyone atmosphere. There weren't words big enough to express how much she had missed it all.

Ben didn't speak as he pulled up at the stop sign where Jolee Road ended. Dead ahead was home. The crush of cars and trucks crowded into their driveway and spilled over onto the shoulders of Stewart Road. An unwelcome sense of dread hit her. She was happy to be home, but all these people. She would have to talk to them. Make small talk. Ask how they were doing. Remember what had been going on in their lives while she was gone. They were sure to ask questions. Questions she dreaded answering.

She didn't want to talk about where she'd been or what she'd done. She didn't want to have to find words for how she felt, either while she was gone or now that she was home. And she didn't want to even think about Scout or John or so many others.

Ben drove his truck onto the grass to get past the jam of vehicles and pulled up between the house and the building that housed the kennels and training facility. He scrambled out before the engine had even finished rumbling to a stop and hurried around to open her door for her.

"I'm sorry about the crowd. You're probably exhausted, and I bet you really just want to spend time with the boys. And me, too, I hope, but it'll probably be a while before we can get everyone to head on out and give us some alone time." He paused, his face suddenly serious. "God, Meg, I missed you so much. It feels like you've been gone forever. Does it feel like that to you?"

Meg slid off the seat onto the running board and put one hand on Ben's shoulder. She pressed a finger against his lips. "I love you, Ben. I always have, and I always will. Missing you —" Her eyes ached with the tears she still couldn't shed. "Words aren't big enough." She leaned down and pressed her aching eyes into the hollow of his neck.

As Ben lifted her off the running board and let her slide down the length of his body, he groaned. Meg felt him swell with need. She clung to him. Just as needy. Desperate to be all the way home. Wanting to be consumed by this man who once had been her whole world.

"Mom?" Her sons' eager young voices called out. "Mommy?"

Yanked back to reality, Meg pushed free of Ben's embrace and stepped back. The boys barreled around the front bumper, and

21

Ben turned away to haul her duffle from the bed of the truck.

"Mommy!" Five-year-old Evan, trailing a bright blue helium balloon with "Welcome Home" emblazoned on it in sparkling silver, flung himself at her. "You're home! You're finally home!"

Meg caught him up in her arms and returned his eager hug. Over Evan's head, Meg saw Rick move uncertainly, his seven-year-old shoulders squared and his blue eyes wide and somber. She had a hard time reading the expression in his eyes. Eyes so like his father's it gave her heart a stab. Was he having as much difficulty believing she was actually home again as his dad? Meg gave her younger son one last squeeze, then set him on his feet.

Rick hung back, so Meg went to him. She fell to her knees and wrapped him in her arms.

"I think you must have grown a foot since I left," she tried to joke away the choking lump crawling up her throat.

"Only three inches, Mom," Rick corrected in his soft, reserved little voice. Evan was the outgoing son. Rick the shy one. Always cautious with his emotions. She hugged him tighter.

"Mom." He buried his face against her

chest and wound his arms tight about her neck.

Meg felt the first hesitant shudder of a sob her son was valiantly trying to hold back. She tightened her arms about his slender, boyish form. "I missed you, too," she murmured into his silky dark hair. "I missed you so much."

The shudders grew until Rick gave up fighting them.

Evan and Rick were so keyed up once the party broke up and everyone had finally departed Meg wondered if they were ever going to fall asleep. They chattered all the way up the stairs and right through the job of brushing their teeth. She got Evan into his pajamas while Rick disappeared into the bathroom to change. Then they climbed into Rick's bed, each with two carefully selected books for the nighttime reading ritual.

She read Evan's books first and then listened while Rick proudly read to her the books he'd chosen. When she'd left for Iraq, Rick had only just begun to read. Yet here he was, reading books more than a grade level above him with fluent ease. She had missed so much.

Her mind began to wander. *How much*

else have I missed? Ben had done his best to keep her up to date on the latest events and achievements through their sporadic email connections and occasional Skype sessions, but there were all those little daily details even the most observant parent forgets to notice. She'd missed Rick losing his first baby tooth, and Ben had sent her a photo of Rick grinning around the gap in his mouth. But the two new oversized adult teeth already most of the way in had been a surprise. It felt like her baby had grown up a lot more than just a year in the time she'd been gone. Three inches taller, big new teeth, reading out loud. What else had she missed?

Evan had begun kindergarten. Rick had become a Cub Scout. What about Ben? Her mind moved from Rick and his story to wonder what Ben was up to while she was tucking the boys into bed. Her eyes grew heavy as the hours of travel began to catch up with her. She forced her attention back to Rick's story. His voice soft, his diction so careful.

Meg woke with a start. She shot up, heart pounding. Where was she?

"I didn't finish my book yet." Rick's blue gaze pinned her with an accusatory, disappointed gleam.

"I'm sorry," she apologized, leaning down to kiss his forehead. "I guess I'm more tired than I thought."

"Didn't you get to sleep on the airplane?" Rick asked, his expression softening. "Didn't they give you a little pillow and a blanket so you could take a nap before the party?"

Meg swung her feet to the floor. "They did give me a pillow and a blanket, but I was so excited about seeing you I didn't sleep much."

Rick shut the book and set it aside. "That's okay, Mom. I'll finish the story tomorrow." He was generous with his forgiveness. He scuttled down under the covers and curled his arm protectively about his little brother. As Rick mumbled goodnight, she tucked the covers around them, straightened, and gazed down at them for several minutes.

Meg hadn't been in a place she could fall asleep and feel safe in almost a year. She'd begun to think she would never feel safe again, but lying in that narrow little bed between her two sons, peace had caught up with her unexpectedly. She reached down to push Rick's dark hair off his face and kiss his forehead. Evan burrowed into the curve of his brother's body, his face invisible. Meg kissed the top of his head instead.

In her bedroom, she stripped off the

rumpled civies she'd been wearing for more than forty-eight hours and dropped them into the hamper, then headed to the shower. As she worked up a lather, then rinsed the shampoo out of her hair, Ben's eagerness earlier that afternoon came back to her in a rush. If her skin hadn't already been pink from the hot water, it would have flushed rosily at the memory of her own response to Ben's need.

Meg shut off the water and reached for her towel. Maybe she should show up in the kitchen with nothing on but the towel? Or . . . Did she even have a sexy nightgown in her dresser? She couldn't remember the last time she'd gone out of her way to wear something provocative to bed.

But didn't she still have that tailored-style red silk shirt that came just to the bottom of her butt? The one Ben had bought for her on a business trip? Slinky fabric meant to tease, with matching and very skimpy briefs. He'd been in Europe purchasing breeding stock for his kennels, yet he'd made time to buy her a gift. Not just any gift but one he'd gone out of his way to find. One meant to tell her just how much he'd missed being away from her.

She'd never actually slept in it because every time she had put it on, it came off shortly after. She smiled. Sometimes before they even got to the bedroom. Where was it?

Ben had his hands in a sink full of soapy dishwater when Meg stepped silently into the kitchen on bare feet. She leaned against the doorjamb and watched him as he scrubbed his sister's chili pot. Beneath the faded blue fabric of his favorite chambray shirt his muscles flexed smoothly as he scraped a few hours of baked-on sauce from its stainless sides. He hadn't heard her come in, so Meg savored the moment to study him. He was a big man, but moved with such grace that she loved watching him work. She always had.

It was how they'd met, in fact.

Meg's brothers CJ and Stu owned the only auto shop on the North Carolina coast just north of Wilmington, and CJ had been a classmate of Ben's. When Ben had purchased a beat-up Ford Mustang that was older than Meg herself, he'd brought it to CJ's shop to restore it and get it running again. Meg had spent hours perched on a stool watching Ben work on that car. Most of the time wishing Ben would notice her as something other than just CJ's kid sister.

Abruptly Ben turned. "Hey," he said

softly. A wicked smile spread slowly across his handsome features as he took in her transformation from squared away warrior to a provocatively dressed wife in red silk.

"Hey, yourself," Meg replied, husky and suddenly breathless. She pushed away from the doorjamb and crossed the kitchen. "We're alone. At last."

The roguish smile disappeared and was replaced by a look of tender longing.

He reached for her, his hands still warm and damp from the soapy water. The heat of them flooded through the thin silk of the shirt. Her breath quickened as the blue of his eyes darkened, and his fingers worked their way under the shirttails until they discovered her bare behind.

Ben's eyes widened. She hadn't found the matching briefs and had decided she didn't need them anyway. The result was better than she'd imagined. Ben was a hard man to surprise.

"Are you just going to stand there and stare?" she asked, trying to control the impatience that been building ever since she'd stepped out of the shower. She pressed herself to him and wondered if all soldiers came home from war with the same shockingly intense need for the ultimate intimacy with their lovers.

"It's been too long." Ben sounded as breathless as she felt. He bent his head and kissed her with lingering tenderness. His lips were soft, urgent, yet without the punishing forcefulness that had left her mouth tingling and sore a few hours earlier. Her heart raced.

As Ben lifted her off the floor, she laced her fingers through the silky length of his overgrown hair and wrapped her legs about his waist. He turned and set her on the kitchen counter.

"You have no idea how many times I've imagined this," he murmured as he began undoing the small flat buttons that ran down the front of her shirt. He bent to kiss the hollow just above her collarbone. Then he trailed a string of kisses down the slope of her breast as the shirt pooled about her waist.

"Imagined what? Doing me in the kitchen?" Meg tried for humor, but neediness made the humor come out ragged.

"Oh, yeah! Here in the kitchen." Ben rested his forehead against hers as his voice dropped to a low, sexy growl. "In our bedroom. In the living room. Out in my office. I imagined doing you pretty much *everywhere.*" Ben covered her breasts with his big, warm hands and squeezed gently.

Meg gasped as passion fired everywhere at once.

Meg shot out of bed. It was the middle of the night. Where was she? The room was cold. Not Baghdad! She shivered. She was home. In her bedroom. Immediately her heart rate eased off its frantic pace. She slid her feet to the floor and stood where she could see the glimmer of moonlight on the waterway and, beyond that, the ocean.

She shivered again and stepped silently away from the bed. The sexy red shirt was probably still on the kitchen counter. She groped blindly in the ink-dark closet she shared with Ben, hunting for her bathrobe. Unable to locate the robe, she settled for a soft chamois shirt of Ben's that came nearly to her knees. She wrapped it about herself and crossed the room to the window.

Ever since that first night so far from home, she'd had daydreams about her first night back home. Daydreams of sleeping in their luxurious king-sized bed where she could spread out and get really comfortable. Sleeping with the windows open and the sound of the ocean lulling her to sleep. Daydreams of sleeping the whole night through without the sound of war at her doorstep. And being able to reach out and touch Ben any time she wanted to.

But it hadn't turned out anything like the daydreams that had gotten her through their year of separation. After a year on an army cot, she wasn't used to sprawling or sharing her bed. Ben seemed too close, too possessive, even in his sleep. His arm draped across her middle, his breath in her hair. It felt claustrophobic.

Meg had gotten used to sleeping the way soldiers have always slept, half on alert and ready to respond in an instant. She'd grown accustomed to having people awake and moving about, on guard while she slept. But home was eerily still with just the little creaking sounds of a settling house and no one keeping watch.

She'd been dozing fitfully, and now that she thought about it, she decided it must have been Ben's dogs barking that woke her. Which was puzzling. There had been a constant cacophony of dogs roaming loose in the streets, day and night, in Baghdad. Stray dogs barked all the time, but she'd gotten used to them. So, why tonight had the barking brought her bolt upright in bed in a cold sweat reaching for a rifle that wasn't there?

Hugging the chamois shirt closer, she stared out over the yard that was so familiar, and yet in a weird way, so unfamiliar. The dogs had already quieted again. She eased the window open even wider to let in the scent of the sea she had missed so much in her long absence. Some stray animal must have gotten them going. Maybe a raccoon moseying about, hunting for something to eat.

Scout hadn't barked unless he was alerting someone that he'd detected unseen danger. He hadn't barked when he'd stepped on a hidden detonation plate either. Meg shuddered and hugged herself harder.

That hadn't been her fault.

"Not my fault." She whispered the mantra aloud in the hushed dark room.

Everyone in her unit had insisted that Scout's death was not her fault. Scout's handler hadn't blamed her either. But she'd clung to her self-recrimination and had a meltdown over the dog's death in her commanding officer's arms. Unexpected and inexcusable desire had flared up between her and John, and she had wanted to lose herself in the passion of it and forget about Scout.

That desire *had* been her fault.

"You all right?" Ben slipped his arms about her waist and bent his head down next to hers.

Meg's heart slammed into overdrive at Ben's sudden closeness. "I'm — I'm fine." It appalled her that she hadn't heard him getting out of bed. It appalled her that her mind had been so full of John and the forbidden things she'd felt in Baghdad that she'd become completely unaware of her surroundings. A shocking breach in good soldiering.

"I thought I heard you crying." Ben pulled her back against his chest and rocked her gently. "What's wrong?"

"I was thinking about Philip." Meg tried to change the subject. "He told me he's getting sent to Afghanistan right after Jake's wedding."

"How come I get the feeling that my big brother is not what you're crying about? Even if he is headed to Afghanistan?"

"I'm not crying." Meg turned in his arms to prove it. She lifted her face toward his. "Marines don't cry." She needed Ben to comfort her. But something kept her from giving in to such weakness.

John had tried to comfort her, and look where that had led. Guilt twisted in her gut.

"Come back to bed with me. Let me hold you."

He kept his arms draped loosely about her, but she could feel the strength in them, and the warmth. They were intimately familiar in spite of the year they'd spent apart. She wished she still felt like the same woman who'd left him behind a year ago.

She and Ben had a special bond. A bond that had been there for almost as long as she'd known him. Since long before they'd fallen in love, married, and brought two sons into the world. None of that should have changed, but somehow it felt like everything had. She'd gone off to war holding tight to the thought of Ben and their closeness, knowing he would be thinking of her as often as she thought of him. Knowing without a doubt that he would be there for her when she returned home.

She leaned into him and pressed her cheek against the pale curly thatch of hair on his chest and listened to the steady beating of his heart. Ben was her safe place. Her lover, her husband. Her soul mate. If only she could tell him everything.

"Make love to me?" Meg whispered, the last word lifting in a pleading question.

"Again?" He sounded uncertain.

Maybe three times in one night was asking too much? Or maybe he suspected there was something she wasn't telling him.

She nodded and flicked her fingernail over the closest flat male nipple.

Ben grunted softly and led her back to the bed. He laid her down and stretched out beside her before drawing the covers up around their waists.

He studied her face in the dim light and touched the skin beneath one eye with the pad of his thumb. "You need sleep more than more sex. Not that I'm trying to talk you out of it or anything."

"Then stop talking and kiss me."

Ben chuckled. "Yes, ma'am." Then he gathered her close and gave her what she'd asked for.

Thoroughly sated and minus the second shirt of the night, Meg's thoughts drifted aimlessly. This time the possessive clutch of Ben's embrace felt welcome and safe as sleep began to overtake her.

When Ben spoke, his voice sounded tight and not at all sleepy.

"Who's John?"

CHAPTER 3

The dogs greeted Ben with wagging tails. Eager for his attention, they nuzzled his thighs with their cold noses. He knelt down and scratched behind their ears, his mind elsewhere. He relived, yet again, the heart-stopping moment that Meg, still flushed with sex and already half asleep, had whispered another man's name.

Who is John? He didn't know anyone named John. Meg had never mentioned anyone named John either. Should he be worried? Especially given the context in which she'd let the name slip.

Impressed with his own stamina, Ben knew he'd satisfied her. She'd been astride him when she came that last time, arching up and crying out his name as pleasure overtook her. Then she'd slumped forward, buried her face against his neck, and told him she loved him.

Yet only moments later, as they sprawled

in sated languor with his arm across her hips and her head on his shoulder, she'd mumbled another man's name.

"I can't do this, John."

What did it mean? Had her mind already been back in a war zone, coping with things no one should ever be asked to deal with? Or did it mean something else entirely?

Ben turned on the water and began hosing down the runs. Normally, this was his assistant Mike Davis' job. Except on weekends, Mike came in around six thirty to feed and water the dogs as well as clean the runs that ran from the rear of the building out toward the marsh and the salty waterway beyond. But Ben, his mind churning out all kinds of explanations for his wife's drowsy utterance, hadn't been able to get back to sleep. Finally, unable to lie still a moment longer, he'd slipped silently out of bed and come out to the kennels before the sun had even begun to lighten the eastern sky.

"Who the devil is John?" Ben asked Columbo.

Columbo perked his ears forward and tipped his head.

"It's not what you're thinking," Ben told the big dog. "She would never be unfaithful. That's not who she is. It's not part of who *we* are, either."

Columbo licked Ben's hand and whined softly.

Who was he kidding? Infidelity was the first thing that had popped into his mind. If Meg had been having an affair during her deployment, she would have been careful not to talk about the guy during any of their Skype chats, and it made sense that he'd never heard the name before. It also made some twisted sort of sense that she'd muttered it unknowingly when she was groggy with exhaustion and mind-numbing sex.

He'd pretty much talked himself out of that obvious conclusion during the hours he'd lain awake. He couldn't believe it. Maybe it was an obvious conclusion to jump to, but that was not the kind of relationship he and Meg had. Meg was not the kind of woman who could cheat on him and still look him in the eye.

A vision of her coming toward him in the kitchen last night dressed in nothing but that outrageously suggestive nightshirt he'd given her years ago replayed itself in his mind. That seductive smile playing about her mouth and desire hot in her eyes. There had been no guile there. Not a hint of guilt. Meg simply could not have been unfaithful to him and behave as if nothing had changed between them.

"So, who is John? And what is he to Meg?"

"John, who?"

Ben whirled about. He thought he was alone with the dogs and his tangled thoughts. "What are you doing here?"

"I was going to ask you the same thing, Boss." Mike hung his backpack on a hook and began to climb out of the wind pants he wore while riding his bike. "You're usually fixing the boys' breakfast about now and rousting them out of bed to get ready for school."

Ben looked at his watch. "Damn!" He handed the hose to Mike and headed for the house.

Meg wrestled with the tangled covers, flung herself onto her back, and then abruptly woke. The smell of coffee filled the air, and a soft murmur of voices came from down the hall.

"But I want to show her my new uniform." Evan's voice piped up more clearly than his father's hushed tones.

Meg rolled over and looked at the clock. How could she have slept so late? It was already the middle of the afternoon in Iraq. Her day there would have been more than half over already. She scrambled off the bed and headed toward the bathroom.

She'd been dreaming in the moments before conscious thought returned. They had been troubled dreams, but the harder she tried to remember what they'd been about, the wispier they grew. Perhaps it was better that way.

She splashed cold water on her face and then studied herself in the mirror. The tender skin below her eyes looked bruised. No wonder Ben had suggested she needed more sleep as he gently brushed his thumbs over the tired-looking skin. But her eyes had looked haunted and in need of sleep for the last two months of her tour. Ever since Scout's death. She folded a facecloth into a square, soaked it with water, icy-cold from their artesian well, and held the cloth against her eyes.

A sudden raucous barking came from outside, and she flinched. *I've got to get over jumping every time Ben's dogs start barking.*

Meg squared her shoulders and looked at herself again, decided her eyes were as good as they were going to get, and picked up her hairbrush. She started to pull her hair back into her usual ponytail, but then changed her mind. She let the silky dark curtain fall around her face again. The effect softened her features and diverted attention from her tired-looking eyes.

She was pretty, but not beautiful as Ben claimed.

Ben liked to tease, and it had become a game she willingly played. Often when Ben was in a frisky, amorous mood, he would tell her she was beautiful while his hands skimmed over her body, telling her the same thing without the words. As desire flared she would reply that she was not as beautiful as he was. And Ben would snort and remind her men were not beautiful. Men were handsome. All the while demonstrating his opinion of her desirability with increasingly suggestive fondling. Aroused and breathless, she'd agree, by then doing a significant amount of fondling in return. Semantics! *I'm still not as pretty as you are handsome.*

Ben always ended the debate with the declaration that they were a right fine-looking couple who made right fine-looking babies before kissing her until her head reeled and every receptive cell in her body was on fire. But occasionally, he'd grow serious and ask when they were going to try for a girl who could grow up as pretty as her mother.

He'd asked that very question just two weeks ago via Skype. They'd played their little game thousands of miles apart without

41

the aid of touching and fondling and still managed to get each other excited. Until he asked her about getting pregnant again.

Meg ran her hand over her flat stomach, watching herself in the mirror. A distinctly unfeminine six-pack gave evidence of the hard active life she'd lived for the past twelve months. No soft curves or even the suggestion of any. She'd lost a lot of weight and probably wouldn't be able to get pregnant right off even if she was sure she wanted to. She swallowed hard and tried to gaze objectively at the woman she was now. She had a warrior's body.

And a warrior's thoughts.

When she'd watched Ben move his hands in a way that suggested giving her breasts a squeeze and responded with an equally lewd gesture of her own after taking a quick look behind her to make sure no one was paying attention, she had been aroused. And she supposed Ben had been as well. But the game had been different, buffered by all those miles and time zones, and strangely unreal.

Then Ben had suggested trying to get pregnant when she got home, and she'd crashed back to reality. He had made her forget about who and where she was for a little while, playing their private little game, but suddenly the transformation from warrior to lover had moved from playful to serious. He was asking her to leave the warrior behind and become a mother again. She didn't know if she could do it that easily. Or maybe at all.

She loved her sons. Reuniting with them yesterday had been sweeter than she'd ever imagined. Holding their innocent young bodies, listening to their chatter, and tucking them into bed had been part of her dreams for twelve long months, and the reality hadn't disappointed. But in spite of that, there had been a distance between them that hadn't been there when she left a year ago. Rick and Evan had not acted as though they felt any remoteness. Ben didn't behave as though he sensed it either. But it had been there. The distance was inside her head, and she didn't know how to fix it.

"Mommy?" Evan called her, his footsteps pelting down the hall in her direction.

Hastily, Meg grabbed Ben's old terry robe from the back of the bathroom door and put it on. "Coming," she answered as she yanked the sash tight.

Evan stumbled to a halt and straightened, clearly waiting for her to notice and admire his new school uniform.

Meg staggered back dramatically. "Evan?

Is that really you?" She dropped to her knees and admired the uniform, patting the shoulders smooth. "That tie makes you look so grown up."

"It's not a real grown-up tie," Evan confided. "It's a kid's tie. See?" He grabbed the knot and pulled the plastic tabs free of his collar. Then he dropped the backpack he'd been holding to the floor and carefully inserted the tie back into his shirt. "But Dad says he'll teach me how to tie a real one as soon as he can buy one my size."

"Well, I think you look splendid." Meg pulled her youngest son to her, gave him a hug, then set him away and lifted the backpack from the floor.

"Evan! Hurry up, the bus is coming," Rick called from the front door.

Meg jumped to her feet and fitted the backpack onto Evan's small shoulders, then gave his butt a pat as he scurried down the hall.

She followed, wanting to give Rick a hug as well, but he was already running down the driveway to where the big yellow school bus waited patiently with its warning lights flashing.

Meg waved from the front door as Evan bolted across the lawn to catch up with his brother. A moment later the boys disappeared into the bus, and the doors snapped shut. She stood in the doorway watching as the bus chugged away down Stewart Road toward its next stop.

She turned away finally and found Ben standing in the kitchen archway watching her.

"You should have woken me up."

"I'm sorry. I guess I should have, but I got a late start." Ben shrugged. "I was hurrying to get the boys in gear and get breakfast in front of them and their lunches packed. And I forgot."

As Meg got closer, she realized Ben looked as tired as she did. Her fault. Keeping him up all night making love. That was hardly his usual routine. "I'm sorry, too. I interrupted your beauty sleep."

"Men aren't beautiful," Ben began. A slight smile lit his eyes and eased the tired look.

"Yeah, they are. And you are. Inside and out." Meg tiptoed to kiss him. He hadn't shaved yet, and his fast-growing beard glistened in the morning sunlight and tickled her face.

Ben wrapped her in a bear hug. He didn't say anything, just held her close. He didn't argue about being beautiful. Didn't tease. Didn't kiss her in return. When he set her away from him again, the brief smile was gone, and his exhaustion showed.

"Want some coffee? I made it strong, the way you like it." He turned and headed toward the counter.

Meg followed.

"Mike asked how come you didn't come home with your unit, and I realized I never asked. I was too busy being disappointed by the delay to think about the reason for you coming home alone." Ben poured coffee into her favorite mug. "Don't guard units get shipped out and come home together, usually?" He glanced at her over one shoulder as he dropped two slices of bread into the toaster.

"They usually do, but I stayed behind to tie up loose ends. John would have, but he was attacked and beaten up pretty bad. They sent him stateside for medical treatment." Meg slid onto a stool and pulled the coffee mug close.

Ben's blond brows drew into a questioning knot. "I'm sorry. Who's John?"

"Captain Bissett. My commanding officer," Meg answered. *He was a lot more than just your commanding officer,* the imp on her shoulder reminded her.

"I thought some guy named Nichols was in charge of your outfit."

46

"He was, but they reassigned him two months after we got there. And then John got promoted and took over."

"Do you usually call your commanding officer by their first name?" Ben's voice sounded curiously flat.

"No," she conceded. Maybe her guilty conscience was reading more into his tone than he'd implied. "Not usually. But Captain Bissett was . . . John was different. He — he . . ." She floundered. Maybe she just needed to tell Ben the truth. At least some of the truth.

"John's father died five months ago. He had a massive coronary and died before they could even reach John to tell him. Of course, he was devastated. I just happened to be the one who was there when the call came through.

"I stayed with him while arrangements were being put in place to get emergency leave. And he talked about his father. He told me about growing up and the things they'd done together. The things they hadn't done so much in the last few years with the reserves being called up so much. John was feeling guilty and upset with himself. I was just being a good listener."

Meg shrugged uneasily. "That kind of stuff changes things. It was kind of hard to go back to being Captain Bissett and Lieutenant Cameron after that. He was just a man in a lot of pain."

"I can imagine," Ben agreed, sliding a plate with freshly buttered toast onto the counter in front of her. "So, you became — friends?"

"After he returned from burying his dad, yeah, I guess you could say that." Meg bit into her toast, chewed, and swallowed. "He still gave the orders, and I still saluted before leaving to carry them out. But in the down times, we got to be friends. I showed him photos you sent of the boys, and he showed me photos of his nieces. Occasionally we made it to the chow hall together, when neither of us was out with a convoy. We talked, sometimes, about what we wanted to do when we got home again."

"How come you never mentioned him before?"

Was that a hint of jealously in Ben's voice? His blue eyes were as unreadable as Rick's had been yesterday afternoon.

Uneasy guilt clutched at Meg's gut. "I didn't realize I hadn't." Surely at some point over the last year she'd mentioned him to Ben. Just not in the last two months. "There were a hundred fifty Marines in my unit. I probably didn't tell you about most of them.

But we were all close. We were family."

"I guess you would. Feel like family, that is. With nicknames like Pudge and Keek. That sounds like the names I called my brothers when we were growing up."

"They don't call it a band of brothers for nothing," Meg said as she reached for a second piece of toast. "Of course, there are sisters mixed in now, too. Meredith got called Boots because she had the smallest boots in the unit."

"What did they call you?"

"Brat."

Ben laughed, spraying coffee. He wiped his mouth. "CJ is vindicated."

"Yeah. Maybe he is," Meg muttered as the similarity hit her. Her big brother had called her Brat for as long as she could remember. Then her thoughts returned to the brothers she'd spent the last year with.

Being in a war zone created a unique, unusually close relationship between warriors. Right now, so soon after returning home, every face was clearly etched in her mind. The way they moved and spoke. Their loves, their hopes, and their fears. Over time that closeness would be lost, but she doubted she'd ever forget them completely. Nor would she ever forget John. Or the way she'd felt when he held her.

Chapter 4

After Meg had gone to their bedroom to shower and start unpacking her duffle, Ben refilled his coffee cup and stood staring sightlessly out the window.

Her remark about her "war-time family" had hit him hard. How much of her life had she left out? What hadn't she shared with him and maybe never would? The twisting in his gut was jealousy, and it shamed him.

On rare occasions, Philip had shared bits and pieces of the wrenching emotions that haunted his life and those of his friends. His confidences reflected the unbelievably close-knit bond that formed between soldiers serving on the front lines. Baghdad had not been the front line by the time Meg got there, but war today was different. Her life had been just as much in jeopardy every day as earlier generations of warriors had been in the trenches of the world wars or the jungles of Vietnam. Of course she would share the same closeness and loyalties with her fellow Marines that Philip had. Ben's jealousy was totally out of place.

He had worried about her constantly and been thankful beyond words that she'd come home unharmed. But now he felt left out. Being able to justify it mentally didn't remove the sting of knowing that for over a year, he had not been the center-point of Meg's life the way she had remained the focus of his. The way they had both been before she'd gone off to war.

Back when she was just a kid, and he'd expended a great deal of effort reminding himself she was off limits because he was five years older, she had already become the focus of his life. Out of high school and working hard, saving up to start his own breeding program and kennels, he had looked forward to the hours he spent at CJ's garage restoring his vintage Mustang. Partly because he loved that car, but even more because Meg would be there working diligently on her homework.

The battered desk where Meg always sat was just beyond the bay allotted to Ben while he worked to restore the Mustang. Far too often he had found himself, hands idle, watching her as she studied. The silky sweep of her hair added mystery to her face and made him think about things he had no business associating with a girl not yet sixteen.

He hadn't realized it at the time, but Meg had returned the longing looks when his attention had been focused on his car. Just as well or he might not have behaved himself, despite the fact that she was his friend's kid sister. The day she turned eighteen, she had asked him out, and he'd reacted like a bashful schoolboy in his surprise.

Ben smiled ruefully at the memory and made his way over to the sink. He turned on the tap, rinsed the coffee pot, washed their mugs out, and propped them all in the drainer. Then he dumped the soggy remnants of the boys' cereal bowls and put them into the dishwasher along with their juice glasses and the knife he'd used to make their sandwiches. A quick wipe-down of the counter with the sponge, and he was done.

He grabbed his slicker in case it rained while he was out in the training barn and headed out the back door. Memories of Meg, the way she'd once been, followed him.

In the months after they'd started dating and before becoming intimate had been a challenge. He hadn't understood her hot and cold behavior. She always seemed to enjoy making out in the back seat of his brother's car, while Will and whatever girl he'd been dating at the time steamed up the windshield, but Ben had been twenty-three and still a frustrated virgin. Not because he hadn't had a chance to get laid, but because he'd loved Meg, and she wasn't ready to go there. Every time he'd tried to push the envelope a little, sliding his hand up under her jersey or pulling her hips tight against his throbbing groin, she'd freeze up like a snow cone, and Ben would go home horny, aching, and confused.

Until CJ clued him in.

Meg's drunken mother's live-in boyfriend had been abusing Meg when she was barely twelve, and that was why she had hung out at the garage so much of the time. Avoiding unwanted advances. After *that* enlightening conversation with CJ, Ben had been more patient. However long she needed, he was willing to wait. Ben had occasionally dated other women while Meg was growing up, but none of the women held his interest beyond a date or two. Meg had already become the center of his world and the only woman he had ever really wanted.

Columbo met Ben at the door and trotted along beside him as they moved through the entry and into the training room. He bent to ruffle the dog's fur and whisper in his ear.

"I found out who John was, and we don't have to worry."

The dog perked his ears forward, looked up at Ben, and wagged his tail.

"Smart dog," Ben told him. Although he knew the dog didn't understand a word Ben said, he made all the right moves as if he did.

"Hey, Boss!" Mike came in from the outdoor runs, bringing the scent of salt air and sunshine with him. "There's a guy from the Wilmington PD in your office waiting to see you."

"Thanks." Ben turned and headed back toward his office. "Now what do you suppose he wants with me?" Columbo whined again. "I haven't broken any laws that I know of. Except maybe a speed limit or two." Ben recalled his impatience yesterday after getting past the accident. He'd definitely broken the speed limit then. Might have run a yellow light on the edge of turning red, too.

As he stepped into his office, a uniformed police officer got to his feet.

"Jerry Brady," the officer introduced himself as he shoved his hand in Ben's direction.

Ben took the proffered hand. "What can I do for you, Officer?"

"This is going to sound like an odd request, but you were recommended to me," Brady began.

"Have a seat." Ben gestured toward the chair Brady had been sitting in when Ben entered and then dropped into his own battered wooden desk chair. Didn't sound like a belated traffic stop. "Shoot." Ben shook his head. "Maybe that was the wrong word to use when speaking to an armed officer of the law."

"Not so far off, actually." Brady sank back into his chair. "It is about a shooting."

"Anyone I know?" Ben's heart raced. *Please, God, don't let it be about Will.*

Brady shrugged. "You've probably heard about it anyway. You remember about three months ago, there was that robbery at the pier, and an officer was killed?"

"Yeah, I remember." Ben breathed a sigh of relief. "My brother told me he knew the guy. Ray Hillman, I think."

"Your brother is the one who recommended I come see you. Ray was a K-9 officer. And we're having some problems with his dog."

"What kind of problems?" Ben leaned

forward in his chair. Instant sympathy for the dog coursed through him. Folks who claimed that dogs had no souls didn't know much about dogs. If the dog had seen his partner killed, the dog would be grieving. Same as a human partner.

"He's been at the police kennels since then, and he's gone downhill. He doesn't eat enough, and he's lost too much weight. Doesn't seem to take an interest in much. When we give him a chance to get out and exercise, he goes just far enough to do his business, then he's back in the crate, his head on his paws. It's breaking my heart looking into those eyes of his."

It was breaking Ben's heart hearing about it. "What is it you're hoping I can do?"

"We asked Ray's widow if they wanted to adopt the dog, but she couldn't bear to look at him. Your brother suggested you might be willing to foster Kip here for a while. See if a change of scenery might help him get over Ray's getting shot."

"Absolutely!" Ben agreed. He'd need to think about the best way to handle the dog, but he was sure he'd find a way. He began running possible canine companions through his head.

"He's in the truck," Brady said, looking immensely relieved. "I'll bring him in."

"I'll go with you." Ben got to his feet and joined Brady at the door.

As they headed toward the entry, Columbo appeared at Ben's side.

"Stay," Ben commanded, holding his hand, fingers down, in front of the dog's nose.

Columbo sat.

"All your dogs roam the premises free?" Brady asked, stepping out into the yard.

"No, only special ones. Columbo is my number one stud. He thinks he's the boss."

Brady chuckled as he approached a pickup truck with the Wilmington PD shield emblazoned on its door and a rack of lights on top that Ben hadn't noticed on his way out. "I should have such a good looking boss." He went around to the tailgate.

A big German shepherd with an inky black face lay despondently in a large wire crate bolted to the truck bed. He didn't react when Brady lowered the tailgate.

"His name is Kip," Brady said as he stepped back to give Ben better access.

Ben leaned across, unlatched the crate door, and said the dog's name. The dog lifted his head and gazed at Ben. Ben couldn't recall ever seeing eyes so sad in all the years he'd worked with dogs.

"Hello, Kip." Ben spoke softly and held

out one hand, palm down, fingers curled under.

Kip whined but didn't move.

"You want to stay with us for a while, Kip?" Ben kept his voice soft and repeated the dog's name several times, waiting for the dog to respond.

Finally, after what seemed like an eon, Kip lowered his head and sniffed at Ben's hand. He whined again and then got to his feet. Ben backed up and invited the dog to come with a hand gesture. Kip jumped down to the ground and sat at Ben's feet, looking up at him as if waiting for a command. Ben gave him the hand signal to go around and sit at his left side. The dog complied without hesitation.

"Hasn't forgotten all his training, I see," Brady said as he reached into the truck bed and retrieved a canvas tote. "His leash and his training toy are here along with the blanket that's been in his crate. I was going to bring something of Ray's but decided that might be counter-productive." He handed the tote to Ben.

"Give me a week at least before you come checking on him. Call if you need daily updates." Ben took the tote.

Brady stuck his hand out, and Ben took it. "Thanks. He's a good dog. A great dog.

It's a shame what happened to Ray, and I'd hate for that to be the end of Kip, too. He might never return to police work, but I'd like to think we can find him a good home to retire in, at least."

"Give it time. He'll recover. Just might take a while. Right, Kip?" Kip turned his head to look up at Ben.

"Well, I've got to say, he's responded to you with more enthusiasm than we've seen since Ray got killed. I guess Will knew what he was talking about when he said if anyone could help Kip, you'd be it. He says you're even better than that guy on television."

"My brother tends to exaggerate."

"You look just like him." Brady shut the tailgate and moved around to open the driver's door. "You guys twins?"

"Identical," Ben said. "Made for some pretty fun pranks when we were kids. He got me into more trouble —" Ben shook his head, then, "But we grew up. Now Will is my hero. Will and my big brother Philip. And my wife. They go out every day and put their lives on the line while I stay home where it's safe."

"The police force and the military need men like you just as much as they need weapons and body armor. Never doubt it. If it weren't for the men and women who train

59

these animals, we wouldn't have the dogs to do things men can't. Canines make a huge difference in the way we do our work, and they save lives every day."

"That's what Will says."

"I envy you. From the way Will talks, you've got three pretty terrific brothers to my one bitchy sister." Brady hauled himself up into the truck. "I'll call in a couple days." He reached across the seat and plucked a business card from his open briefcase. "In case you need to reach me." He slipped the card into Ben's hand. "My cell's on it. Try that first."

Brady shut the door and started the engine. Ben and Kip watched as Brady drove down the drive and crossed over Stewart Road and onto Jolee Road.

"Well, Kip?" Ben squatted down to wrap an arm about the dog's neck. "Now I've got two troubled warriors to worry about."

Kip licked Ben's cheek.

Meg towel dried her hair as she walked past her bedroom window and glanced out.

Ben and a uniformed police officer stood at the back of a big pickup truck with a light-bar mounted on its roof. Curious, Meg inched closer to the window. It wasn't Ben's twin brother, Will. Wrong uniform for one thing. Wrong vehicle for another.

Ben leaned forward and unlatched the gate on a big dog crate. After a few minutes, Ben backed away. A dog leapt gracefully to the driveway and sat down in front of him.

Meg's heart clenched. The dog was darker than most German shepherds, and his ears were a tad longer. She swallowed against the sudden lump in her throat. The dog looked just like Scout. He had the same bushy patches of blond-colored fur above his eyes and held himself with the same taut concentration. She knew Ben was speaking to the dog by the way the dog tipped his head, his full attention riveted on Ben's face. Then the dog stood and walked around to sit at Ben's left side.

The men spoke for a little longer, and then the police officer got into the truck and drove away. Ben and the dog watched him go for a minute before Ben crouched down and put an arm about the dog's neck. The dog licked Ben's face.

Tears stung Meg's eyes, but she blinked them back.

Was she ever going to get away from her nightmare?

CHAPTER 5

Meg had her duffle emptied and her gear sorted. Dirty laundry in the washer. Clean stuff refolded and arranged in her dresser. Personal belongings stowed. She adjusted the pillows on the bed and smoothed a wrinkle from the spread, then headed to the boys' room. In spite of their late start, their beds were made and the room tidy. As she wandered through the rest of their modest home, she found everything was tidy. Ben tended to be a neatnik, but she'd expected more of a mess left behind in the wake of yesterday's party. She checked again for stray glasses or a forgotten cookie at least, but there was nothing. Even the kitchen was squared away: coffee pot rinsed, mugs drying in the rack, breakfast dishes in the dishwasher.

She didn't know what to do with herself. She felt unsettled and a little out of place, which was ridiculous. This was her home, for Pete's sake. What had she done before her deployment?

I spent the days in the kennels, helping Ben train the dogs and keeping the books. Sweat popped out on her forehead, and a wave of nausea hit her. The last place she wanted to be today was out in the kennels. Especially with that dog that just got dropped off.

"Damn you, Scout. You shouldn't have sat down."

I should have called him back.

Guilt flooded through Meg, nearly doubling her up. It had been two months. When was this aching wave of grief and self-reproach going to ease up? It hadn't been her job to call the dog back. She wasn't his handler. She was home now and surrounded by dogs. She would see them every day, circling the training pens with Ben and Mike or galloping in the field out back, jubilant with freedom from the daily round of lessons or nosing through the salty marsh checking out the scent of any animal that had passed through.

"Get over it," she ordered herself sternly.

Idleness didn't suit her, and wandering around a spotless house with nothing to do didn't help either. Meg decided to make a batch of cookies for her boys.

When was the last time she'd baked cookies? At least a year ago. Probably a lot longer. She began hauling ingredients out of the cupboards and set to work.

By the time the school bus deposited Rick and Evan at the end of the driveway, there were three different kinds of cookies either already boxed up in plastic containers or still cooling on the racks spread out on the counter. The Crock-Pot in the corner by the stove had sweet and sour chicken in it along with the snow peas she'd dug out of the freezer and the water chestnuts she'd found in the cupboard. Meg was punching down a dark round blob of pumpernickel bread dough for the last time, and a coffee cake Ben's mother had given her the recipe for graced the cut-glass cake plate that had been a wedding gift from Ben's godmother when the boys burst through the door.

"Yay! Mommy's home!" Evan dropped his backpack on the floor by the door and flew across the kitchen to wrap his arms about Meg's waist.

She hugged him in spite of her floury hands and kissed the top of his head.

Rick hung his backpack up on the hooks Ben had installed, surveyed the results of her cooking spree, and then looked at her with a growing smile. "My favorite kind," he said, scooping a still-warm spice cookie off the cooling rack. He hesitated and looked at Meg with a questioning look in his eyes. "Is it okay if I have one?"

"I made them just for you," she assured him, wondering at the new maturity he'd acquired while she was gone.

"What about my favorite kind, Mommy? Did you make my favorite kind?" Evan hustled from one counter to the next looking for the double chocolate chippers.

"Would I make Rick's favorites and not yours?" Meg asked her younger son while ruffling the hair on his head. "Go wash your hands, and I'll fix you a snack."

Not quite as mature as he'd seemed a moment before, Rick had already devoured the cookie he'd snagged before asking permission and was reaching for another when he heard Meg mention washing hands. He immediately drew his hand back and moved to the sink where Evan already had a stream of water running.

"Good grief! Have I walked into a bakery by mistake?" Ben halted just inside the back door and lifted his nose to sniff the air. "And my favorite chicken in the pot, too?"

"I wanted to make sure you were all happy to have me home again." Meg finished smoothing out the bread dough and dropped it into the previously greased pan.

She covered it with a clean dishcloth, set the timer, and then paused to push a stray lock of hair out of her face.

Ben lifted his brows expressively. "You didn't need to go to all this trouble to ensure that." He grabbed a knife, cut himself a generous slice of coffee cake, and bit into it.

"Now I know where Rick gets his manners from," Meg said laughing. For the first time since she'd walked into the house yesterday afternoon, she felt lighthearted. She crossed the kitchen and lifted her face to Ben's to be kissed. He swallowed and complied. He tasted like cinnamon and smelled like the out-of-doors and dogs. Some of Meg's easy pleasure fled.

"Sorry." Ben pinched her butt playfully. "I couldn't help myself. It's been a while since I tasted anything I didn't cook myself. And I don't bake anyway."

"I refuse to believe your mother didn't keep you supplied while I was gone," Meg said, desperate to hang on to the feeling of belonging and normalcy.

Ben set the bundle of mail he'd had tucked under one arm on the corner of the counter and wrapped both arms around Meg. "She did drop off a few things. But we never got to smell them baking." He got suddenly very serious. "It's good to have you home, Meg."

Meg looped her arms about Ben's neck. "It's good to be home."

He kissed her. Not with the pent-up passion of yesterday, but with a gentleness that touched her in a way passion couldn't.

"Ewwww!" Rick and Evan echoed their joint disapproval as they turned away from the sink, hands still damp, ready for the promised snack.

"Someday they'll get it," Ben whispered against her lips before setting her away and retrieving the mail.

Meg put two glasses of juice on the breakfast counter as the boys scrambled onto their stools. "Just two," she admonished as Evan slid the plastic container with his double chocolate favorites in his direction. "And only one for you, mister," she told Rick. "You've already had one."

She plucked Rick's backpack off the hook and began sorting through the papers inside.

"Those are for Dad," Rick said as Meg began to read through a request for chaperones for an upcoming field trip. "Hey, Dad! Can you go to the corn maze with us again?"

Meg slumped onto an unoccupied stool. "Why not me? I'm home now. I can go. I'd love to go."

"But . . ." Rick looked at his father, then at Meg. "But Sam asked if Dad was going again. Dad always goes."

It sounded more like Rick wanted his father to be a part of the adventure, and his friend Sam was just an excuse. *It's not a big deal,* she told herself as she handed the papers to Ben.

"But you can come too?" Apparently Meg hadn't hidden her disappointment well enough. Rick looked to his father for confirmation. "Right, Dad? You can both come?"

"It's okay, Rick. I haven't even checked my schedule. I might not be free."

Meg got up and walked out of the kitchen. Actually, she didn't have a schedule. For the next thirty days she was on leave. No schedule. Nothing she needed to get done. No one needed her. Not the Marines. Not Ben. Not even the boys.

CHAPTER 6

Meg read the page over and over again and still couldn't figure out the logic behind Rick's math homework. She was good at math. It was one of the reasons Ben had enlisted her help with the bookkeeping after he'd made a mess of the kennel ledger. She analyzed the diagram on the example problem. She knew what the answer was, but she couldn't figure out the method they were using to arrive at it. All this new math was driving her crazy.

"We're supposed to do this part first." Rick pointed at the first column of numbers, then at another illustration that made no sense at all to Meg.

"Ignore the picture," Meg advised. "Just add the numbers. You know how to carry. Right?"

"What's carry?" Rick looked up at her, his brow furrowed.

"It's like when you add a five and a seven.

The answer is twelve, but there's nowhere to put the one, so you put it at the top of the next column," Meg answered patiently. *What were they teaching kids these days?*

"But it's not a one, Mom. It's a ten."

"Yes. I know that, but if *you* already know that, then why do you need these pictures?" She tried to keep the frustration out of her voice.

"Never mind, Mom. I'll ask Dad to help me when he gets in." Rick shoved the homework assignment into his notebook and stacked it with his spelling book.

Meg felt like someone had punched her in the stomach. Her son was going to ask his father for help? Ben, the guy who couldn't keep his bankbook balanced! How could Ben do this stuff any better than she could?

"I can help you. Just be a little patient with me while I try to figure out this new math. I just got home, remember?"

"Don't feel bad. I stink at math, too," Rick consoled her.

"But I don't stink at math." Frustrated anger rose in Meg's gut.

Her protest got ignored in the noisy arrival of Ben bursting into the kitchen with Evan hard on his heels. Rain slatted against the windows and followed them into the kitchen. Ben scuffed his wet boots on the doormat, removed his dripping wet rain jacket, and hung it on a hook.

"Hurry up, Kip." Evan held the screen door open and made urgent come gestures with his free hand.

Kip? Who was Kip?

Then the dog Meg had seen jump down from the bed of the truck the day before trotted into the kitchen and shook. Rainwater spattered everywhere. Ben chuckled, and Evan laughed out loud.

"Sorry about the water, Mommy." Evan beamed up at her. "Kip's sorry, too. Right, Kip?"

The dog looked up at the sound of his name. He gazed first at Evan, then at Ben as if waiting for further instruction.

Rick slid off his stool and hurried across the kitchen. "Where did he come from?" Rick dropped to the floor in front of the big dog and offered his hand for a sniff the way his dad had taught him. The dog sniffed Rick's hand, glanced at Ben, then back at Rick.

"This is Kip," Evan introduced the dog excitedly. "He's a police dog. A really brave police dog. He saved a lady's life."

"Sit," Ben ordered in a soft voice.

Meg backed up hastily. Her heart raced. Her head pounded. Instead of a dog with

71

rain-wet fur plastered against bones that were too prominent, Meg's brain flashed a vision of Scout, his fur orange with dust, backing up and sitting. And then the explosion.

She bolted from the kitchen. Her heart thundered in her ears. She didn't realize her eyes were clenched shut until she tripped over the ottoman and landed in a heap on the living room floor. She buried her head between her knees as a wave of dizziness washed through her. She hugged her knees and willed herself to stop shaking.

"Meg?"

Meg tensed. She swallowed hard, pressed her lips together, then, resolutely forced her eyes open and looked up at her husband. He was on his knees in front of her, blond brows drawn together in bewilderment. Concern deepened the blue of his eyes.

"Why did you bring him in here?" she asked, trying desperately to keep the panic out of her voice. Ben had often brought dogs into the house, and she'd never questioned it before. No wonder he was confused. She hadn't told him about Scout. Maybe she should have. But Ben loved dogs so much she hadn't wanted to distress him. Besides, talking about Scout might bring up the subject of John again.

Ben reached out and tucked a stray curl behind her ear. "He needed people. I didn't think you'd mind. But he can go back to the kennel if his being here distresses you."

"N-no." Meg strove to get a grip on herself. "H-he can stay. I just — I just had a little flashback. I'll be okay." *Please, God, give me the strength to be okay. I need to be okay for Ben and for the boys.*

"Are you sure?" Ben cupped her chin with his hand. He tipped her face up and looked intently into her eyes. "You're sure you're okay with him being in the house?"

"I'm okay with it." Thank God her voice came out firm and positive. She wasn't going to burden Ben with her nightmares. Not if she could help it.

"Want to talk about it?"

Meg shook her head. No way could she talk about it. Not without breaking down again. She wasn't sure she wanted to talk about this dog either, but she had to say something to reassure Ben. "T-tell me about the dog. Kip, I think Evan said? Is he really a hero?"

"He did what he was trained to do. Not sure if that makes him a hero or just a well-trained canine." Ben stood and reached a hand down to pull Meg to her feet.

"Why is he here?" Meg straightened her

shirt and picked at a loose thread to avoid looking at Ben.

"His human partner was killed in the line of duty. Kip is not adjusting well. Will suggested they bring the dog to me to see what I could do with him."

Ben peered at her intently. Meg could feel it, even though she hadn't yet met his gaze. She forced a smile and looked up. "They brought him to the right place, then. If anyone can help him, it would be you."

"We'll see about that." Ben's shoulders relaxed visibly. "Some dogs never recover. But he's too valuable not to give it a try."

"Hey, Mom!" Rick bounded into the living room with Evan and the dog on his heels. "Watch this." He turned to the dog and pointed at his brother. "Hold!"

Kip immediately pushed Evan to the carpeted floor and placed his paws on Evan's chest. Evan giggled and wriggled, but the dog kept him pinned to the floor.

"Off," commanded Rick, imitating his father's quietly authoritative voice. "Sit." Kip removed his paws from Evan's chest and sat. Evan was still giggling, thoroughly enjoying the game. Kip looked up at his young commander, his tongue lolling as if pleased at a job well done.

Ben watched the interplay between his

sons and the dog with a smile of pride on his face. "Maybe all Kip needed was to get out of the police kennels and spend some time with kids."

Conflicting emotions tore at Meg. Watching her sons following in their father's footsteps, imitating his gentle but effective way with canines should have filled her with delight. If only she was watching them learn how to whittle, or sail a boat or any of the other things their father was so adept at. But the presence of the dog stole her sense of satisfaction.

She didn't hate the dog. At least she didn't want to hate the dog. She just wished he didn't look so . . . so much like Scout. *It's not the dog's fault. I can't hold his genes against him. If only he'd stayed out in the kennels.*

"Can we keep him, Dad?" Rick and Evan piped almost in unison. Evan had one arm wrapped about the dog's neck. Kip hesitated and then gave Evan's cheek a quick lick. All three looked up at Ben. Ben looked at Meg.

CHAPTER 7

Scout tipped his head and looked back at his handler, clearly pleased with himself for finding the hidden object he'd been sent to find. Eager to have his reward, the bright green ball he loved, he backed up and sat as he'd been trained to do.

Meg bolted upright in bed. Her heart thundered in panic. *Smoke billowed out, stinging her eyes. Bits of debris rained down around her, and the big green transport vehicle rocked with the sound of the explosion.*

"Meg?" Ben's voice sounded alien and out of place in the echoes of Meg's nightmare.

Meg shook her head to clear it. There was no smoke. No explosion. And no Scout.

"Are you all right?" Ben sat up and cupped her shoulder with his hand.

"I'm — I'm good."

"You don't sound good." He wrapped both arms about her.

She tried to stifle the trembling so he wouldn't notice. "Just a bad dream, but it's over. I'm good."

Ben lay back down, pulling her with him. Panic rose in her chest. Every instinct told her to bolt from the bed and get out of here. Away from Ben and . . . and what? And go where? There was nowhere she could go to get away from the nightmare in her head.

She forced herself to relax in Ben's arms. *Breathe in. Breathe out,* she told herself. *Breathe in. Breathe out. Relax.*

"Want to talk about it?" Ben asked.

"No."

"Maybe talking would help. Get the nightmare out in the light and face it. You always said I was a good listener."

"It won't help."

She felt him sigh but couldn't decide if he was disappointed, hurt, or just tired.

"I just want to forget." She turned into him, burying her face against his chest. If he was feeling hurt because she wouldn't share what was obviously bothering her, she still wanted him to know she loved and trusted him. Silently she begged him to accept that there might be things she couldn't bring herself to talk about. At least not yet.

"I know," he murmured as he began rubbing her back.

You don't know. You weren't there.

Gently he massaged the nape of her neck, then her shoulders, then her back. His caress was soothing and undemanding and not meant to be arousing. She wished it was. Meant to be arousing, that is.

When Ben touched her with passion, the echoes of war receded. With his mouth on hers and his sensitive fingers urging her to arousal the wrenching memories she'd brought home with her fled. When he pounded into her, his need as urgent as hers, none of the guilt and anger could claim her. In those sensuous, heart-racing, mind-blowing moments, she could forget everything.

Breathe in. Breathe out. Relax. Don't think.

The trembling subsided, but the memories persisted. Meg gave up the mantra and slipped her hand between them. When her fingers slid beneath the waistband of his pajama bottoms, Ben sucked in a sharp gasp. The hand that had been rubbing her back froze. For several long moments Ben was ominously still. Then he relaxed and began trailing his fingers slowly down her spine. He welcomed her intimate touch with soft sounds of pleasure, not questioning why.

When Ben's alarm went off, Meg didn't stir. He turned off the annoying buzz and kissed her before he rolled out of bed. She pretended to be asleep. It was easier to feign sleep. That way Ben wouldn't ask about the nightmares. He padded into the bathroom and closed the door. Meg rolled onto her stomach and buried her face in his pillow. His scent lingered in the rumpled linen. She inhaled and relaxed.

She woke some time later, surprised that she had fallen back to sleep. A dead sleep, totally devoid of dreams. She glanced over at the alarm clock and then scrambled off the bed in a rush.

When she reached the kitchen, it was empty. The boys had left for school, and Ben was gone. Presumably out to his kennels. Meg poured herself a cup of coffee from the machine Ben had thoughtfully left on warm. Once again the kitchen was spotless, the counters cleared and wiped down, dishes stacked in the dishwasher. Even the floor had been swept. There was nothing left for her to do.

Tomorrow would be different. Tomorrow was Saturday. Was the Saturday morning ritual of waffles and cartoons still followed? Or had that changed in the months she'd been gone, too? There was so much Meg had missed out on this past year. She felt like a stranger in her own family. How long was it going to take before she got up to speed again?

She still had twenty-six days of leave. Twenty-six days to relearn the life she'd left behind and the things her menfolk did or didn't do.

But besides that, what was she going to do with herself? She sat at the counter staring at nothing and considered the question. She got off the stool and went to consult the calendar on the wall. Ben's meticulous entries noted a dentist appointment for the boys, Cub Scouts for Rick and swim lessons for Evan, and an eye exam for himself. His brother Jake's wedding was written large with a heart drawn around it. And the Harvest Fair.

The fair! A thought percolated into Meg's head.

Every year their little parish of St. Theresa's held a huge and successful fair that drew people from all over the county. And every year except last year, Meg had set up a craft workshop just for kids. She ran her forefinger over the squares, counting the days between now and then.

Planning for the fair would have been months in the making, but maybe whoever was running it would welcome her return. Aunt Bea was probably still in charge? Meg would have to call the church office and find out. She had less than three weeks if it was still possible at all. Something to do, and being part of her community, was just what she needed.

Meg hurried into the hall and reached for the rope attached to the attic hatch.

What sort of craft could she think up for little kids to do this year to make holiday gifts for their parents? There were always the tree ornaments with the children's photos inserted. She'd done those every year, first with an ancient Polaroid and more recently by hauling her digital camera and a printer to her Elf's Workshop.

No adults were allowed except the helpers, in order that the gifts would be a surprise for the moms and dads. Meg would have to think fast and be creative to come up with a new idea for the kids. Tree ornaments were all well and good, but by now, hardly a surprise to anyone.

She yanked the hatch down and stood back to let the ladder unfold. Then she climbed the dusty steps into the dim attic interior. Where were those totes?

Hadn't she left them parked next to the chimney? Apparently not. A neat line of clear plastic bins stood on the far side of the chimney, but those, she knew, held outgrown clothes or stuff that was out of season. The boys would need their winter jackets soon, if nothing else.

Meg hauled the bin with winter outerwear to the top of the steps and then wrestled them through the opening and down to the hall below. She sorted it right there in the hallway, dumping hats, mittens, scarves, and jackets in a heap. When she'd finished, she shoved the nearly empty bin back up the ladder and into the attic.

Then she went in search of a flashlight to take a more thorough look around the attic for the missing craft totes. They were bright teal blue, bought on sale just for the storage of her Elf's Workshop gear. They couldn't be that hard to find. Half an hour later, she stood in the middle of the attic, her hands on her hips, her hair straggling into her face, and her teeth gritted in frustration.

Where were those totes?

"You did what?" Anger exploded in Meg's head.

"I didn't think you'd mind." Ben ran his

fingers through his blond hair, leaving it standing on end. His brows bunched together in puzzlement. "You weren't here, and she said she wanted to make sure there would still be an Elf's Workshop."

"That was *my* thing." Meg bit down on her lips to keep from screaming. She couldn't believe what she was hearing. Except she could believe it, and she didn't want to. Anne "The Snake" Royko had taken over Meg's pet project! And there had to be some ulterior motive. The Snake never did anything that didn't benefit herself. *Ever!*

Long before Meg even knew Ben, back when he was still a jock in high school, he'd dated Anne Royko. The only reason Meg knew that was because her big brother CJ was one of Ben's friends. Anne had gloried in being seen on the arm of the school hero, but shortly after Ben had been injured and sidelined for the remainder of his senior year, she'd transferred her devotion to the son of a wealthy banker in downtown Wilmington. A rich little "daddy's boy" with entrée into the country club and elite circles Ben could never aspire to.

The moment my back is turned that Snake comes sucking up to my husband with the outrageous excuse that she's concerned

83

about my project! Hah! I don't believe it for a minute.

The fury in her brain probably had smoke coming out her ears. Meg took a deep breath and dragged her anger into submission.

"So where are the boxes now?"

Ben shrugged one shoulder, his face plainly showing his discomfort and confusion.

"She didn't bother to return them?" Meg clung to her temper by a thread.

Ben shrugged again and shoved his hands into his pockets.

"And you didn't ask?"

Ben frowned and looked beaten. "I didn't want to ask. I didn't want to give her another excuse to come by the house."

Meg opened her mouth to ask why, but then shut it again. She'd been right! The Snake had wanted something else. She'd wanted *Ben.*

Anne Royko's brief marriage to an up-and-coming news anchor had left her a wealthy widow with no need to tie herself down to any one man. She was rich, beautiful, and sexy — a flirt with a reputation for casual affairs, and it didn't seem to matter to her that some of her conquests were married.

"Why not?" Meg couldn't help herself. Her own dark night of temptation lurked uncomfortably in the back of her mind, but guilt over one moment of temptation in Iraq didn't measure up to infidelity here at home. In her house! Why had Ben not wanted the woman here? Had something happened he was ashamed of and didn't want to repeat? Or was he afraid he wouldn't be able to resist the temptation of an all-out assault on his virtue?

"She came on to me," Ben admitted, his voice tight with something that could have been either guilt or distaste.

"And — ?"

"And nothing. I just didn't want her here." Ben yanked his hands out of his pockets and gestured vaguely, taking in the room, or perhaps the whole house. "This is our home, Meg. I didn't want her in it when you weren't here."

Ben had never lied to her before, and he'd been faithful to her for years. Long before she even had a right to expect his fidelity. Through all her absences and commitment to the Marines. Why had the thought even popped into her mind? Was she projecting her own guilt onto him?

Meg forced herself to let go of her unfounded suspicions and crossed the room.

85

She wrapped her arms about Ben's waist. "I'm sorry. I didn't mean it the way it sounded. I'm just pissed that she took over my project. It's my stuff. I paid for it, and the idea was mine, too."

Ben laid his cheek atop of her head and hugged her. "Maybe the boxes are still at the church. I'll take a spin by there on my way back from Mom's this afternoon and check. She was a lousy chief elf anyway."

After Ben had gone out again to return the tables he had borrowed from his mother for Meg's coming home party, Meg sat at the kitchen counter. Paperwork with the unmistakable imprint of the Marine Corps was spread out before her. Decisions to be made. Stay in or resign her commission? If she left, what did she want to do with her life? Her career? If she stayed in, the chances of being deployed again were weighted against her. And if she went, how did she feel about leaving Ben vulnerable to a siren like Anne Royko? Could she even trust herself?

Chapter 8

When Meg heard the screen door slap open, she looked up from the casserole she was putting together for dinner. She wiped her hands on a towel, hurried to open the kitchen door, and found Ben struggling with the doorknob while balancing two bright teal plastic bins in his arms. He eased past her, kissing her on the way by, and plunked the bins down in the middle of the kitchen floor.

Will followed with another bin. "Hiya, kiddo." Will dropped his bin on top of Ben's and gave Meg a peck on the cheek. "What's for supper?"

"I'm a lieutenant in the United States Marine Corps. I think it's time to stop with the kiddo thing." Meg planted her hands on her hips and tried to keep a stern look on her face. But Will just grinned at her, and she couldn't help grinning back. "Did Ben invite you for dinner, or did you invite yourself?"

"I invited myself, and Ben took pity on me."

"Well, since you're here, Rick is working on one of his Cub Scout projects, and he's having trouble. I never heard of the kind of kite he's trying to build, so I can't help him. Maybe you can check it out and fill me in."

"Sure thing. Is he in his room?" Will tossed his jacket to Ben as he headed for the hall and disappeared around the corner.

"I think Will is really enjoying being a Cub Scout den father," Ben observed as he hung his own and Will's jackets on the hooks by the door.

"I thought he was an assistant troop leader?" Meg watched while Ben unlaced his boots and removed them.

"He still is. But when Jerry Hudson's company transferred him to the west coast, someone had to step in and take over as a den father or mother. Rick begged Will, and you know how persuasive Rick can be. Will was a little nervous about taking over without much warning, but he's good with the boys. And he's good at organizing and keeping them in line. And they like him."

"He should find a wife and have kids of his own."

Ben chuckled. "He says he's looking for

your clone."

"I'm a one of a kind," Meg replied, enjoying an unexpected spurt of amusement.

"And thankfully, I found you first." Ben pulled her in for a kiss.

"I'd have picked you anyway," Meg assured him, returning his hug. The two men could not have looked more alike, yet their personalities were so different. Will was the extrovert while Ben was more reserved. Both were warm-hearted and had a ready sense of humor, but Will's tended to be more boisterous while Ben's was sly and offered with diffidence. Except for the airline attendant from Raleigh that he'd been engaged to, Will had never dated a woman longer than six months tops, while Ben, on the other hand, had been committed to Meg since the day she'd turned eighteen. Will was a great guy, but Ben was for keeps.

"I'm glad to hear it." Ben kissed her again and then squatted down to inspect the bins.

"Where were they?" Meg asked as she joined him.

"Mom had them." Ben snapped the clasps off the first one. "She found them sitting all by themselves in the rec hall at church when everything else had been cleaned up and taken out. She recognized them as yours, so she took them home with her own stuff. She said Aunt Bea asked about the workshop this year, but Mom didn't know if you'd be home in time to pull it together."

Meg noticed that the plastic clasps that held the lid on one of the bins were broken, and there was a crack down the side of the bin.

"Actually," Ben confessed, "Mom reminded me that she told me a year ago that she had them. Somehow I forgot."

Meg glanced at Ben.

"Sorry." He bunched his shoulders in apology.

Should she interpret that to mean he'd been trying to put Anne Royko out of his mind? Including wiping her workshop gear off his radar? Just what had he meant by "she came onto me?" Had he been tempted? Had he been doing his best to bury guilt?

Meg shook her head and turned her attention back to the bin. Ben was too transparent. It was her own guilt that was making her see things that weren't there — making her read intent that had never entered Ben's head.

She opened the tote. The contents had been dumped carelessly into the bins. Odd bits of colored paper mixed with crayons and colored markers, pipe cleaners, and holiday trimmings all piled messily into the bin with no thought to their possible reuse another year.

Meg clenched her teeth. This wasn't Ben's fault. Except, he *had* given the stuff to The Snake in the first place. So maybe it *was* his fault. Partly his fault at least. Meg struggled to hold onto the feeling of contentment that had been percolating through her just moments ago.

Ben began removing the contents, flattening the sheets of colored paper into a stack and collecting the markers into a pile.

"Most of it seems salvageable." Then he began pulling at the loose ends of red and green yarn. "Or maybe not."

Meg pulled the bottom bin free and opened it. It was just as bad as the last one. Her project two years ago had been Snow Dudes, made from white sport socks. Now the remaining packages of socks had all been opened and tossed back into the bin with no thought to order or keeping them clean and dry. Bright colored feathers purchased to adorn their heads were clumped together, broken and matted with some unknown substance. Meg lifted it cautiously to her nose and sniffed. Coffee. The Snake had spilled coffee on the feathers and didn't even have the sense to toss them out.

Meg slumped onto the floor and glared at

the mess in front of her. It was a good thing Anne Royko was not sitting in Meg's kitchen at this very moment, because Meg would have scratched her eyes out. Or worse. Another woman might have cried at this point, but not Meg. Fury rose in her so sharply that she had to clamp her mouth shut before she took it out on Ben.

She'd put Ben through a lot over the years and especially over this last year. She'd left him to hold down the fort, run his business, be mother and father to their boys, and manage every other aspect of their family life on his own. The fact that he'd been conned into turning over Meg's fair project should be the last thing on her list of things to gripe about.

Meg got to her feet and went to wash her hands. She turned back to Ben who was still struggling to sort the contents into salvage-able piles. "Just toss it."

"All of it?" He looked up, eyebrows arched. He patted some of his piles as if checking to make sure they were still there.

"I'll buy new stuff."

"The socks at least," he said, bundling them into a plastic shopping bag he'd found tangled in the mess. "They can be washed. I'll wash them."

"Fine!" Meg bit the word off short. Her

anger was all out of proportion to the issue. Had she brought more than guilt home from the war? She'd heard military wives complaining that their newly returned soldier-husbands tended to have short fuses over seemingly nothing. *Am I no better?*

"Fine," she said again, tempering her voice this time. "I'll wash the socks. And two of the bins are worth keeping. Just toss the broken one and all the stuff inside."

She turned back to the casserole.

Ben came up behind her and wrapped his arms about her waist. "I'm sorry. I should have known better."

Meg shrugged but didn't say anything. He *should* have known better.

"Forgive me?" He squeezed her a little and kissed the back of her neck.

"Yeah."

"Say it like you mean it."

Meg turned in his arms and snaked her hands behind his head. "I forgive you." She pulled his face down to hers and kissed him.

"That's more — like it," Ben said a little breathlessly when she let him go again. "I was planning on taking a shower. Want to join me?" He winked at her as he moved toward the door.

Meg frowned. "With your brother here? I don't think so! I can only imagine the ragging he'd dish out."

"I'll make it a cold one, then." Ben disappeared down the hall.

Meg finished the last of the casserole and bent to slide it into the waiting oven, all the while mulling over satisfying possibilities of retribution for Anne Royko.

First thing the next morning, Meg called Beatrice Quinn, the town manager's wife, to find out if it was too late to get the Elf's Workshop set up for this year's fair. Mrs. Quinn looked so much like Andy Taylor's aunt of Mayberry fame that everyone in Tide's Way called her Aunt Bea whether they were related to her or not. She'd been running the annual St. Theresa's fair with a bustling efficiency that belied her age for as long as Meg could remember.

Aunt Bea was delighted to hear Meg's voice, stopped to thank God that Meg had returned home in one piece, and then told Meg it was never too late for the Elf's Workshop. They would find a place to fit her into the program and a nice location in the church hall.

Next, Meg booted up Ben's kitchen laptop and logged onto the Internet to look for a new project idea she could pull together in just a couple weeks' time. As she scrolled through one of the craft sites she'd found, Kip wandered into the kitchen and sat by the back door watching her. Maybe he needed to go out. She got up to open the door, but the dog sat gazing at her with a probing yellow stare.

If only his face wasn't so unusually dark. If only he didn't look so much like Scout. The hair on the back of Meg's neck prickled, and her heart felt like it was being squeezed. Kip could have been Scout's littermate, and the uncanny resemblance unnerved her. Meg went back to the computer and did her best to ignore the watching dog. Eventually, he settled down and dropped his head onto his front paws, but his unblinking gaze continued to follow her every move.

It was a relief to find an idea she liked and gather up her purse and get out of the house.

First stop, her mother's trailer.

In addition to being a drunk and a slovenly housekeeper, Mary Ellen Grant was a packrat. A packrat with a penchant for saving every glass jar that ever came her way from plain peanut butter jars and faceted jelly jars to an endless array of jars in all sizes and shapes. The project Meg had found online involved turning ordinary glass jars into pretty luminaries by covering their outsides with colored paper with holes punched in whatever pattern a child could create. Tea light candles were cheap at the Dollar Store, so if she could talk her mother out of a significant portion of her horde, this would be a great Elf project and easy to pull together in a short time. Even toddlers could punch holes in colored paper to decorate a light for their moms.

Guilt tugged at the back of Meg's mind. Her mother had not been at the homecoming bash the Camerons had thrown for Meg. But since Mary Ellen Grant was an alcoholic, and Meg could never count on how she would behave, her absence had brought more relief than concern.

Mary Ellen was still her mom, though, and Meg loved her. Her mother could no more help being who she was than kittens could help being adorable and curious. *I should have come to see Mom the first morning after I got home instead of waiting nearly a week. And I only came today because I want something. What kind of a daughter have I become?*

Her mother's trailer was not a place she visited often, or enjoyed being at. There were too many bad memories associated with the place, but that was a lousy excuse to justify avoiding her mother. *I'll visit first and then ask about the jars.*

As she pulled into the rutted patch of bare dirt that served as her mother's driveway, Meg's gut tightened. *I'll try to visit more often, Mom. I promise.*

Meg climbed from the car and heaved a sigh. She picked her way carefully over the rutted dirt to the rickety metal stairs. The railing had been recently replaced. CJ or Stu must have been by to fix it. *At least my brothers are watching out for Mom.* Meg shrugged off the weight of self-reproach and knocked on the door.

"Mom?" Meg knocked again.

"Is that my baby girl?"

Meg could just make out her mother's response, muffled as it was by the still-closed door.

Then the door swung open, and Remy McAllister stood holding it for her to enter.

Meg swallowed her shock. Remy McAllister! The last person Meg had ever wanted to see again.

His slow smile and the calculating glint in his eye hadn't changed a whit.

Meg felt the blood drain from her face. Her stomach churned, and she had to fight for her composure. She wanted to turn and run. But she wasn't a defenseless kid anymore. She was a Marine. Marines didn't back down from anyone. Least of all, this sorry piece of trash that called himself a man.

She squared her shoulders and stepped past McAllister into the claustrophobic interior of her mother's squalid trailer. Her mother tottered toward her, clearly already drunk even though it wasn't yet ten o'clock in the morning.

"Baby Girl." Her mother enveloped her in an embrace that reeked of gin. "Where you been? How come I haven' seen you 'round?"

Meg returned her mother's hug, then freed herself and stepped out of the alcoholic miasma. "I was deployed, Mom. Out of the country."

Mary Ellen Grant pinched her brows together as if trying to recall why Meg would have been out of the country. Then she smiled again. "You're a Marine. I remember now. But you're home." She reached for Meg's hands and checked her out. "And not hurt. Praise be." Mary Ellen sank onto the couch and patted the space next to her.

As casual as if I was out on a date and missed my curfew. Meg sat on the chair opposite her mother.

"You've been gone so long." Mary Ellen lifted her nearly empty glass to her lips and drained the rest of her drink. Then she looked around as if trying to recall where she might have left the bottle.

Meg heard McAllister move behind her but refused to turn and acknowledge his presence. He reached over her shoulder to refill Mary Ellen's glass. Instantly a jumble of memories full of helpless panic and revulsion raced through Meg. Disgust rose up in her throat and almost choked her.

She grimaced, doing her best to ignore McAllister and respond to her mother. "It was a long time, Mom. Too long. I just got back. That's why I haven't been by to see you." Did CJ and Stu know how bad things had gotten with their mother? They hadn't mentioned it at the party. The subject of their mother hadn't come up. Probably because CJ and Stu were as relieved by her absence as Meg had been. Another wave of guilt washed over her.

"Well, surely you weren't where all those nasty bombs are. They don' send women to those places." Mary Ellen took another swallow of her drink and cradled the glass lovingly in her hand, comfortable and secure in the hazy world she'd created for herself.

The door behind Meg shut, and the weight of a man's footsteps descended the metal stairs. Her shoulders relaxed for the first time since he'd opened the door at her knock. She didn't know where he might have gone or for how long. She was just happy for the reprieve.

"How long has McAllister been back?"

"Remy?" Mary Ellen's face took on a soft glow. "A month. I think. Maybe a little longer. He's stayin' this time. I just gotta get myself straightened out. But he's staying. He promised me."

Meg's vow to herself to visit her mother more often had just become exponentially harder to keep. She was all grown up and not cowed by any man, but McAllister wasn't just any man. He was a nightmare from her past.

The sooner Meg got what she came for and got out of there, the better. If the jerk had a job, she'd come back to see her mother when he was at work. But right now, she couldn't wait to leave.

"I came to ask if I could have some jars."

"My jars? You want my jars?" Mary Ellen tipped her head and looked at Meg as if she'd asked for her life savings rather than a collection of worthless jars.

"I've got a project." Meg began to rise and then forced herself to stay sat and tell her mother all about the fair project she had in mind.

Mary Ellen listened to Meg's plan wearing an expression of vague interest, but then shrugged good-naturedly. "Sure thing. I knew them jars would turn out useful someday." She took another swallow from her glass. "Take however many you need." She looked past Meg and then back at her as if she'd forgotten McAllister was no longer lurking in the background. "Remy can carry 'em to the car for you."

Meg jumped to her feet. "No need. I can handle it myself. Thanks, Mom." She bent to kiss her mother's cheek and bolted for the door before her mother could summon McAllister to help with the lugging.

There was no sign of the man when Meg stepped out of the trailer and made her way toward the shed. *Thank you, God!*

When she opened the rusted door to the storage shed behind her mother's trailer several cockroaches scurried out of sight, and a box filled with old newspapers nearly toppled out on top of her. Meg shoved the newspapers back and reached for the bigger box underneath, checked to make sure it contained the jars she had come for, and hauled the box out to her car. She dashed back, grabbed two smaller boxes of jars, hip-checked the shed door shut, and hurried to her car. Only after she'd turned back onto the paved road and was out of sight of the trailer did Meg notice she was trembling.

She started to pull into CJ's auto garage but changed her mind. No need to stir up trouble for her brothers if they didn't already know about Remy. She had to get a grip on herself.

Meg bit her lip. If only she'd told Ben about Remy a long time ago, she could have gone to him to talk it out and get past it. Seeing Remy like that had rattled her more than she liked to admit.

I can deal with this. Put it into perspective, for Pete's sake. He can't hurt me; just bury it and forget about him. Don't burden Ben with this now after all these years.

CHAPTER 9

Meg drove on past her brother's garage, still arguing with herself. She had plenty of new nightmares she wasn't sharing with Ben. He'd only feel even more hurt if she dragged out a bunch of old ones she'd never told him.

Ben was her hero, and he'd understand. But he would be sad that she hadn't trusted him enough to be honest about why intimacy had scared her when they'd first started dating. Just as she knew he was upset now because she couldn't find a way to share her wartime nightmares with him.

As she approached the junction of the road to the beach and home, the shiny silver New York transplant that was Joel's Diner caught her attention. The parking lot was nearly empty, typical for middle of the morning, middle of the week. Maybe another cup of coffee and a slice of peach pie would help to put the unnerving memories of Remy McAllister into perspective and out of her mind.

The bell over the door jingled as she entered, and Margie Barnes pushed through the swinging doors from the kitchen.

"Welcome back." Margie hurried around the counter to envelop Meg in a warm hug. When they parted, Meg slid into the nearest booth, and Margie plunked herself down on the other side of the table. "I'm sorry I didn't get to your big party, but I was down for the count. I had two wisdom teeth pulled, and whatever they gave me made me dizzier than a carousel. And sick. So how ya doing?"

"I'm okay." Meg's stock answer. "But I've missed Joel's peach pie." Joel's Diner looked like it was plucked off the streets of Long Island, New York, but the menu was all North Carolina — including grits, hot dogs with everything but grits, and peach pie.

Margie scrambled to her feet. "Coming right up. You want coffee with that?"

"Black," Meg replied to Margie's retreating back.

Margie was already hustling around the end of the counter toward the pie rack. "You home for good now?" she called across the counter as she slid a slice of the sweet, juicy pie onto a plate.

"I better be," Meg answered. "I'm trying to decide —"

"Hang onto that thought," Margie interrupted. "I gotta get some clean mugs from the kitchen."

Margie returned to the table a few minutes later, balancing a tray that held two slices of pie and two steaming mugs of coffee. "I'm taking my break so we can do some catching up. You were saying you had a decision to make?"

Meg took a bite of her pie and then set the fork down. "I'm trying to decide what to do next. My hitch is up in a couple months, so I can get out if I want. But then what? I always planned to be a cop. But eight years as an MP, and I'm done with that."

Margie eyed her with a frown. "I never really got why you were so intent on being a cop in the first place. Besides, signing up for a stint in the Marines seemed like a big price to pay just to get an education in criminal science. Especially when you don't need a degree to get into the police academy."

Meg looked at her friend and realized how much of her past she'd kept buried, even from her best friend. And Ben. She glanced away toward the kitchen where Joel and his assistant were prepping for the lunch crowd, then back to Margie.

"Back when I was really little — maybe three or four — Mom hooked up with a police officer from Wilmington. He was younger than she was, but he was really sweet. Probably the nicest man she'd ever had in her life except maybe CJ and Stu's dad. I never knew . . . "Meg stopped. She'd never told anyone but Ben about not knowing who her own father was, either. But she guessed most of the town probably knew anyway. "I never knew who my daddy was. CJ didn't know either. I guess — well that's no never mind.

"When Bobby Daniels moved in, he became the daddy I never had. I loved him, and I followed him everywhere whenever he let me. He called me his little partner and took me down to the station sometimes. He took me to the Sweetheart Dance when I was in first grade, and I loved that he wore his uniform and looked so important. It made me feel important. I guess that's when I decided I was going to be a police officer, just like him."

"Bobby Daniels?" Margie frowned. "Do I know this guy?"

Meg shook her head. "Not likely. He moved away a long time ago. He loved my mom, but they argued a lot. He didn't like her drinking, and she didn't like him being a cop. Eventually they broke up, and he left."

"And you never heard from him again?" Margie's pie was gone and her coffee mug empty, while Meg's was barely touched. Margie prided herself on knowing everyone in town and everything about them. Digging all this new information out of someone she thought she knew obviously had her undivided attention.

"Not long after he left Mom, Bobby gave up the police force and joined the Marines. He's been all over the world, but he still sends me cards, and he never misses my birthday. I've only ever seen him a couple times since he left, though. He showed up when I graduated from college, and he came back for my wedding. He's why I figured joining the Marines to get an education was a good idea."

"Too bad he and your mom couldn't make it work." Margie made a face. "I probably shouldn't be saying this, but that new guy she's taken up with is a piece of work."

"He's not so new, either. We've got a history, too," Meg blurted out before she thought about what she was revealing.

Margie's eyebrows flew into her black

fringe of bangs, and her blue eyes widened. "You're kidding. Right?"

"I wish." She should just shut up right now. But she wanted to talk about it and get past it. Margie wasn't a gossip, and she did care.

"You know you can trust me." Margie tapped Meg's knuckles. "Right?"

"Yeah, I know." Meg sighed. "McAllister was boyfriend number who-knows-what. He dropped into our lives when I was ten. Stayed a couple years and got run off when he got a little too friendly with me."

Now Margie's jaw dropped, and her eyes, which had been round before, grew even rounder. "He what?" She leaned across the table and grabbed both of Meg's hands. "He didn't — I mean, he didn't — who ran him off?"

"CJ."

"I can't believe you never told me."

"I never told *anyone.*" Meg couldn't believe she was telling anyone now, but once the catharsis began, she couldn't seem to stop. "I felt like it was my fault, and I was ashamed."

"How could it possibly be your fault? How old did you say you were? Like twelve or something? That's sick!"

"Yeah! I know that now. But at the time I

thought I was to blame. Like I asked for it or something. I was still pining after what I'd had with Bobby when Remy McAllister took up with my mother. He was tall and handsome, and I was as fascinated with him as Mom was. He taught me how to shoot my first gun. Even Bobby hadn't taken me to the gun range.

"When I hit puberty and McAllister didn't bother to hide the fact that he enjoyed ogling me, I was flattered. At first." Meg felt the flush rushing into her face, but the embarrassment fled at the look of sympathy on Margie's face.

She'd been a kid. What did she know about what was appropriate and what wasn't, back then?

"And then what? You aren't going to stop there and just leave me hanging, are you? What happened? And how did CJ come to be running the bas— the guy off?"

"I grew up," Meg stated flatly. Boy, had she grown up. Her mother might not have noticed that Remy had begun to show an unhealthy interest in her daughter, but Meg had. As the months passed, and McAllister's interest became more intense, her uneasiness had grown along with her sense of guilt.

"It was just little things at first. Things I didn't like, but didn't know how to tell my mother about. I felt like I'd asked for it somehow. One time I found him sitting on my bed when I came back from the shower with nothing on but a towel. And I thought maybe I should have known better than to walk around the house almost naked. He didn't touch me, but I could see that he was aroused, and I just knew I'd done something to make that happen. He left when I asked without doing anything, but after that I was afraid of him. I took to hanging out at CJ's auto shop after school so I wouldn't have to be alone in the house with him again."

Disgust clouded Margie's expression. "Did he ever touch you?"

"Yeah. That's when it all blew up, and CJ told him to leave. He didn't rape me, if that's what you're thinking. He just groped me. I was washing dishes, and he came up behind me. I panicked when he shoved his hands up under my sweatshirt and squeezed my breasts. He had me pinned against the sink, and he was twice my size. But then he started rubbing himself against my backside, and I started screaming at him to get away from me.

"CJ charged into the kitchen and was ready to call the cops. But McAllister threatened to report my mother's drinking problem to the authorities and made us believe he could get me taken away and put into the foster system. If I hadn't been so frightened, it might have seemed funny. CJ looked like a bantam rooster standing up to the biggest cock in the yard. But then Stu appeared, and it was two against one. CJ told McAllister to disappear. Permanently."

"And he went? Just like that?"

"He went," Meg confirmed. But not without leaving emotional scars that followed Meg into adulthood. Into her relationship with Ben.

"Does Ben know?"

Meg shook her head. Her guilt over what she'd thought was her fault in attracting McAllister's unwanted interest had been her secret. Until now.

She'd grown up eventually. Ben had patiently taught her the joy of intimacy when it was with someone you loved, and in the end, McAllister's behavior hadn't ruined her or the life she now had with Ben.

"I didn't want Ben to know. I was still ashamed about the whole thing."

Margie reached across the table and covered Meg's hands with her own. "I'm so sorry you had to go through that. It would have scarred me for life, I think. Have you seen McAllister yet? Oh, of course you have.

Otherwise how would you have known who I was talking about? So what are you going to do about him shacking up at your mom's again?"

"Nothing."

"Nothing? Are you kidding me? The man should be in jail."

"But he makes Mom happy. And not much else does except booze."

"I wouldn't want to be in the same room with him, no matter how happy he made my mom," Margie declared with a ferocious scowl. "You are more charitable than I would be."

"Not really. It's just something I'd rather forget. I wonder what Stu and CJ are thinking, but I'm afraid to ask. I don't want to stir up a hornets' nest and have them get in trouble."

"I guess you're right. Statute of limitations has run out, and decking the guy would just get them tossed in jail. But it would still gall me to have the creep living right under my nose, knowing what he did to you and got away with."

"I can't say I like it very much either. I couldn't wait to get out of my mother's trailer. But he can't hurt me anymore, so I'm determined not to let it bother me. I can't tell you how good it feels to be able to tell someone, though. Thanks for listening."

Margie slid out of the booth and came around the table to plunk herself down next to Meg. She wrapped her arms about Meg and hugged her for a long time without words. Then she got to her feet and began gathering up the empty plates and coffee mugs. "Anytime." Two men in jeans and hard hats came in and hiked themselves onto stools at the counter. "I gotta get back to work. But really. Any time you need to talk, you know where to find me." She gave Meg one last hug and hurried off.

Meg grabbed her purse and got up to leave. The two men turned and saluted her. She forced a pleasant smile, wondering what made them think she deserved a salute. She didn't know them, but maybe Ben did. It was a small town.

In the car, she mulled over all the stuff she'd told Margie. Suddenly her inability to tell Ben about John and what had almost happened in Iraq clicked into place. She'd flaunted her developing body around Remy McAllister because he'd liked what he was seeing, and she'd liked that he noticed. She hadn't meant for it to be anything more, but when he tried to take that admiration to its logical conclusion she had to accept some of the blame.

Had she come on to John, too? Had she done things to make him think she was receptive to his advances in spite of her being married?

A woman in a man's world had to be especially careful to keep to herself, and for the most part Meg had done just that. But after John had lost his dad, and she'd sat up keeping him company while he awaited arrangements for emergency leave and transport home, those barriers had been breached. She'd gotten into the habit of spending time alone with him in the command post and heading over to the chow hall with him. Her behavior had definitely set the stage for John to think she might be interested in more.

She could never tell Ben. Especially since she had enjoyed John's company and attention. As innocent as it seemed at the time, she'd gone past the unspoken boundaries. And what had happened in the end was all her fault.

She dropped her head onto the steering wheel and tried to blot out the surge of memories. Running to John when the horror of Scout's death had overwhelmed her. John's arms around her, offering solace against the pain. His mouth on hers, warm, sweet, and exciting. That momentary escape from the reality of war and destruction. Ben would never understand.

"Hang in there." John's big hands gripped her shoulders hard. His fingers dug in, bringing her back from the brink of shock. "You've been through worse. A lot worse. It wasn't your fault, Marissa."

"No-nobody calls me that," she protested. It was her fault. She should have known. She should at least have had a gut instinct. She pressed her hands against his chest to stop their trembling. Fine way for a Marine to behave. Breaking down over a stupid dog. She sucked in a shaky breath and tried to get a grip on herself.

"Marissa fits you." John's voice was gentle and filled with compassion.

"I'm just Meg. I've always been Meg." Meg sounded tougher. Less delicate. Better able to cope with harsh realities and the unthinkable. She had to pull herself together. This trembling, near-tears stuff had to stop. She tugged at the kerchief she wore around her neck to protect her face from sand on the road and began brushing debris off her uniform.

"Sorry," she muttered, looking down, searching for her missing helmet.

"Don't apologize," John said gently. "That's what friends are for." He bent and reached behind her, then straightened and dropped her helmet back onto her head. He squared it away with both hands, then pressed one thumb beneath her chin and forced her face up toward his. The brim of his cap shaded most of his face, but didn't hide the glint in his eyes or the beginnings of a smile lifting the corners of his sensitive mouth. "You were there for me when I needed a shoulder to lean on. It's my turn."

She stared back up into those shaded sea-green eyes, suddenly struck by the unusual color and the expression in them.

"Marissa?" His face was closer than it had been a moment before. The smile was gone. The glitter in those extraordinary eyes was gone, too. He was going to kiss her. She shouldn't allow it.

Her hands slipped up his chest to his shoulders. "John?" This was so wrong. She should get away. Run away. Run far and fast.

But she didn't run anywhere. She just wanted to forget.

"I just wanted to forget, John. I didn't mean —"

Meg woke, startled by the sound of her own voice. She was on her side. Ben curled behind her, his arm tucked across her belly holding her close against his body.

The dream faded quickly, but the fact it

116

had been about John didn't. What had she said? Had Ben heard her?

His breathing was steady and slow. He seemed to still be asleep.

Meg waited until she was sure, then lifted his arm and slid out of his possessive embrace. She grabbed her robe from the back of the bathroom door and slipped into the hall. The house was quiet. Moonlight filtered in the front windows, slanting in eerie patches across the living room, glinting off the glass fireplace door, creating long shadows. Then one of the shadows moved.

Meg froze. Heart pounding.

Scout lifted his head off his paws and looked up at her.

"Scout?"

The dog tipped his head. Meg started to reach out to him. Then she remembered.

Scout was gone. Scout was the reason John had been comforting her that day. Comfort that had led to something else. To John breaking all the rules. To her kissing him back with so much pent up passion it had shocked her. Shocked her back to reality.

Kip tipped his head and whined softly in his throat. Meg bolted from the room. Her heart tripped erratically as she turned the deadbolt and slipped out onto the porch.

Tiptoeing as if fearing someone might hear, she made her way to the swing that hung in the corner. She curled up on the swing, unfolded the fleecy blanket draped over the back of the seat, and pulled it around herself.

As her heart rate slowed and her thoughts began to settle, the truth hit her.

It hadn't been her passion that had shocked her back to sanity. It had been the touch of John's hand. The warmth and urgency even through the bulky layers of her uniform, cupping her breast, caressing her so intimately. Too intimately. Just like Remy McAllister back when she was only twelve.

She'd encouraged them both, then panicked when they responded to her invitation. Did that make her a tease or just plain stupid? And what about her promises to Ben?

What is wrong with me?

Margie could explain away the fiasco with McAllister. Meg had been just a kid then. She hadn't known much about men yet. She hadn't understood what McAllister might want if she led him on. But she couldn't claim innocence with John.

John knew she was married. She was a junior officer. John would never have crossed those boundaries if she hadn't sent him the wrong message.

If she hadn't clung to him, kissing him as if there was no tomorrow.

What else was he supposed to think?

Meg hung her head. Shame flooded over her like a tsunami. She'd hurt John, and she'd failed to honor her promise to Ben. Her promise that Ben would be the only man she would ever want.

Tears that ached to be shed were as far away now as they'd ever been. When was the last time she'd cried? When Bobby Daniels left? But she'd been six then. Had she cried when her grandmother died? She didn't think so, but maybe she had. In any case, she'd deserved the right to tears then. She didn't now.

She deserved to live with this penance of guilt. She deserved —

"Meg?"

Meg sucked in a stifled cry of alarm.

Ben came toward her across the shadowy porch. He was barefoot and wearing nothing but a ragged pair of cutoff shorts. "What's wrong?"

Chapter 10

Meg stood in front of the mirror at Francine's Frocks staring at herself, not happy with what she saw. Francine's was the only place to buy a dress in Tide's Way, and she didn't really want to have to drive all the way downtown to Wilmington. She didn't really want a new dress, either, but she had a wedding to attend. Jake's wedding. She had lost so much weight over the last year that everything she owned hung on her.

She had met Zoe Callahan for the first time at the welcome home party and had liked Jake's fiancée right off. She was so perfect for Ben's baby brother.

Jake was a gentle, loving man who'd been shafted by his first wife and left holding the bag with three daughters and an ailing mother-in-law. But he'd never lost his sunny disposition, nor had he ever complained about his abandonment, although it must have hurt him deeply. Meg had never once heard him say a single disparaging thing about the woman he'd married right out of high school, giving up all the dreams he'd had for himself and a great deal more trying to make things right after getting her pregnant.

Zoe Callahan was everything Marsha Jolee had not been. She doted on Jake's girls, she cared deeply for the mother-in-law suffering from Alzheimer's, and she loved Jake to distraction. That had been obvious. Ben had told Meg about the courtship and the events leading up to Jake delivering Zoe's baby in the middle of a hurricane via Skype a month ago. He'd grinned happily as he'd told her how totally in love his brother was, but how long it had taken Jake to see his feelings for what they really were. The whole family was thrilled for him.

Jake deserved his happiness. He deserved Meg's best effort to show up at his wedding, cope with being seated near the front of a packed church, and get through a chaotic reception afterward. Meg knew about the tiny preemie that had been born beside the road some years back — an event Jake had just happened to come upon on his way home from the station one night. And she knew some of the anguish Jake had felt when the lifeless little body in his hands had been unable to survive despite all Jake's efforts to revive it. He must have been scared to death when Zoe went into labor, and he was the only one on hand to help her. Yet he'd held it together. With no power, no coaching, no training, and just candles for light he'd held it together. And it wasn't even his child. Zoe called him her hero.

Jake was one of Meg's heroes too. If he could hold it together, then so could she. She could square up to her issues with crowded places and noisy receptions and be there to rejoice with him. But she needed a new dress.

Back in the little changing room, she removed the shimmering gold dress and hung it back on the hanger. The color was all wrong in spite of her desert-tanned skin. Or maybe because of it. The last dress she'd brought in to try on was a bit pricey, but Meg slipped it on anyway and stepped back out to the big mirrors.

She ran her hands down the teal blue silk, turned a bit, and studied her reflection again. She was way too thin. Odd that Ben hadn't commented on it. He'd once told her he liked women with a little meat on their bones. Of course, at the time she'd been plump with pregnancy and feeling ugly about that. Ben was such a sweetheart. He always seemed to know the right thing to say. Or not to say.

Like last night when he'd followed her out to the porch to ask her what was wrong. He must have heard her talking in her sleep. Why else would he have been awake? Why else would he have come after her? How else had he known anything was wrong?

She should have told him right then. He'd asked, and she knew he'd have listened without interrupting. Until she confessed her feelings for the man who'd been there to offer her comfort when Scout had been killed; her moment of weakness might always stand between her and Ben like a hedge of brambles. It would prick her constantly.

She should have told Ben. She should have trusted him. Except, what if the hedge of brambles became a wall of bricks? What if Ben was hurt beyond forgiving?

Fear shouldn't have stopped her. She should have told him, but she'd let the moment slip between her fingers. She was a coward and a tease.

"What do you think?" The clerk stood beside her, eyeing the view in the mirror. She smiled and nodded her head. "I think it flatters you."

Meg glanced at the clerk blankly for a moment, then back at the mirror. *Right. The dress.*

Ben liked blue. He'd like this dress. *He'll like me in it.*

"Shall I ring it up for you?" The clerk was eager for the sale.

Meg checked the price tag again and then made up her mind. "Sure."

She hurried back into the dressing room to take the dress off and pull her jeans back on, trying not to think about her unforgivable lack of honesty with Ben.

Ben finished writing the last check, shut the checkbook, and dropped it back into the big center drawer on his desk. He glanced out the window to the driveway, but Meg's Honda wasn't back yet.

She'd gone out to buy a dress for Jake's wedding hours ago. Perhaps she'd had to drive all the way into Wilmington to find one she liked. He thought she looked good in anything. Or nothing. But she tended to have a hard time deciding when it came to buying clothes.

Maybe it had something to do with wearing uniforms so much of the time. One didn't have to think about them. Just pull on the uniform decreed for the current activity. Someone else did all the deciding. It was a skill he hoped she'd soon have to re-learn. He'd never tell her what she should do, but he prayed she'd choose to leave the military now that her commitment was up. He was more than ready to have her home permanently.

That day at the airport, with her back in his arms where she belonged, he'd been certain that now she was home everything would be fine. But now he was beginning to understand that a year in a war zone had changed her. Had changed them. He didn't know if they could survive another deployment.

He finished sealing the checks into their respective envelopes, placed stamps in the corners, and stacked them into a neat pile, then got up to carry them out to the mailbox.

Mike was working with one of the dogs out in the training field. Ben could have taken one of the other dogs out to work with, but he needed to get away. He needed time to think. He started to return to the kennels to get Columbo for company, then changed his mind and headed toward the house and Kip.

Kip sprawled in front of the door on the porch. His head was on his paws, but his eyes and ears were alert. He watched Ben approach but didn't move until Ben said his name.

"Come, Kip," Ben commanded from the foot of the stairs.

Kip got to his feet and came down the stairs obediently. Without any signal from Ben, he circled Ben and sat at Ben's left side, looking up, expecting the next command.

"You're a good fellow. Aren't you?" Ben reached down to run his hand over the coarse black and tan fur of Kip's head and shoulders.

Kip tipped his head.

"Maybe we should try you with guns? See if you've turned gun-shy. Or if it's just missing your partner that's your issue. What do you think?"

Kip's ears slanted forward as if he understood every word. He probably only understood two of that last exchange. Gun and partner. And maybe not partner.

"Missing Ray still?"

Kip shot a glance in several directions as if expecting his missing partner to appear.

"I guess that would be a yes." Ben started walking back toward the kennel. Kip trotted along at his side without urging. Back in his office, Ben unlocked the gun safe, retrieved his favored Glock handgun, then reached for a box of blanks. He filled the clip, shoved it into the gun until it locked into place, and then put the box back and locked the safe again.

Discharging weapons, even loaded with blanks, tended to cause alarm for folks who weren't expecting it, so Ben decided he and Kip would head out to the beach. It would be pretty much deserted at this time of year and this time of day.

Columbo, who'd met them at the door and carefully checked Kip out, accompanied them back to the door. "Sorry, Columbo, not this trip." Ben patted the big dog's head and ushered Kip back out into the parking lot.

Normally he would have put Kip into one of the crates bolted to the floor of the truck bed, but instead, he opened the passenger door and invited him to get in. Kip leapt nimbly onto the passenger seat and sat looking out the windshield with an expectant, tense set to his shoulders and body. Was he thinking they were going to find Ray? If that was the case, he was going to be disappointed.

Ben rambled on sociably as if he were talking to another human on the drive toward the beach. Kip glanced at him from time to time, but mostly kept his vigilant gaze on the road. He jumped eagerly from the truck when Ben opened the door for him. Ben reached under the driver's seat and retrieved a coil of rope with a snap hook on the end.

"Can't have you bolting for parts unknown if you take exception to the gunshots," he told Kip as he snapped the hook onto Kip's collar.

The dog lifted his face into the wind and sniffed. Ben sniffed as well. "Smells good, doesn't it?" Ben loved the scent of the sea and loved that his kennel was close enough for the scent to reach the house. But it was so much more pronounced here. There was a light breeze off the water, and little waves lapped noisily along the shore. He headed toward the sandy path that led through the dunes to the water.

A bright blue plastic barrel disguised with a wooden enclosure drew the dog's attention first. He sniffed carefully, then left his own calling card and trotted off to the next item of interest. That happened to be an old-fashioned anchor planted in the packed sand that spilled out of the dunes at the entry to the path. After sniffing thoroughly, Kip chose not to pee on the anchor. He looked back at Ben as if checking to make sure he was still following.

The sun was warm, but the breeze felt cool. Ben zipped his jacket all the way up as he followed Kip through the dunes to the beach. They walked through the soft sand to the hard-packed, still-wet shore and turned to follow along the tide line. Kip ran ahead as far as the rope would let him, but kept returning to check on Ben before trotting off again.

Kip didn't mind his feet getting wet, but he apparently had no desire to swim. Ben smiled. If Jake's golden had been along, she'd have made a beeline into the water. And once done with swimming, she'd have rolled in the sand, coming up looking like a sugar donut. Just as well Kip wasn't interested in getting soaked with seawater and bringing salt and sand back into the house. Meg wouldn't have been pleased.

Ben let his mind drift back to last night.

To Meg's mumbling in her sleep. *No one called her what?* He wondered. And what was it she didn't want to remember? What was it she could tell John, but she couldn't tell her own husband? *Is she afraid I won't understand? Or is it just a warrior's disdain for a civilian's lack of firsthand experience?*

She had almost told him. At least Ben thought she had been on the verge of telling him something when he joined her on the porch swing. But then she hadn't. Maybe he'd imagined her hesitation. Ben wished he knew more about this guy John and just what he meant to Meg. Beyond being her commanding officer and friend.

Ben pushed his hat back and ran his hand over his hair. He squinted into the glitter of sunlight glancing off the water.

He'd been so sure everything would go back to the way it had been before Meg left. He should have known better. He'd read enough about the transition from warrior to civilian, from a war zone to peacetime. But somehow, he hadn't believed it would intrude on the relationship he and Meg had always enjoyed. Maybe for other couples, but not them.

Even before they'd become lovers, they'd shared just about everything. From the mundane details of their individual days to politics and world events. Their hopes and dreams, their triumphs and their fears. They had shared everything. Well, nearly everything. She had never talked to him about her mother's boyfriend, either. Maybe there were other things . . .

Ever since her first night home things had been different, and he didn't know what to do about it. She was eager to share her body with him, more than eager it sometimes seemed. But whatever was going on in her head, she kept to herself.

Kip nuzzled Ben's hand. Ben had stopped walking, and the dog had come back to see why.

"It feels like she's shutting me out," Ben told the dog.

Kip gazed up him and wagged his tail once.

"She's hurting, but she won't let me help." Ben put his hat back on and began moving toward the dunes. Kip followed. "She won't even tell me what's hurting her."

Saying it aloud, even to the dog, suddenly made Meg's silence feel a lot more ominous. The uneasy feeling that had begun to grow in his heart solidified into dread. Ben felt suddenly afraid. But afraid of what?

Maybe it was nothing. Maybe it was like when you suddenly realize your toddler in the next room is unnaturally quiet, and you don't know what he's up to. Your heart races, and your mind comes up with all the worst possible scenarios until you finally get up to go look and find him sitting amidst a pile of stuffed animals flipping the pages in his favorite book. Everything was just fine, and it was only your imagination that had taken a flight into disaster. *Maybe I'm read-*

ing too much into Meg's silence.

She just returned from a war zone, and she's probably just trying to sort things out. She'll be okay. We'll be okay. I just need to be patient and be there when she needs me.

"I need to stop taking it personally," Ben told Kip. "Meg's always been fiercely independent and determined to face life head on. You knew she was a Marine? Right? It takes someone really tough to be a Marine." He ran his hand over the dog's head and down over his back. "Like being a working K-9. You have to be tough, too. And it's time for you to face life head on, just like Meg. Time to face life without Ray."

Again the dog scanned the area intently. Ben squatted in front of the dog. "Ray's gone, Kip. It's just me. You and me and the critters who inhabit this beach. Want to see if we can scare a few seagulls?"

Ben removed the Glock from the small of his back and racked the slide to load a round into the chamber. Kip eyed the pistol and lowered his head. Ben made sure he had a firm grip on the loop on his end of the rope, then raised the muzzle toward the sky and pulled the trigger.

Kip cringed but didn't run. *Good dog. Police dogs don't run when guns go off.*

Ben pulled the trigger again, three times

132

in quick succession.

Kip whimpered and shoved his face into Ben's crotch. *Not so good. Police dogs can't flinch at the sound of gunfire.*

Ben kept firing. A lock back on the gun signaled that Ben had emptied the clip.

Kip shivered all over, his face still buried against Ben's jeans.

This wasn't a good sign for an eventual return to police work, and it wasn't a good thing for a service dog either.

Ben pushed the gun back into his jeans and then sat down. He gathered the quivering dog into his arms and held him.

Maybe he'd been too precipitous with the gun thing. Kip had been doing well since Officer Brady had dropped him off. Hopefully today's little experiment hadn't set him back too much.

"I had this other idea," he told the dog conversationally. "If you weren't up to returning to the K-9 unit, you might be a candidate for a service dog instead."

Kip stopped shivering but kept the top of his head butted firmly against Ben's chest.

"You know Mike, right? The guy who works out in the kennel? His brother Ron came by a few weeks back, and you wouldn't believe the change in him.

"Ron's a disabled vet. He's got a chest

full of ribbons to prove he was a good soldier. But they sent him into combat one too many times. He wasn't much good when he first got back. Jumping when he heard loud noises and all. Wanting to spend most of his time in his room. Kind of like you."

Ben continued telling the dog the story of Ron Davis. It didn't matter that Kip couldn't understand. He understood the reassuring sound of Ben's calm voice, and that's what mattered.

"So then he got himself a service dog. He went off to this place in Florida where they train dogs, smart dogs just like you, to help these soldiers out. Kind of like guarding their back, if you know what I mean."

Kip raised his head from Ben's chest and plopped his butt between Ben's feet. Ben ruffled his fur.

"So anyway, I got this idea. Actually, it was Mike's idea. Not all the dogs we breed and train make it into police work. They're not all as good as you were." He grabbed Kip's head between both hands and ran his fingers through the dog's fur, down the sides of his neck and back. Kip thumped his tail against the sand.

"It occurred to me, this might be the perfect answer for you if you end up not going back to police work."

Kip thumped his tail once, then looked back down the beach in the direction they'd come. He was over his fright at the firing of the gun. Ready to go home. So was Ben. Meg would be home by now for sure. Ben got to his feet and dusted the sand off his jeans. He took the lead off Kip and coiled it up.

"Let's go home, shall we?"

Kip bounded down the beach. Ben followed, still thinking about the plan to train service dogs.

After Ron had returned from a four-week stay in Ponte Vedra, Florida, accompanied by a happy-looking mutt wearing a camouflage vest and a bright red bandana, the change in Ron had been incredible. Instead of hiding out in his room over his aunt Emmy Lou's antique shop, he was more likely to be in the shop greeting customers with Lola glued to his side. Or out walking along Jolee Road waving at friends and acquaintances. Ron's favorite hangout had become Joel's Diner, one of the busiest places in Tide's Way. Always with Lola at his side.

When the vest was off, Lola was full of mischief and play, but once it was on, she was all business, guarding Ron's back and restoring his ability to function in the world around him. Lola had been a rescue from a shelter according to Ron. They had saved each other, he liked to say. Ron had even gotten a job and was enjoying his work driving a delivery truck for the *Wilmington Star* with Lola riding as his co-pilot.

Ben could train dogs to do that. There were always a few dogs that didn't end up qualifying for K-9 work, but they were still smart, healthy animals. And there were plenty of shelters around with too many good dogs who just needed a life outside of a cage and someone to care about. He and Mike had already begun making plans. But first they needed to enlarge the kennel to provide space for the new program. And another building to house the veterans who came to train with their new companions.

Ben had applied for a second mortgage, or he would be applying for one as soon as he got Meg's signature on the paperwork. He hadn't told her about the new venture yet, though. There hadn't seemed like a good moment to bring it up. She hadn't once visited the kennels since she'd come home, and he wasn't sure why. She used to be one of his best trainers in her spare time. And she'd kept his books for him. Maybe he'd bring it up tonight.

He called Kip to heel when he reached the path back through the dunes. A few minutes later they passed the old anchor guarding the beach and arrived back at the truck. Ben unlocked the door, and Kip leapt up onto the seat. Ben went around and climbed into his own seat, then looked across the cab at the dog.

He had considered the possibility that even if Kip could not return to police work, he might be a perfect candidate for a service animal. But that wouldn't work if he continued to cringe at the sound of gunfire. Loud, unexpected noises were exactly the sort of thing good service dogs protected their wounded warriors from.

Ben ruffled the dog's fur. "What are we going to do with you, Kip?"

CHAPTER 11

Ben did like the bright teal dress. He'd first commented on it while it was still hanging shapelessly on the hanger. But if the appreciative gleam in his eye was anything to go by, he especially liked her *in* it. She'd been busy straightening the boys' ties and getting them out the door, or Ben would probably have grabbed an opportunity for a hands-on demonstration of his approval. But that treat was still ahead of them, once the ceremony was over and the party began. The thought turned her on.

And thankfully, distracted her from the claustrophobic feeling of being seated on the groom's side of the church, only two pews from the front. It had been years since Meg had been in the big church downtown, and it was bigger and more overwhelming than she remembered.

The back of her scalp twitched uncomfortably. Escape was impossible. With Rick and

Evan on either side of her, she was stuck in the middle of the row. Her sister-in-law Kate's family was to her left, and Jake's formidable godmother, Ben's Aunt Catherine, was on her right, blocking any speedy exit should panic overtake her. It would have been nice to have Ben's presence for security, but even that was out of reach. He was one of Jake's groomsmen.

You're not in a war zone anymore, she chided herself sternly. *Get a grip. Think about dancing with Ben at the reception. Don't think about two hundred people packed in behind you.*

Meg glanced across the aisle toward the row of pews at the far right side of the big basilica. Three smartly dressed older ladies whom Meg never met were probably from the guild in charge of preparing the altar and arranging the flowers. Several more people Meg didn't know sat right behind them, but Emmy Lou Davis was seated right up front. Emmy Lou loved weddings, and she always managed to snag a seat with a good view wherever she went.

Meg's eye went to the man sitting next to Emmy Lou. She didn't recognize him at first. Then she did. Good God! Emmy Lou's nephew was even thinner than Meg was and the ravages of war even more obvious on his face. Meg hadn't seen Ron Davis since high school. His brother Mike worked in Ben's kennels, and he'd kept Ben and Meg informed about Ron's military career. But the reports Mike had shared hadn't prepared Meg for this gaunt shell of a man. Ron had been a linebacker for the high school football team and must have weighed nearly twice what he did now.

Then Meg noticed the dog.

Again, the hair on her scalp prickled. The mixed breed dog clearly had a lot of lab in her. She had the kind of face that usually included a lolling tongue and a friendly welcoming expression. But at the moment, the dog was hyperalert. Her floppy ears were pricked forward at attention, and her eyes were sharply vigilant. She wore a vest with the words, *Please ask to pet,* and *Service Dog* stenciled clearly on the side along with a number of patches Meg couldn't make out.

"That's Ron's new service dog," Ben whispered, leaning across his Aunt Catherine to put a hand on Meg's shoulder. Meg nearly jumped out of her skin. She hadn't seen Ben approach. "I've been meaning to tell you about Ron. And Lola. I saw you checking them out."

Meg swallowed hard and tried to regain

her sense of calm. "What about Ron? Is Lola the dog?"

"Later." Ben gave her a quick kiss. "Sorry, I didn't mean to startle you. Gotta go." He gave his aunt a kiss as well and then strode to the front of the church to join Jake and the rest of his groomsmen.

Trying to calm her jangled nerves, Meg studied the four men standing to the right of the priest. They were so alike in appearance, yet so different in personality and life story. Jake was the youngest, the baby of the family. Spoiled by his siblings growing up, he'd made some pretty big mistakes when he was in his teens, yet when he'd had to, he'd grown up into the kind of man any mother would be proud of.

Ben was the quietest and the most patient of the brothers. Ben's twin Will was the garrulous, outgoing half of the duo. They looked so alike it fooled almost everyone, even those who knew them, until one of them opened his mouth.

Philip, the oldest of the four brothers, was Jake's best man. He'd joined the Marines two days after graduating from high school and had spent most of his adult life in one overseas post or another. He had a reputation with the ladies, but according to Ben, had never found the one he wanted to settle down with. Looking at him now in his dress uniform, it was easy for Meg to see why women vied for his attention. His height and long legs set off the bold blood stripe down the side of his blue trousers, and his chest was certainly broad enough for the sea of colored ribbons decorating it.

In less than a week he'd be going into harm's way again. Meg's heart shuddered at the thought. Where did her mother-in-law find the strength to love him and then let him go? Again and again? Meg looked down at her own sons and knew it must be the hardest thing Sandy Cameron ever did.

As she glanced back up and caught Ben watching her, she had a sudden revelation. If it was hard to let your son go off to war, what was it like to let your *wife* go? What had it been like for Ben while she was away? Somehow that aspect of her career had never struck her so poignantly. It was one thing to be the one going into harm's way, but what was it like to be the one left behind? Suddenly Ben's patience with her, his unstinting love, and his support seemed so much more than she could ever deserve or live up to.

Ben pursed his lips, then mouthed the words *I love you,* but a frown clouded his brow.

He's worrying about me. Meg forced a bright smile onto her face and blew him a kiss.

The weather being nice and the area around the altar being limited, photos of the entire family together had been saved for the riverside gardens at the reception venue. Meg didn't envy the photographer. She didn't envy herself, either. She was squashed in between Ben and his sister, her sons and two nieces fidgeting in front of her, and the rest of the groomsmen so close behind she could feel Will's tuxedo brushing against the back of her dress. But this was family. She was safe here. She forced herself to relax and glanced around at the happy faces jockeying to find their place in the family photo.

The Camerons were a handsome lot. Jake had never looked so happy as he cradled two-month-old Molly in the crook of one arm, and Molly's mom, his new bride Zoe, tucked securely against his side.

Jake's daughters, with grins as wide as their dad's, crowded in front of the happy couple. To Zoe's right, her equally big family jostled for their place in the family photo: her dignified white-haired father, her sister and maid of honor, four handsome black-haired brothers, one wife, one fiancée, and more aunts and uncles and cousins than Meg could count. Now there's a challenge, Meg thought. Just try getting this whole big crowd to smile at the same time.

"Say cheese," someone called out. Everyone dutifully muttered the magic word and smiled. As soon as the moment had passed and the photographer nodded his approval, the cluster broke apart like it had exploded. The kids all hurtled toward the tables laden with appetizers of every sort where other guests were already helping themselves.

"They're eager to check out what's been laid on for refreshments," Ben chuckled in Meg's ear.

"I'm surprised you aren't right on their tail," Meg shot back. Ben was always hungry, and it had been almost three hours since lunch.

"I can wait." He slid his hand around her waist. "Did I tell you how much I like your dress?" He pulled her around to face him, his hands warm and exciting through the silky fabric.

"You did." She grinned up at him, feeling more relaxed than she'd felt all day. "But if you keep touching me like that, I can't answer for the consequences."

Ben drew her closer until their bodies

were touching. He winked as he lowered his head and then kissed her with deliberate thoroughness. "Like that?"

"Benjamin. Joseph. Cameron!" she gasped, trying to catch her breath. It sure was easy to get her turned on lately. Was that normal? Was she normal? They were in the middle of a big family wedding, for Pete's sake, in one of the most posh venues in downtown Wilmington, and all she could think of was jumping Ben's bones.

Ben glanced beyond her. When he looked back down at her, he winked. "Think you can get your mind out of the sack for a moment? There's someone I want you to talk to." He gave her butt one last suggestive pat then set her free.

"I wonder who put my mind there?" she quipped, trying to collect her thoughts and calm her racing pulse.

"Me, I hope. Come on." He held out his arm.

Meg took the offered elbow, glad for something to hold onto. After more than a year in combat boots, she was out of practice in heels. The cute little shoes the clerk at Francine's had insisted were perfect for the dress had four-inch heels and nothing but thin, crisscrossed straps for support. Way out of Meg's league, but she'd let herself be persuaded. She followed Ben's lead, keeping her eyes on the ground, on the lookout for anything that would send her toppling into embarrassment.

Her heart clenched. There was that dog again. Sitting obedient and alert, wearing that distinctive vest. The dog watched their approach, glanced quickly up at the man to make sure Meg and Ben were welcome, then back to Meg and Ben.

"You remember Ron?" Ben glanced at Meg as he reached out to shake the other man's hand.

"If it isn't little Meggie," Ron Davis said, shifting his free hand from Ben to Meg. "All grown up. And if you don't mind my saying so, looking like a million bucks."

Meg shook his hand, feeling confused and a little off-kilter. Ron sounded like the boy she'd gone to school with. Like the jock she'd once cheered on the football field. But he looked like someone who'd been a prisoner of war. Someone who would never sound that cheerful. There was no way she could repay the compliment.

"Thanks. I don't mind you saying so, but Ben might." She angled a look at her husband who was making a gesture, asking to pet the dog.

Ron gave the required permission. "Say

hello, Lola."

Ben squatted and took the dog's proffered paw. "Good to see you again, Lola. I see you're on your best behavior, taking care of your buddy." The dog gave Ben's cheek a lick. Ben patted her head, then straightened.

"Lola is a service dog," Ben explained to Meg.

"I noticed." Meg had noticed a lot more than the dog. She was still trying to balance the war-weary look of her former school-mate with his cheerful, easy smile.

"Mike went on and on about how terrific Lola was and the difference it made in Ron's life," Ben continued as if he hadn't heard the sarcasm in her voice. "I didn't believe it until I ran into Ron at Joel's."

"I didn't believe it either," Ron added with a laugh. "At least I didn't believe the differ-ence a dog would make in my life until I tried it." He looked directly at Meg then, and she saw a glimmer of the haunted soldier she'd expected earlier. "I was a total mess until I met this wonderful girl here." He bent and gave the dog a quick hug.

"I heard you were wounded," Meg said, trying to understand how a dog could make such a big difference.

"Yeah, that too. I got a medical discharge six months ago after nearly a year in rehab.

But all that's left of that is an artificial leg and a bit of a limp. I can live with that. It was the PTSD that nearly did me in. That's what Lola helped with. But you don't want to hear that sorry tale."

Meg fought to find a small smile, even as her chest tightened. Too many soldiers with PTSD. She'd heard too many stories. Hers wasn't nearly as disturbing, but right now she didn't think she could cope with Ron's or anyone else's.

"Well, if she helps, then I'm glad you've got her," Meg finally said.

"Say hi to the lady, Lola."

Lola lifted her paw obediently. Meg could have sworn the dog was grinning. She hesitated. Another dog. Another sad soldier. The dog waited patiently. Finally, Meg reached down and took the dog's paw, shook it briefly, and straightened.

"Shouldn't we be headed into the reception?" she said to Ben. "They'll be introducing everyone and expecting us to march in together. Like everyone doesn't already know everyone anyway."

"Well, the Callahans don't know all the Camerons and vice versa," Ben said, smiling. "It was good to see you, Ron. You coming in?"

"No," Ron said a bit too quickly. "Lola

and I are going to go check out the river-walk. It's not every day we get all the way to this side of town, and the day is perfect." He gave Meg a hint of a salute and turned to walk away.

"So why did you want me to talk to Ron?"

"I wanted you to meet Lola."

"Why?" Meg glanced back at the war-ravaged man limping toward the riverwalk with his dog.

"It's an idea I had, but — you're right about being on hand to get introduced." Ben gestured to the now empty terrace. "I'll tell you about it later."

CHAPTER 12

Meg woke feeling stiff and disoriented. Then sat up in a rush when she realized why. She'd been sleeping on the sofa. The quilt that had covered her slid down around her waist, and she had nothing on but her bra and her panties.

What had happened to all the tantalizing promises Ben made about how he was going to take her dress off a little bit at a time, then make love to her? He had removed the dress. But they hadn't made love.

By the time they'd left the reception it was so late the boys had fallen asleep on the way home. Ben carried them in from the car and settled them into their beds one at a time, telling Meg she was next. Wandering into the living room to wait for the promised seduction, she'd pictured him removing the boys' shoes and slacks, wrestling to get their spaghetti-limp arms out of their dress shirts, and pulling the covers up before kissing each on the forehead and closing their bedroom door.

The strappy high heels had begun to pinch hours earlier. By midnight they just plain hurt. She'd sagged down onto the sofa to remove them. When Ben still hadn't appeared, she'd rolled down the pantyhose and discarded them as well. The important piece of clothing — the sexy blue dress — she'd left on for Ben to remove. But that's the last thing she remembered.

Kip lay curled in the middle of the room. He lifted his head when she stood up and watched her with an alert, unwavering gaze.

"Go back to sleep," she hissed. "It's too early to be up and about."

Kip put his head back onto his paws but didn't close his eyes.

Meg folded the quilt and draped it over the back of the sofa, then, carefully skirting the still watching dog, padded barefoot into the hall. On her way to the master bedroom, she detoured into the boys' room. Evan burrowed down in a little ball with just the top of his head showing. Rick sprawled across his bed with the covers shoved aside and half on the floor. She tiptoed in and pulled the blanket back onto the bed and tucked it around her sleeping son. Then she went to find their father.

Ben slept exactly like his older son when there was no one else to share the king-sized bed. He sprawled diagonally across the expansive mattress. Blankets draped partially over the bottom half of his body and mostly on the floor. His blond hair, while so much lighter than his son's dark locks, spilled over his forehead and into his eyes, just like Rick's. The only difference in their position was that Ben was hugging Meg's pillow to his chest.

For a moment, Meg stopped to wonder if Ben had slept hugging her pillow the entire time she'd been away. But then Ben stirred, and one eye opened.

"What time is it?" he asked sleepily.

"Four," she answered, crossing to the bed. "Where's my dress?"

"Dress?" Both eyes were open now.

"The blue dress? The one I wore to Jake's wedding?"

Ben smiled slowly. "I hung it up."

Meg glanced toward the closet and saw that he had, indeed, hung the dress up. He'd arranged it carefully on the padded hanger it had come on and hooked it over the closet door.

"I didn't think you wanted to sleep in it," Ben murmured, his voice still heavily laced with sleep.

"No, but I was looking forward to having you remove it." Meg lifted the sheets and blanket off the floor just as she'd done in Rick's room and climbed in beside Ben.

"I did remove it," he reminded her as he rolled onto his side and gathered her into his arms. "You just weren't awake to enjoy the process."

"You were going to tell me about the dog, too."

"It's four in the morning. Unless you're still in a mood to make love, then let's go back to sleep. We can talk about dogs in the morning." He ran one hand provocatively down her side, past her waist to her thigh where he let it rest, the heat of it radiating into her.

"Now there's an idea . . ." She moved to reciprocate.

Abruptly, a loud beep erupted from the pager on Ben's side of the bed.

Meg froze, her heart jerking into panic.

"Damn!" Ben rolled away to shut the pager off.

Ben had taken a hiatus from service as a volunteer fire fighter while Meg was out of the country, but this weekend, he'd stepped in to cover for Jake while he was on his honeymoon.

Ben rolled back and kissed Meg on the

neck right below her ear. "Hold that thought. I've got to go, but I'll be back. Promise."

He rolled off the other side of the bed and stood up. Meg's heart slowed its initial frantic pace, but adrenaline still flowed in her veins, leaving her flushed and breathing hard.

"Be careful, Ben." Meg sat up and watched her husband thrust his legs into a pair of jeans.

"I'm always careful." He grabbed a T-shirt out of his drawer and pulled it over his head. Then he shoved his feet into the old boat shoes he saved to wear down to the firehouse and headed for the door. But before he got there, he turned back, came over to the bed, and pulled Meg into his arms for a hug. "Keep the bed warm for me."

Ben hadn't returned while Meg was still in bed. Nor by the time Meg and the boys were ready for church. He still hadn't returned when she arrived home again after mass. The boys had been invited to spend the afternoon with friends, and Meg had the house to herself.

She made herself a sandwich and sat down to go over the paperwork for resigning her commission again. After staring at it awhile and still not sure what she was going to do, she pushed it aside.

Kip got up from the welcome mat by the back door and came to sit by her stool. Meg gazed down at him. If he wanted out, he'd be staring at the door, not her. She checked his dishes, but both were still half full.

"What?" she asked the dog.

Kip blinked.

"If you're looking to play, you'll have to wait for Rick and Evan to come home."

Kip watched her intently.

Meg started to reach out to pet him then drew her hand back. He looked so much like Scout. *That's not his fault,* the logical side of her brain reminded her. This time she did touch the dark head.

A pang of longing, grief, and guilt shot through her. She pulled her hand back. "It's not your fault," she said aloud to the dog. "But you're not him. I'm not ready for this."

She turned her back on the dog and pulled another stack of papers out of the folder of things that needed taking care of.

She owed her niece a check for the dance marathon she'd participated in for breast cancer. Ava's best friend's mother had organized the event, and Ava's little group had danced non-stop for five hours. Time to pony up, but the checkbook was out in Ben's desk. She hadn't been out there since she got back.

Suck it up, Marine. Time to get past this and get on with your life.

Meg slid off the stool and marched purposefully toward the door.

Almost as soon as she opened the door to the building housing Ben's dogs, the breeding and whelping rooms, and an indoor training ring, Ben's favorite stud Columbo ambled over to greet her. His entire body wiggled in welcome, and he made happy little noises in his throat. A year ago, she'd have knelt right down and gathered the eager animal into her arms and let him lick her face. But right at the moment, it was all she could manage to pat him on the head to acknowledge his exuberant welcome. He didn't seem put off by her cool greeting as he followed her into Ben's office with his tail wagging.

Ben's desk was as meticulously neat as he kept everything inside the house. She plunked down in the battered old chair he loved and pulled out the middle drawer, grabbed the household checkbook, and dropped it onto the desktop. Quickly she wrote out the check, logged it into the register, and shut the book again. Then she leaned back and pulled the drawer open to replace it, but before she could put the book back, she noticed a thick sheaf of important looking documents with the masthead of the local bank.

She drew the packet of papers out and replaced the checkbook. Then she began reading through them.

Meg pounced as soon as Ben let himself into the kitchen. "Are we in money trouble?"

Ben rubbed his eyes, trying to shake off the smoke and exhaustion brought on by twelve hours on his feet fighting a nasty warehouse fire.

"Of course, not." He shrugged out of his windbreaker and hung it on the hook. Then he shucked his battered boat shoes and parked them beneath the jacket. "Why would you think we were?"

"Because I found these in your desk." She shoved a sheaf of papers at him.

His eyes stung, and his body ached. He glanced down at the papers she thrust into his hands. The mortgage application and accompanying documents he'd left in his desk. The project he hadn't found the right time to bring up yet. "Can we talk about this later? I really need to get cleaned up and get some rest."

"I want to know why we're applying for a second mortgage," she insisted, ignoring his request.

Can't she see I'm ready to crash? My feet are being sucked down like I was walking in quicksand, and my head is packed with cotton wool.

"I thought the kennel was making money. It was when I left. What changed?"

"Nothing's changed. We are making money." Ben rolled his shoulders, trying to work out the kinks.

"Then why do we need to borrow more?"

"It's all connected to Ron's dog and the plan I have. I meant to talk to you about it last night, but you fell asleep." God! What he wouldn't give for a shower and a nap. His brain was numb with exhaustion. No way he had the energy to explain his plan so she'd see how great it was.

"So let's talk about it now." Meg's voice was unusually strident. She wasn't usually like this, and it confused him. *Or maybe it's me. Maybe I missed something, and I'm just too tired to remember.*

"It's a great plan, Meg. You'll agree. I know you will, but I gotta get some sleep first. Please, can't we discuss this later?"

"I've been home for more than two weeks.

money issue? You can't take a mortgage out without my signature, so if it's all that important, I'd have thought you'd have brought it up before now."

If only he could pull her into his arms and hug her and banish this angry stranger she'd turned into. But he stank of smoke, and she didn't look like she would welcome a hug even if he wasn't smoky and sweaty and disgusting.

He slumped onto a stool and set the paperwork on the counter. "I want to enlarge the kennels and set up a separate training facility."

"For what?" Meg planted her hands on her hips.

"To train dogs like Ron's dog, Lola."

Meg opened her mouth to say something and then shut it again. A crease appeared between her eyes.

Ben rolled his head to ease the pain shooting up the back of his neck. "There are always dogs that don't make the cut for police work. You know that."

"Yeah, but what does that have to do with expanding? You usually find good homes for them."

The unusual quietness suddenly penetrated Ben's fog. "Where are the boys?"

"At Sam's. Playing," was all the explanation she offered. "What do washout dogs have to do with Ron and Lola and needing a second mortgage?"

"If you had seen Ron when he first got discharged you'd understand better, but it's like this." Tiredly, Ben launched into an explanation of programs that had cropped up all over the country, most of them non-profit and not run by any government entity. They trained dogs, many of them rescues, to become service dogs for veterans suffering from PTSD.

"Ron is like a new man," Ben explained. "He was hiding out at his aunt's house like a hermit until someone convinced him to give this program a try. His brother drove him down to Florida to a place in Ponte Vedra. He was there for four, maybe five weeks. I can't remember exactly how long, but he came home a very different man than he'd been when he left. Ron'll tell you he still has a long way to go, but, Meg, you wouldn't believe the difference in him. It was the first time I'd seen Ron smile since he got out."

"I still don't get what that has to do with us and you wanting to borrow more money." Meg folded her arms stubbornly across her chest and rested her hips against the kitchen

160

counter. At least she didn't look quite as aggressive as she had a few minutes ago.

"I want to try training the dogs who don't become police K-9s to become service dogs instead."

Meg's brows rose. She glanced at Kip who'd been watching the entire heated exchange as if he'd been at a tennis match. "And dogs like Kip, too?"

"And dogs like Kip, too," Ben agreed. "And probably a few from rescue centers as well. But I need a bigger facility. I need a place for the veterans to stay when they come to learn how to live with their dogs once we're ready to pair them up. And for that I need money I don't have."

He had been so excited about this whole idea, but at the moment he was too tired to inject much enthusiasm into the argument. And Meg appeared totally dubious. It wasn't like her to question his running of the kennel. *Where is all this opposition coming from?*

She shook her head again. "I don't think this is such a good idea."

"Don't make your mind up until you have a chance to think about it." Ben saw all his plans slipping away, but tired or not, he wasn't about to give them up so easily.

"Thinking about it isn't going to change

my mind, Ben." Meg shoved herself away from the counter and went to the sink, turning her back on him. For a moment, they just stood there, not speaking, not even engaging. She grabbed a glass from the cupboard and filled it. But then set it on the counter without drinking any of it.

"If I decide to get out of the military, I need to figure out what else I want to do with my life. I haven't got another job lined up, and there won't be a second paycheck until I do. We can't afford to go borrowing more money right now."

"We can afford it. Even if you don't have a paycheck, we can afford it." His head pounded with exhaustion, and his patience was wearing thin. "Please, let's talk about this later. I really need a couple hours of shuteye. Then I'll show you all the numbers, my working budget, and everything." He got up off the stool and started for the door. Then he turned back and placed a hand on Meg's shoulder. She stiffened under his touch, but he didn't take his hand away. "This is really important, and I'd like to discuss it when I'm not so beat I can't think straight. Can you, please, try to understand?"

She looked up at him with her mouth pressed into a thin, hard line. He didn't kiss her. That look told him she wouldn't let him if he tried. "I'll see you in a bit." He turned and walked out of the kitchen.

"I'm not going to change my mind." Meg's voice followed him down the hall.

CHAPTER 13

Her leave was almost up, and Meg had an appointment with her CO at Lejeune. She didn't know what to tell him. Extend her reserve service or put in for a discharge? What next?

What she'd told Margie about not wanting to pursue a career in police work had been true. Either as a Marine MP or in civilian law enforcement. She had just never put it into words before, and the realization once the words were out of her mouth had been a little shocking.

She should be talking to Ben about it instead of Margie, but somehow it all seemed tied up in not knowing what she did want to be. And admitting it to Ben would be like telling him everything he'd sacrificed for had been a waste of time. So she'd talked to Bobby instead. Bobby had advised her to look objectively at the toll her deployment had taken on her and Ben and the boys. With the country constantly stepping up to deal with ever-increasing threats and hotspots, there wasn't much chance she'd stay home if she stayed in. Unless she managed to change her MOS. But that would require another whole commitment of service. Another whole span of years she couldn't call completely her own. Or Ben's.

But if she got out, then what?

Before she'd left for Iraq, Ben's helper in the kennels had been an older man, past retirement age, but still hanging on to his part-time work with Ben and the dogs. When she hadn't been on duty at the base, she'd taken up the slack. In what now felt like another lifetime, she'd loved being in the kennels, working with the dogs. Keeping Ben's books for him. But Iraq had changed everything.

While she'd been gone, Marshall had decided it was time to retire and moved to Florida where he now lived with his sister in Fort Pierce. Ben had hired Mike Davis, and Mike had taken over not just Marshall's place, but Meg's as well. Just turned thirty, he was full of energy and ideas, and now that Meg was home, there seemed to be no need for her to help out anymore. Not that she felt like she was ready to go back to working with the dogs. But even if she wanted to, Ben didn't need her.

Bobby had pretty much ordered her to level with Ben about her indecision. But then she'd found the mortgage paperwork, and they'd argued. Or at least *she* had. When Ben had finally come in, dog-tired after fighting a fire for nearly twelve hours, she'd ignored the weary, red-rimmed eyes and slumped shoulders. She'd forged on, demanding answers. And then hadn't liked the ones he'd offered.

After an evening of avoiding discussion on either issue, they'd gone to bed with an unspoken and uneasy truce between them and slept on opposite sides of the bed for the first time ever.

Which brought her right back to the unresolved question of what to do with herself if she left the military. What did she want? Even Bobby hadn't been able to help there. Instead, he'd reminded her that she was part of a team, and she needed to share her concerns with the other half of that team. In other words, share her confusion with Ben.

But there was no way Ben could under-stand. He'd never left home. He'd never experienced the things she had. No way could he understand the guilt and nightmares. Or the anxiety that boiled up inside her every time she thought about Ben's dogs.

Ben wouldn't know what to say about her indecision either. He'd always known what he wanted in life, starting with her. Or maybe starting with that Mustang he'd been fixing up in her brother's shop when they first met. He'd decided she was the woman he wanted to spend his life with even before she was a woman. He'd been her friend while he waited for her to grow up. He'd been a patient and careful lover, claiming her heart, her virginity, and eventually her hand in marriage.

Even when he was in college double majoring in business management and animal husbandry, the heavy load of course-work had been aimed at owning his own kennel and raising dogs for police work. He'd set his course and never looked back.

He just wouldn't understand the current chaos in her mind.

Meg tried to recall the zeal she had felt all those years ago when she wanted to go into police work because of Bobby. Discussing it with Margie had been like telling a story about someone else. The passion that had once been there for Meg was gone. She felt like a raft with no sails, drifting on an uncertain sea of obstacles toward a goal she couldn't see. Or to no goal at all.

Staying busy was impossible. For a brief flurry, she'd devoted herself to preparing for the church fair, but all that was done now, and she was just waiting for the event to happen. Ben seemed to thrive on being up early and getting the boys off to school. He enjoyed fixing dinner and assumed it was his turn at least half the time. He still took care of his own laundry and ironed his own shirts along with Rick's and Evan's school uniforms. All of which left her wondering what her role in the family was anymore.

Meg had been to parents' night at the boys' school, and there had been carefully penned notes to her as well as Ben, but at home Rick always turned to Ben for help with his homework. To be honest, the first day Rick *had* asked her for help with his math, she'd been lost. Her! Marissa Ellen Grant, math champ four years straight in high school, and she couldn't figure out what he was supposed to be doing on his second grade homework page. Ben had never been more than just average at math, but he seemed to get it.

Rick hadn't asked for her help again.

Only Evan seemed to accept her back into

his life as if she'd never been gone. Kindergarten didn't have homework she didn't understand. Life was a lot less complicated when you were only five.

Hoooooooonnnnnnnnk!

Meg jerked her attention back to the road. Heart thumping, she clamped her hands hard about the steering wheel and glared at the rearview mirror and the driver who had just leaned on his horn. A flood of adrenaline coursed through her body. Without even thinking about it, she assessed the traffic, checked her speed, knew she was where she should be, and knew she had been driving safely. What did this idiot want? The other car loomed ever larger in her rearview mirror.

She jerked the car onto the shoulder and jumped out, ready to tell the guy off. But he just swerved around her and continued on. She stood there, hands clenched and ready to fight. But there was no fight. More cars sped by, ignoring her as if nothing had happened.

Finally the effects of the adrenaline charge began to wear off. Now her legs felt shaky, and she leaned back against the fender of her car. The light but steady traffic on Route 17 continued to zip by her as she recovered from her out-of-control reaction to being honked at by an impatient driver wanting to pass. Finally, feeling steady again, she climbed back in her car, but instead of rejoining the flow of traffic, she pulled into the derelict, overgrown parking lot of a closed-down farm stand.

She'd been warned to expect a lot of things. Heart pounding alarm when someone slammed a door or a car backfired. The need to check behind herself frequently when she walked through a parking lot or stood at the ATM. Nightmares and waking up in a sweat, reaching for a rifle she no longer kept beside her cot. She thought she'd been coping okay with that stuff. But she hadn't expected this well of bottled-up frustration that burst out of nowhere.

Like the way she'd gone after Ben when he got back from the fire yesterday afternoon. Anyone with eyes in their head could see the man was beyond tired. Her initial instinct had been to put her arms around him and hold him. But then she'd remembered the papers in her hand, and she'd ignored his exhaustion. She'd attacked him with questions when all he'd asked for was a shower and a nap.

She'd been angry, but she didn't even know what she was angry about. And when he'd begged her to think about it, she'd flatly told him she wasn't going to change her mind.

But she knew nothing about this service dog program. Meeting Ron at Jake's wedding was the first she'd heard of it. She should have agreed to talk to Ron and Mike. She should have agreed to think on it at least. Just because looking at Kip filled her with despair and guilt didn't mean that Ben's idea wouldn't be right for someone else.

Besides, Ben had always been careful about money. She'd been totally unfair to lash out about that. What was the matter with her? That rudderless raft she was drifting on appeared to be well armed with cannons with which to fire on any would-be rescuers. She had to get a grip.

The debriefing with her CO had done nothing to clarify things in Meg's mind. She'd ended up telling Colonel Jenks she hadn't made up her mind about re-upping yet. In ten days she'd be reporting in to part-time duty again. Maybe by then she'd know what she was going to do.

Meg stood on the sidewalk juggling her car keys, debating whether or not to make a stop at the PX before heading home. There were things they could use, but she didn't know if she wanted to cope with the crowded PX just now. It had already been an unsettling day.

"Hey, Lieutenant!"

Meg whirled to see Captain John Bissett limping toward her. Her heart jerked in recognition. The last time she'd seen him, he'd been strapped to a stretcher headed to Landstuhl, Germany.

He took off the cap he was wearing as he approached. "Good to see you. You're —" He broke off to check her out. "Wow! You clean up nice."

Before Meg could bring her hand up to a proper salute, he stuck his hand out.

"You're looking pretty good, too." She took the offered hand. It was as warmly enveloping as it had been when he was offering her solace after Scout died. She snatched her hand back and decided to salute after all. "How long since you got out of sick bay?"

Captain Bissett hesitated as if counting in his head. "Eight days. I was lucky. It wasn't as bad as it looked. How are you doing?"

"I'm doing well, sir. I'm just —"

"Knock off the *sir* stuff, will you? I'm out of uniform and off duty. Besides, I thought we were friends."

Butterflies fluttered in Meg's gut. He *was*

a friend, and she wanted to keep it that way. Memories of how that friendship had almost gotten off track and the fact that she'd not told Ben the whole truth about John was her guilt, not John's.

"You headed straight home?" Bissett consulted his watch. "A few of the guys from our unit are meeting up for supper. It'll be good to catch up and see how everyone's doing."

"Well, I —" She should head home. It was Ben's pizza night so she didn't have to cook, but they'd be expecting her.

The captain shook his head and looked disappointed. "I guess you have a ton of things you need to do. Maybe another time . . ."

Meg didn't have a single thing she needed to do. That was the whole problem lately. With a spurt of defiance, she made up her mind.

"Where is everyone meeting up?"

"There's a new place off base, but not far. Not so crowded, at least for now, and the food's great. Where's your car parked? If you want I can drive you to it or bring you back to get it after dinner."

Considering her car was halfway across the base, she accepted his offer and climbed into his obviously new Corvette Stingray.

173

"Nice car," she said, running her hand over the leather seat. "This what you spent your combat bonus on?"

"It made a nice down payment. I needed something. My sister got the Camaro I used to drive when I deployed, so I didn't have any wheels."

"Didn't care for a Humvee?" she asked. Meant to be a joke, but once said, not so funny. Too many days spent in military Humvees in places they'd both prefer to forget. "Sorry, dumb question."

He ignored the question and her apology. "You mind getting your hair mussed?" He raised his eyebrows at her and ran a hand over his own closely cropped head.

When she shook her head, he put the top down. The engine purred to life, and he pulled away from the curb.

They hadn't even left base, and already Meg regretted her impulsive decision. She should have gone home to her husband and sons. Pizza night or not. The boys would ask where she was, and Ben would be expecting her even if she turned up a little late. But there was no way to change her mind gracefully.

She dug into her purse to grab her cell phone to call Ben and let him know why she'd be late. She punched the on button and discovered it was nearly dead. She should have remembered to charge it before she left home. Instead of taking a chance on getting a call through, she texted Ben to say she was having supper with some of the guys from her unit. He would understand.

Ben faced the wall, pretending to be asleep. He had no idea where Meg had been until nearly two in the morning. Her trip to Lejeune was supposed to have been just three appointments. One with her CO, one with the recruitment officer in charge of extensions and retirements, and one with the medics.

He'd discovered her text message after he'd tucked the boys into bed and figured she'd be coming in any minute. Then the minutes had stretched into hours, boosting concern to outright worry. When his own bedtime had arrived, he'd called her, but gotten no answer.

He'd considered calling Will. Even if he wasn't on duty, he'd be able to find out if there had been any accidents between here and Lejeune. But then Ben had decided if something had happened to Meg, he'd already have been notified. So he'd gone to bed. To do nothing but toss and turn and check the alarm clock every five minutes.

The sound of Meg's car crunching into the driveway alerted Kip and erased the need for worry. As the dog got up and trotted out to the kitchen, Ben pushed himself up against the headboard and waited for Meg to appear in the bedroom. She had some explaining to do.

But Meg didn't come directly to the bedroom. Eventually, he slumped back down to wait in comfort. By the time her footsteps came tiptoeing down the hall, he decided to feign sleep. Two a.m. was not a good time to start a fight, and he was still hurt and angry that she hadn't bothered to keep in touch or answer her phone when he called.

At some point in the midst of his worried pacing, Ben had begun to wonder which of her combat buddies she might have had dinner with. He kept telling himself that Meg would never cheat on him, but the name John kept popping up. John, her commanding officer. John, who'd been wounded and come home ahead of her. John, the name she kept mumbling in her dreams.

Meg slipped almost soundlessly into their bed. Ben tensed, waiting for her to roll toward him and wrap her arms about his chest. But she didn't do either. He waited for her to speak. *Say something, Meg. I'm not really asleep. Say something. Say you're sorry you're so late. Or just say I love you.*

Meg folded her hands across her chest and did her best to still the anxious beating of her heart. If Ben were awake, he'd have rolled over by now. *Right?* She strained to listen to his breathing, trying to determine if he was awake or asleep.

Maybe he was waiting for her to make the first move. Or maybe he really was asleep.

She should never have had that second beer. Or the third. She'd been in no condition to drive home, so when the only other woman in the group had insisted Meg go back to her place for a cup of coffee before she headed back to Tide's Way, she hadn't been able to argue with the logic. The restaurant they'd eaten in didn't stay open late, and there really wasn't a better option, but she should have called Ben when she first got to Meredith's.

She hadn't meant to fall asleep on Meredith's couch.

Maybe she should be the first to reach out. If Ben was angry, he had every right. He'd probably been worried out of his mind.

Meg rolled onto her side and faced Ben's broad back. He didn't move. As she slid her hand across his abdomen, his stomach

177

muscles didn't even twitch. He was asleep!

Surprise hit her first. He was asleep? He hadn't worried about her after all? It was the middle of the night, and he hadn't wondered where she was or what might have happened to her?

It's because I've been gone for a year. He's gotten used to falling asleep in this bed alone. The thought unsettled her. Somehow she'd imagined him the way she'd seen him the other night. Hugging her pillow and pretending it was her. Missing her as much as she'd missed him.

She inched closer, pulling her knees up under his thighs and pressing her cheek against his back.

"I'm sorry I didn't call," she whispered to his sleeping back. "My phone was dead." She kissed the warm smooth skin between Ben's shoulder blades. "I love you, Ben."

Then Ben's big hand moved to cover hers where it splayed across his chest.

CHAPTER 14

"So." Ben sloshed the remainder of the coffee around in the bottom of his mug and kept his eyes on the swirling brown liquid. "How'd it go yesterday?"

Meg wished she'd followed her instinct to tell Ben everything while she thought he was sleeping. It would have been easier to admit to her confusion and indecision in the dark. But with daylight streaming in the kitchen windows it just seemed so much harder.

"I met with Colonel Jenks." She turned away to refill her own coffee mug. "I told him I hadn't decided what I was going to do yet."

"And that kept you out 'til the middle of the night?"

"I sent you a message. I went to supper with some friends from my unit." Her voice sounded defensive even in her own ears.

"Two o'clock in the morning is a little

more than dinner with friends. I was worried. Didn't it occur to you that I might be afraid something had happened to you?"

Guilt swamped Meg with regret. The heat flooding her cheeks just added to it. When she'd woken up on Meredith's couch she'd been in such a rush to get home that the possibilities that might have occurred to Ben to explain her absence hadn't been foremost in her mind.

"I should have called. I'm sorry. Time kind of got away from me. I drank a couple beers too many, and by the time we broke up, I didn't think I should be driving home right away. So I went back to Meredith's place for some coffee, but then I fell asleep."

Ben looked at her with an unreadable expression on his face. "Meredith doesn't have a phone?"

"I thought you'd be asleep." She'd thought no such thing.

"Well, I wasn't asleep, and I was damned worried. Next time, call. I don't care how late it is, and I don't care if you wake me up. Just call so I'll know."

Meg nodded. She'd been in the wrong. She should have just come home for pizza night and ignored John's invitation.

"So . . ." Ben drank the last of the coffee in his mug. "Back to my original question.

How did it go with the CO?"

"He told me I needed to get my decision squared away so I can fill out whatever paperwork needs filling out when I go in ten days from now."

"What's happening in ten days?"

"Whatever I decide, I still have to report in for my two days a month until my hitch is up."

Ben looked at her as if he was trying to make up his mind about something, but he didn't speak.

"Bobby said I should talk to you about it."

"When did you talk to Bobby?" Ben looked surprised, and Meg suddenly realized she hadn't even mentioned talking to Bobby during their tense standoff two nights ago. "How is he doing? Or should I ask where is he doing it?"

"He's fine. He's in San Diego."

"Beating a new bunch of recruits into shape, no doubt. I assume you called him?" Ben rinsed his mug and put it in the dishwasher.

"I hadn't talked to him since I got back, and I — I called him because I didn't know what I should do. We talked about the possibility of me getting called back to active duty again if I stay in, and what that would mean for you and the boys, and for us as a couple."

"I'm glad to know I'm part of this decision," Ben said, his voice suddenly tight with an emotion Meg couldn't decipher.

"Of course, you are. You've been part of *all* my decisions."

Ben's eyebrows rose. "Really? I don't recall being consulted when you signed up for the Marines."

"We weren't married then."

"But we were dating. We were a couple."

"CJ had a baby on the way. I couldn't let him help pay for my college education. That wouldn't have been fair to him or Sarah. It just seemed to make sense at the time to let the government pay for it. But you already know all this, Ben. Why are you holding that against me now?"

Ben hesitated, trying to think over his words before responding. "I'm not holding it against you. But you wanted to join the police force back then. You could have just applied to the academy."

"Bobby said a degree would offer me more options."

Meg sounded defensive, but whether she was defending her own decisions or those of the only man who'd ever stood as a father figure in her life, Ben couldn't guess.

"Well, he had a point. But where are you going from here?"

Before Meg could answer, Ben grabbed her hand and drew her toward the living room. "If we're going to have a lengthy discussion about this, we might as well be comfortable."

Kip followed them into the living room but didn't lie down right off. Meg took the ottoman, perching on the edge as if prepared to take flight at any moment. Ben's heart sank. The coming discussion was not going to be easy, and he might not like what she had to say.

"Okay, so let's talk about it. I'd like to feel like I'm not the only person you haven't consulted." He probably wasn't the *only* person she hadn't talked to, but he should have been the first, and it irked him that he wasn't. It also scared him.

Meg looked down at her hands twisting in her lap. The bad feeling in the pit of Ben's stomach intensified. She was going to re-up. And in another nine months or a year, she'd go into harm's way again. He'd spend another whole year alone and terrified she might never come back. How did military spouses do this all the time?

"I don't want to be a police officer anymore."

"Marine MP or civilian?" This was news and the last thing he'd expected to hear her say.

"Either." Meg glanced up at him. A world of confusion swirled in her eyes. No wonder. The whole reason for the degree and being an MP had been aimed at a career in criminal justice.

"Do you have any idea what you *do* want to do?"

Meg shook her head.

"You know, you don't *have* to work, in or out of the Marines. I make more than enough to support us without you finding a new career and heading out every morning. You could just —"

"But what would I do with myself? I'm not used to having nothing to do. And what does doing nothing say about who I am? Where's the reward for doing nothing? What defines who I am?"

"I kind of thought being my wife and the boys' mother defined who you are."

"Does being my husband and the boys' father fulfill you? What would you do all day if you didn't have the kennels and the training programs and all those dogs?"

Ben studied her while his brain cranked out possibilities. *What is she getting at?*

"Those dogs put dinner on the table and

buy shoes for the boys."

"But they define you. You love dogs. Who is Ben Cameron if he isn't the whiz who can train any dog to do just about anything?"

"That doesn't define who I am. You do. You and the boys," Ben snapped back. She was getting under his skin, getting him angry. It wasn't a feeling he liked.

Meg snorted. "Right! You expect me to believe that? Being with your dogs is your whole life, Ben. It has been for our entire married life. Even before the kennel and the breeding facility were a reality, you were working toward creating it. It's you. It's who you are."

Ben swallowed hard. Swallowed his frustration and tried to see his life's work from her point of view. Could he give it all up if she asked it of him? She'd been having issues with the dogs. Their barking brought her out of a sound sleep with a look of horror on her face, and he'd seen her flinch during the daytime, too. Even Kip's presence seemed to make her uneasy. He had no idea where the antipathy came from, but he'd thought it was temporary. And maybe eventually, she'd have been his right hand for the new project he wanted to start to help train and pair service dogs with troubled veterans.

"It's who you are, Ben," she repeated. "It's your whole life, and you love it."

"It's a big part of my life," he conceded, "and I do love it, but it's not who I am. I'm just Ben Cameron. Sandra and Nathan Cameron's son. I'm your husband, and I'm Rick and Evan's dad, and I'd like to be a father again. I'd love to get you pregnant and try for a little girl. That's who I am. And that's what defines my presence here on this earth. I might love my work, but I love you more. I'll give up the kennel if that's what you need. If that's what you want. But it's the people in my life that make me who I am, not my career."

Meg's eyes widened. Surprise? Or maybe shock. The idea of giving up his dogs shocked him, too. But he would do it. For her. If it meant that much to her.

"My desire to have you in my life came long before the dogs did, Meg. What makes my life good is fixing breakfast for the boys in the morning and tucking them in at night. It's having them hug me and tell me I'm the best dad in the world. It's cheering for them at their soccer games even when they suck that defines me as their father. Not how I pay for the roof over their heads.

"It's loving you and being your husband

that makes life worth living. Caring for you and being there for you. It's making love to you and knowing there is no other woman in the world who can make me feel the way you do. That's what defines who Ben Cameron is. You want me to sell the kennel and move on, then that's what I'll do. But mostly I just want to do whatever I need to so I can help you figure out who you are and what you want. I just pray it's still me you want around when you get it all straight in your head."

Meg looked a little more than shocked by this speech, but she rallied quickly. "And what would you do with yourself if I said sell it?"

"Peddle used cars. Teach high school English. It doesn't matter."

"It *does* matter. It matters because you'd be giving up the one thing you love most," she shot back.

"*You're* the one thing I love most," Ben shouted. He shut his mouth, horrified that he'd raised his voice. Worse, they were arguing. And it was not a good argument. He sucked in a ragged, settling breath and tempered his words. "*You* are my life, Meg. And I just want to be *yours.* Wherever that might take us."

Meg's beautiful, expressive eyes widened,

and a sheen of tears suddenly filled them. She hadn't cried since she returned. Not about the nightmares. Not about the friends she'd lost. Not about the things she'd seen and experienced. But he'd brought her to it by telling her he loved her? Why should that make her cry? His heart shuddered in alarm.

"I don't know, Ben. I. Just. Don't —" Meg bolted off the ottoman and headed for the kitchen door. Kip scrambled to his feet and trotted after her. Ben stayed rooted to the chair, shocked into immobility.

The kitchen door rattled as Meg yanked it open, then slammed as she let herself out of the house. His life was crashing down around him. The love of his life had been home for weeks, and everything was supposed to be back to normal by now. But nothing was normal.

Not the way she yelled at the boys when they'd done nothing to deserve it. Not the stone wall she erected whenever he tried to talk to her. Not her reaction to the dogs. Not forgetting to call him when she was going to be late. And definitely not their love life.

He swallowed hard and thought back to her first night home when she'd come into the kitchen wearing nothing but that sexy red nightshirt. If he hadn't already been as horny as a toad that would have done it. Making love to her on the kitchen counter had been the craziest thing he'd ever done. Well, if you didn't count the back seat of that old Mustang, anyway. But she'd reveled in the abandoned lovemaking. She'd demanded more. Almost more than he'd been able to get himself up for. It had seemed, at the time, that their love life had picked up right where it had left off a year earlier.

Except it hadn't. Meg had never been so desperately needy as she'd been since she returned from a war zone. He didn't know why that should be, or why he hadn't realized until this moment that her behavior wasn't what he'd come to expect from her. God! He wished Philip hadn't just deployed to some faraway place. He needed to talk to his big brother.

He needed to talk about a lot of things that weren't the way they'd been before she left. Things he would probably never understand because he'd never been in the military and had never experienced the things she had. But what if it was worse than that?

What if she didn't love him anymore?

Now he was the one with tears in his eyes. What if Meg had fallen in love with this guy John? What if she didn't want to be married anymore? What then?

Meg marched out of the house in long angry strides. She'd forgotten to grab her purse, or she'd have jumped into her car and driven somewhere. She had no idea where, but somewhere. Anywhere away from the unsettling scene that had just unfolded in her living room.

The fact that Ben had raised his voice had shocked her more than his offer to sell the kennel. Ben never raised his voice. Not to her or the boys. But she'd managed to drive him to it with her stubborn refusal to talk about what really ate at her. She'd built a wall between them that she didn't know how to dismantle.

His declaration that she was still very much the center of his life. That she defined who he was stabbed through the careful layers of unfeeling she'd erected. He was trying so hard to understand and be whatever she needed him to be. And all the while she was being ornery, angry, and as closed in on herself as a hedgehog on the defense. All prickly spines for Ben to get caught on and hurt.

There had been a world of hurt in his eyes when she'd shouted him down after he'd gotten control of himself and told her *she* was his life in an achingly gentle voice.

"I can't be your whole life!" Meg whimpered as she marched through the ragged uncut grass beyond the manicured lawn behind the house and toward the dunes. "I don't even know who *I* am anymore."

The damp ground wet through her sneakers quickly. She hadn't brought a jacket either, but she had been far from cold when she'd stormed out of the house. The fall air nipped at her. She hugged herself and marched on, eventually coming to the long wooden boardwalk that traversed the dunes and ended at the waterway.

She stepped up onto the boardwalk, noticing for the first time that Ben had replaced all the old boards. The fresh yellow wood was solid beneath her feet, and there was no longer the hollow clunk of loose boards hitting stringers as one walked over them. She wondered vaguely when Ben had found time between doing all her work and his own.

Not only had she insinuated that being his wife was not fulfilling her, but she'd said it knowing she hadn't even been doing her job. Ben still fixed breakfast every morning and got the boys off to school. More than half the time he put them to bed and oversaw their homework when she got frustrated. She hadn't swept the floor in days or dusted in even longer. The sheets on all the beds needed changing. Winter bedding needed to be hauled out and put into use now that fall was almost over. The pears Ben and the boys had picked never got put up, and the garden overflowed with weeds. There were a ton of things she could have been doing if she'd just looked around a little.

What had she been doing with her time? No wonder she didn't feel fulfilled being a wife and mother. She wasn't showing up for the job at all.

Meg reached the end of the boardwalk and stepped up onto the pier that extended out into the water whatever the tide.

I'm a mess. I'm useless. I pretend to be me, but I'm not. I'm no one.

At the end of the pier, Meg dropped down and shoved her legs over the edge. The tide was out, or she'd have pulled off her sneakers and dangled her feet in the water. Sitting here at the end of the pier, her feet soaking in the salty water eddying around them, had always been a peaceful place for her. But not today. Today, nothing was peaceful.

She shivered again as a gust of wind tugged at her shirt. *Under-dressed and over-*

sensitive.

As she sat there, doing her best to wash her problems out of her mind, she became aware of a presence. Not the kind of presence that makes the hair on one's neck stand up, but something else. Meg glanced around and caught her breath.

Kip sat just a few feet away, watching her through those intent yellow-brown eyes. The blond tufts above his eyes twitched. Then his nose. The rest of him remained totally still.

She'd gotten used to his resemblance to Scout, but her heart squeezed anyway.

The first couple days Kip had followed Ben everywhere, but at some point, he'd transferred his attentiveness to her. After Ben decided to let the dog sleep inside the house, she'd gotten used to seeing him curled up on the end of the couch. When she roamed aimlessly in the night Kip watched her. The dog had taken on the job of escorting the boys to the bus stop and meeting them at the end of their school day, but most of the time, he'd lurked in her vicinity. Watching her every move. Those intelligent yellow-brown eyes appeared to be looking into her soul. What did he see?

Her heart thudded and her head screamed in protest, but she stretched out her hand anyway and made a soft clicking sound in her mouth. Obediently, Kip got up and came over to sit beside her.

"What's with you?" Meg asked the silent, watchful dog.

His ears slanted forward, and the bushy eyebrows twitched in recognition of her question.

Another gust of wind made Meg shiver again. Kip leaned toward her, his furry shoulder brushing softly against her bare arm. Almost against her will, Meg reached her arm about the dog's neck and drew him closer. The heat of his big body seeped through the thick coat of fur and into her. Kip sidled in closer, leaning into her.

For one crazy, disjointed moment, Meg was back in Baghdad, leaning against Scout, drawing comfort from him in a place where nothing was familiar and everything was dangerous. Then Kip whined.

Meg scrambled to her feet. Kip stood.

"I know you mean well," she told the dog, her heart banging painfully. "But I just don't know if I can bear it." Kip tipped his head. His eyes looked sad.

She turned away from the dog and retreated over the pier toward the boardwalk. Stepping back down onto the new boards Ben had installed, she glanced back. Kip still sat where she'd left him.

Meg wanted to leave him there, but she couldn't. He didn't belong to Ben or to her. He belonged to the Wilmington Police Department, and it wasn't a responsible action to leave him out here not knowing if he'd chose to come back to the house or take off somewhere else.

She took a steadying breath. "Come," she said, tapping her left thigh with the tips of her fingers.

Obediently Kip got up and came to her. He licked her hand briefly, and when she stepped out for home, Kip stepped out with her. It felt as though with that quick lick, Kip had offered her a truce. He wouldn't intrude on her when she didn't want him to, but he'd be there if she did. Somehow it didn't seem as terrifying as it had been a moment ago.

Casually, she let her fingers ruffle through Kip's fur. He glanced up at her and gave a brief wag of his tail.

She wasn't being disloyal to Scout if she befriended Kip. And maybe Kip needed her more than she'd needed Scout. Maybe she could help give to Kip what she had not been able to give Scout. A new life. New purpose.

The heaviness in her heart eased, and she

sighed. Kip whined softly as if he'd heard the sigh.

Meg stopped walking and Kip sat. He looked up at her, his yellow-brown eyes guileless and expectant.

"Okay, Kip. Here's the deal. You need something. Maybe a new someone. I don't think *I'm* that someone. I don't know if I could even *be* that someone. Or for that matter how long you'll be around. But maybe together we can figure out where we're going next. Sound fair?"

Kip tipped his head and whined again. A soft, agreeable sound deep in his throat.

Meg dropped to her knees and gathered the dog into her arms. He licked her chin. She buried her face in his fur. And then, without warning, the tears she had not been able to shed since she came home began to slide down her cheeks and into the dog's fur.

CHAPTER 15

Meg rehearsed her apology to Ben all the way home. She'd been a bitch lately. Maybe Ben couldn't ever know or really understand where she'd been or what it had been like, but he was trying to understand. He was trying to put their life back together, but she wasn't helping.

Considering everything he'd put up with over the years they'd shared, she owed him a whole lot more than she'd given him in the last two weeks. First she'd jumped down his throat over turning over her fair project to Anne Royko. He was a guy, and he'd never get it anyway, and Anne's brother was one of his best friends. Ben was just too honest and faithful to see through Anne's subterfuge. Even if he wasn't married, Ben would never even think of going after another man's wife, so he wouldn't get it that Anne didn't care if Ben was married or not. She wanted what she wanted, and a little thing like adultery wouldn't get in her way, but Ben wouldn't believe it of her.

Then there was the whole dog project Meg hadn't given him a chance to explain. In spite of his exhaustion the day of the fire, a flare of excitement had lit his eyes when he started to tell her about it and why they needed to put a second mortgage on the house. The idea was important to him, or he never would have considered going that deep into debt. But she'd flat out told him she would never reconsider without ever giving the project any careful thought. Never mind she hadn't taken the time or interest to listen to his proposal, which translated into she hadn't cared how he felt about it.

Every time Ben asked her what was wrong, she stonewalled him. Sucking back into herself like a snail, shutting him out. She'd even been using sex to avoid answering questions when they were alone at night, which wasn't fair. Ben tried so hard to figure out what was bothering her and how he could help, and she just kept avoiding it.

When he declared that she was his whole life, she knew it was something most wives would give their right arm to hear their husbands tell them. So what had she done? She'd walked out on him. Bitch didn't even begin to describe her behavior since she got home. Maybe her CO was right. Maybe she did need to see the company shrink and crank her reactions down a notch.

But first, she was going to start by telling Ben, *I'm sorry.* Maybe there were things Ben would never understand, but not telling him what bothered her didn't give him a chance.

Rick and one of his Cub Scout friends were racing across the back meadow trying to launch a kite as Meg emerged from the path leading to the waterway. She waved, but Rick didn't see her. He was focused on the bright green kite twisting and dipping at the end of its tether.

The boys were home. If Evan was tagging along on his father's heels as was the norm, her apology would have to wait until after the boys' bedtime. There were too many things to discuss. Things a little boy did not need to hear his mother talk about. But she could whip up Ben's favorite coffee cake before she started in on supper.

Ben's mother had given Meg the recipe along with a number of others Ben loved when they'd first married. Meg's mother-in-law hadn't suggested that the only way to a man's heart was through his stomach, but she stood firmly by her belief that taking the time to prepare his favorite things didn't hurt.

Meg should take a leaf out of Sandy Cameron's book and go out of her way to do something nice for Ben instead of doing all the taking.

She climbed the back stairs, crossed the deck, and let herself into the house. Kip, close on her heels, zipped in past her and hurried to his water dish. Meg washed her hands and began assembling the ingredients for the coffee cake. She was dusting the pan with flour when Evan came around the corner dressed in one of her camouflage utility uniforms.

"I'm gonna be a soldier for Halloween," he announced with a grin.

Shock rocketed through Meg and left her breathless. A vivid kaleidoscope of images raced through her head. Philip in his Marine dress blues standing up with Jake at the front of the church. Meg's sudden realization of how Sandy Cameron must feel every time she had to let her son go off to war. One of Meg's best friends, his face contorted with burns, begging her not to tell his mother what he looked like. A flag-draped coffin being loaded into a plane to bring another mother's son home. The young Marine Meg had barely known, barely old enough to even be in a war zone, crying for his mother while clutching Meg's hand as blood oozed from dozens of shrapnel wounds.

"No, you're not!" Meg screamed at her son.

Evan looked shocked. "But, Mom?"

"But nothing. You are not going trick-or-treating dressed up like a soldier."

"But you're a soldier," Evan protested, his eyes awash with tears.

"And you aren't," Meg snapped. *And you never will be if I have anything to say about it.* "Go take those clothes off this instant."

Evan left the kitchen with his head down and his footsteps dragging.

Meg leaned against the kitchen counter shaking all over. So much for great intentions. Not only hadn't she apologized to her husband, but now she'd brought tears to her son's eyes. He was only a little kid. He couldn't possibly know the gory images that had flashed through her mind when she'd seen him wearing her uniform. How did Sandy Cameron do it? How did Ben?

Meg pushed away from the counter and tucked the hair that had tumbled into her face behind her ear. Then went in search of Evan.

Ben leaned against the headboard reading a book when Meg came out of the bathroom wearing nothing but her damp towel. He carefully marked his place and set the book aside as she turned out the lights. She stood a minute beside the bed before dropping the towel on the floor and slipping between the sheets. Ben didn't move.

Meg rolled onto her side and slid her hand across the sheets until it came to rest on Ben's bicep. "I'm sorry."

"I figured that's what the coffee cake was all about." Ben rolled toward her. He pushed his palm up her arm, cupped her shoulder briefly, then curled his fingers about the back of her neck.

"It was supposed to be a peace offering," Meg agreed. But she owed Ben a whole lot more than a coffee cake. It was just so hard to find words. She didn't understand half of what she was feeling herself. "I haven't been very nice lately, and I'm sorry."

Ben didn't respond. Didn't turn her apology down, but didn't help her either. He waited, his fingers still laced into her hair. As her eyes began to adjust to the pale shafts of moonlight coming in the windows, she could see the strong planes of his cheekbones and the glitter of his eyes as he studied her, patiently waiting, as always.

"I'm just — I don't know what I want."

Ben drew her toward him, pulling her head into his shoulder. She resisted for a moment, thinking it would be easier to explain if she weren't tucked intimately against his side, listening to his heartbeat. But then she gave in and let him envelop her with his warmth and strength.

"That part I got," Ben said into the hair on top of her head. "I'm just not sure where I fit in. Or *if* I fit in. And that scares me."

Meg pulled free of his embrace and propped herself up on one elbow. Ben let her go, but trailed his fingers down her back.

"You're my husband. And my best friend."

"But I get the feeling that's not enough. You need or want something I'm not. Or something I can't give you."

The anguish in his voice cut deep into Meg's heart. The confusion and angst that had been growing inside her since she got home often consumed her, but Ben was her rock. He had been for too many years to count.

"It's nothing you're doing or not doing. It's me." When she reached out to touch his face, he captured her hand and held it tight in his.

"I don't want to go away again, but I don't know who I'll be if I'm not a Marine. And if I stay active, chances are I'll have to go. But if I'm not a Marine, then what am I? I don't really know anything else. I haven't got a real career like you. I don't —"

No point in beating a dead horse. She'd already covered this ground, and Ben already knew she no longer felt drawn to a life in law enforcement.

"You could get out, apply for your GI Bill benefits, and go back to school," Ben suggested.

"And study for what? I don't know what I want to be."

"Maybe it will come to you later."

"I'm a good Marine. A damned good Marine. I've spent years being good at that. I know my place there and what's expected of me. Here there's nothing. Well, not completely nothing. I'm still your wife and a mom. But every day I rattle around this house feeling trapped and useless. When I was on active duty, I had a job. People depended on me. And I was good at it. All except for that once —" Meg broke off suddenly. Ben didn't know about Scout. She hadn't planned on ever telling him because she knew how distressed he'd be. He wouldn't blame her the way she blamed herself, but he'd still be distressed.

She slid back into the curve of Ben's arm and settled her head against his chest. The steady beat of his heart thrummed rhythmically beneath her ear. He was the most non-judgmental man she knew and the most forgiving. His patience and understanding had gotten her through some of the most difficult times in her life, but how could he possibly get her through this? He hadn't been there. Hadn't seen the carnage hidden roadside bombs left behind. Ben would never understand just how hideous her nightmares could get.

Ben welcomed Meg back into his embrace. "No one's perfect, Meg." He slid his fingers into the masses of silky hair he loved so much and massaged the back of her head and neck. If he kept his mouth shut and just waited, perhaps she'd finish what she'd started to tell him about some failure she felt responsible for. Then maybe he'd understand what haunted her. The silence stretched out. Then again, maybe not. Not yet, at least.

"Why do you feel like there's nothing you're good at here?"

"You don't need me."

Her bald statement caught Ben in the gut like a sucker punch. He stopped kneading her head and leaned back to peer into her face. "I'll always need you."

"It doesn't feel like it."

Now it was Ben's turn to lurch up onto one elbow. Her hair splayed out around her head like a silky dark halo. This time her tears weren't just a sheen wavering in her eyes. This time, they were leaking from her eyes and running down her cheeks. His Meg never cried. Never.

He dipped his head and kissed her damp eyes. Then her cheeks and finally her mouth. He tried to put all his aching passion into the kiss, yet let it be gentle enough so she wouldn't mistake it for lust.

Meg hiccoughed on a sob.

What had he done? Why the tears? What was wrong?

He collapsed on his side and pulled her full against him. "Meggie. Meggie," he crooned. "I've needed you for as long as I've known you. How can you doubt it?"

Meg sniffled back another sob. She squeezed her hand between them and rubbed ferociously at her eyes. "I know you need me. But you *don't* need me."

"You're not making sense." He helped to wipe away the tears that so distressed her with the pads of his thumbs. Confusion ran rampant in his head. "How can I need you and not need you?"

Meg waved one hand wildly in the air. "Around here. You don't need me around here. I get up in the morning, and everything is already done. You feed the boys and get them off to school before I'm even out of the shower. You don't even leave any messes for me to clean up. The house could be in a magazine, for Pete's sake.

"Rick won't let me help with his homework, and Evan says he wants you to go to his T-ball games, not me. Rick wants you to take him hunting, but I'm not allowed to go. It's okay if I fix supper, but it's okay if I don't. Every time I think to do laundry the hamper is empty, and you've already done it. You don't need me for anything."

Shock hit Ben first, then dawning understanding. All the things that had filled her days during the year she was deployed were gone. The daily routine that had dominated her life as a soldier had ended abruptly. She had no reports to file, no convoys to escort, no orders to carry out. She'd gone from sixteen-hour days of exhausting, demanding duty to nothing in the twenty-seven hours it had taken to travel from a war zone to home. And while she was away, he'd become so accustomed to taking up the slack on the home front that he hadn't realized he was still doing everything around the house.

Meg chuckled, but it sounded watery and uncertain. "Most women would kill for a husband like you."

"Most men would kill for a woman like you." Whatever she was going through right now, Ben prayed it was just temporary. He'd always felt like the luckiest guy on the planet to have a wife like Meg.

To start with, she was drop-dead gorgeous with a silky mane of rich chocolate-colored hair, eyes so dark and compelling he felt like he was falling into them, and a smile that could light up a whole auditorium. She was a squared away Marine with a hard-earned commission and sterling efficiency reports. She'd given him two incredible sons, and when she made love to him, he felt like he owned the world. *What more could any man want?*

"I'm a mess."

"You're not a mess, and I need you more than I can ever find the words for." He kissed her again, trying harder to make his point.

If his wife was having a little trouble fitting herself back into civilian life, that was to be expected. But now that he knew how she felt, he could try harder to make it easier for her. "How about we move the alarm clock to your side of the bed? You can wake me up, then go roust the boys out and get them moving in the morning."

"It's more than that. I just . . ." Meg trailed off.

"You just what?"

"If I get out, then what will I do with myself?"

Ben hesitated. Maybe he should say it, but . . . "You were always good at working with the dogs. I could use you out in the kennels."

He'd definitely had her in mind for his new venture into training service dogs for returning vets with issues. She, more than anyone, especially more than he, would understand some of those issues. Seemed like a perfect fit. A woman his dogs had always responded to helping to train dogs to respond to the nightmares both waking and sleeping that tormented returning soldiers. Her boots-on-the-ground experience should have made it a perfect fit. Except she hadn't been near his dogs since she returned and clearly had issues even with Kip.

"I thought the things you learned as a Marine might fit into my new project. You'd be good at that, too."

"I got Scout killed."

She what?

"Who's Scout?"

"The bomb dog that was attached to our unit. I got him killed."

Meg loved dogs. She'd written that there were a couple attached to her unit, but she wasn't the handler, so how could she have gotten the dog killed?

"He —" Meg gulped back another sob.

Ben pulled her more firmly into his embrace.

"He found a bomb that I should have found first."

If she had, then she'd be dead instead. That shocking possibility was too painful to even think about. "Isn't that what the dogs were trained to do?" Ben forced himself to ignore the unspeakable image of his wife getting killed or dismembered by a roadside bomb.

"I was trained to look for them too. That was my job. It was why I rode along on those convoys. Only I missed one. And because I missed it, Scout got killed."

Images and possibilities scrambled in Ben's brain as he tried to sort out her story. He prayed she wouldn't notice just how ragged his breathing had become.

"Tell me about it."

CHAPTER 16

Meg hadn't told him. Not all of it, anyway. Feeling like it was past time to get the nightmares that haunted her out in the open, Ben had more or less commanded her to tell him the rest of the story, but she hadn't.

All he knew now that he hadn't known before was that she felt responsible for the death of a trained military bomb-sniffing K-9.

Ben stared down at the papers scattered across his desk, but didn't really see them. Columbo got up from his place by the door and came over to shove his nose under Ben's hand and whimper. Ben patted the dog absently.

Meg had been deliberately vague about her actual duties while she was deployed. Now that Ben knew she'd regularly accompanied convoys of supplies through streets that were routinely booby-trapped with IEDs, he understood her reticence. She'd been doing her best to shield him from worrying over things he couldn't do anything about.

And the dog she'd told him about, the one she'd said reminded her of Ben's dogs and made her feel like it was a little bit of home in a faraway place, had been a K-9 specifically trained to sniff out bombs. Ben had probably known that all along, but just hadn't thought it through. Why else would dogs have been there in the first place? But he'd never really considered it in conjunction with Meg's avoidance of the kennels since her return. Even if he had, not knowing about Scout, he couldn't have made the connection.

But now he did.

Which meant putting the whole service dog project on hold.

Ben focused on the papers in front of him. Sketches of the building he'd planned to build. Outlines of the program he'd been developing. A list of things that needed to be looked into. Trips that had to be made and consultations with others who'd already gotten into the field.

He gathered up the scattered notes and drawings, tapped them into a neat stack, and tucked them back into the file. Then opened the big drawer and shoved them inside. Under the checkbook. Under the kennel ledger. All the way to the bottom of the drawer.

He'd deliberately left the kitchen a mess after fixing his own breakfast, then woken Meg in time to get the boys off to school and come out to the kennel to help Mike clean the runs and put the dogs out to exercise. He hoped she was finding some solace in setting the kitchen to rights and fixing lunches, but it wasn't going to be enough.

His wife was in turmoil. And God help him, he didn't know how to help her.

He didn't do helpless well.

Patience he was good at, and he could wait when he needed to, but right now, he wanted to fix this. He didn't want to wait and watch while his wife spiraled down into depression if that was where she was headed. He didn't want to see her sink into a hole she couldn't dig her way out of. A hole that sucked the life out of everything, like the one that had kept Ron in its depths for so long. Especially if the unswerving devotion of a dog trained for the job couldn't help.

Meg pulled into her mother's driveway and

climbed out of her car. Aunt Bea had been so excited about the Elf Workshop project Meg came up with that they'd both decided more jars would be needed. Aunt Bea was helping to collect more, but Meg had come begging again.

Remy hung over the fender of his big Dodge Ram, tinkering with something under the hood. He lifted his head when she pulled in and watched as she crossed the yard to the trailer.

"Hi, Remy." She waved briefly as she neared the truck. She'd debated what she should call the man. Mr. McAllister seemed formal and maybe imparted some kind of advantage over her. Remy, she'd decided, put them on a level playing field.

"Marissa." He touched the brim of his faded Yankees hat.

"Meg," she insisted. "No one calls me Marissa." Except John. And Ben on the day of their wedding.

"Meg," Remy repeated agreeably. His gaze swept over her as it always had, but today appeared to hold no hidden agenda. Ogling any decent looking woman was just how he was made. He went back to working on his truck.

Meg continued on to the trailer, but before she got there, her mother appeared.

"I washed them all up for you. They're inside." Mary Ellen held the door open and invited Meg into the trailer. Her mother appeared sober. Or more sober than usual. She squatted beside the boxes she'd lined up by the door and opened the lid on the top one. At least two dozen jars of varying shapes and sizes sparkled in the sunlight streaming in the door.

Meg suddenly realized the whole living room seemed cleaner than last time. What had changed?

She glanced back at the big truck in the driveway and what she could see of the man working on its engine. Was Remy at the bottom of this? She recalled the dreamy quality of her mother's voice the first time they'd discussed Remy's return.

Her mother straightened, and she too glanced out the door toward the man and his truck. Then she looked back at Meg.

"I — I went to an AA meeting," Mary Ellen whispered in a hesitant voice.

Meg's gaze jerked back to her mother.

Mary Ellen pushed a strand of faded blonde hair behind her ear and looked at Meg with an odd half-proud-half-fearful expression.

Meg gaped at her mother, then shut her mouth quickly before Mary Ellen could take it for disbelief. "That's — that's good. Really good, Mom."

Mary Ellen smiled. "I'm going to keep going, too."

Astonished beyond words, Meg gathered her mother into an embrace. "I am so proud of you."

Mary Ellen hugged Meg back for a moment longer, then pushed free. Her mother's expression took on a hint of apprehension. "I was wondering . . ." She glanced away, down at the sparkling jars, then out to Remy and his truck and finally back to Meg. "I was wondering if I could help with the Elf Workshop?"

"You are not going to believe it," Meg announced as she strode into her brothers' auto repair shop.

CJ looked up from the bench where he was tinkering with some intricate piece of automotive machinery. "Hey, Brat! I'm not gonna believe what?"

"When was the last time you were down at Mom's trailer? Or maybe I should ask when was the last time you saw her?"

"Not in a while." He had the grace to look ashamed. "I haven't been avoiding her, but just — Why?"

"Then you didn't repair the railing on her

front steps?" Meg had assumed it was CJ or maybe Stu who'd done it, but maybe she'd been wrong.

CJ shook his head. "Hey, Stu?" he raised his voice and called out to their brother.

The legs sticking out from under a late model Chrysler bent, heels digging against the cement floor. Stu and his creeper inched their way out from under the car. "Yeah?"

"You haven't been over to Mom's lately, have you?"

Stu shook his head. "Nope. Probably should check up on her though. Why?" He sat up and scratched his head. "Something wrong?"

Both brothers looked at Meg.

"Not unless you call taking in an AA meeting something wrong."

Stu and CJ both gaped at Meg. She knew exactly how they felt.

"The trailer has been cleaned up, too. And she was sober this morning."

Stu got to his feet and reached for a rag to wipe his hands on.

"Praise God," CJ muttered, his voice still registering shocked disbelief.

Stu crossed the floor toward them. "I'm not gonna hug you. I'm a mess." He glanced at his hand. "Not even gonna offer you my hand. Are you kidding about Mom?"

Meg shook her head. "I wouldn't kid you about a thing like that." She hesitated, then said, "Remy's back. Now don't get in a lather, CJ. I think maybe he's the reason behind the AA meeting. And the clean trailer. And being sober."

"Mom's really sober?" Stu still struggled with disbelief.

"For today, anyway. And she asked if she could help out with my Elf Workshop at the church fair on Saturday."

CJ studied Meg with a worried question in his brown eyes. "How are you with McAllister being back?"

Meg thought about her answer. Too many conflicting thoughts racing through her head left her not really sure how she felt about it. "If he's the reason Mom has suddenly decided to get sober, then I guess I'm good with it." That much was certainly true. So long as the man kept his hands off Meg, she could deal with it. The leering she'd already come to terms with, and she was determined not to let herself get sucked back into the past with all that doubt and bad karma.

CJ continued to gaze at Meg thoughtfully.

"I'm all grown up now, CJ. He can't hurt me anymore."

CJ's shoulders relaxed. But then he shook

a finger at her. "Just so long as you promise to tell me about it if he starts anything this time."

"The Marines taught me how to defend myself. You've got nothing to worry about. Trust me."

The Marines had taught her how to defend herself and so much more. But they hadn't taught her how to find her way back to living the life of a civilian. It seemed like everyone was pulling their lives back together except her.

Captain Bissett had finished his rehab and would be headed back to active duty soon. Ron had his dog and a job and had found his way back into society. Her mother, with or without Remy's help, had finally admitted she had a drinking problem and sought help. Meg's brother-in-law had found the courage to love again and had a new wife and a new daughter.

It wasn't that Meg lacked courage. She had plenty of that. And she didn't have an injury to overcome. She couldn't claim PTSD either. She just had a short fuse and a too-short list of things she wanted to do with her life.

Maybe she *should* consider getting pregnant again. Ben wanted another child, and she loved her boys. But what if that still wasn't enough?

"I just don't know." Meg thumped the steering wheel in frustration.

Someone thumped on the car door. Meg jerked in her seat. Her heart raced into the red zone again. She looked out the window.

Evan stood there dressed in a yellow slicker and tall black rubber boots.

Meg opened the door and slid out. Her heart still pounded, but this time she was not going to take it out on her son.

"What's up?" She squatted down to Evan's level. "It's not supposed to rain, is it?"

He produced a cheap plastic fireman's hat from behind his back and plopped it on his head. "Is it okay if I'm a fireman like Daddy and Uncle Jake?"

"You make a very fine fireman. Daddy will be so proud."

"And Uncle Jake, too?"

"And Uncle Jake, too." Meg pulled Evan into her arms and gave him a hug. Then set him away and checked him out again. "But I think you could use a pair of turnout pants. And I think I know where we can find some."

"Are they yellow like Daddy's?"

"Yellow. Just like Daddy's." Meg took

Evan by the hand and started for the house. "Let's go see if we can find them."

"I need a ticket, too."

"A ticket?" Meg stopped and looked down at Evan in confusion. "What kind of ticket?"

"Like the one that hangs on the back of Daddy's hat."

"Ah!" Now she got it. "That's called an ID. It's so the fire chief knows exactly which firemen he needs to take special care of when they are busy helping to put out a fire. And I'm sure we can make you one for your hat. Come on, race you to the house."

Evan took off, clumping along as fast as he could with the oversized black boots. Where had those boots come from? They were clearly not Evan's. Had Rick worn them last year while she was away and already grown out of them? Another stab of regret. She had missed so much.

Chapter 17

Meg shoved a wayward strand of hair out of her eyes and bent closer to help the little boy glue his design onto his jar.

"It's an angel," Danny informed her as they worked.

Meg hoped Danny's mother wouldn't be required to guess what the random series of punctures was supposed to represent. The boy had chosen black construction paper to depict the night sky, and Meg had assumed the arrangement of holes were just stars.

"Mom loves angels," Danny rattled on, daubing twice as much glue as required onto his creation. "She says they're God's messengers, and they bring good news. She says they talk to her at night sometimes. That's why I wanted my lumiary to look like night time."

"Luminary," Meg corrected. That explained the black paper! Too bad the voices that spoke to Meg at night weren't all just angels bearing good news.

Halloween night had been nothing but fun for Evan and Rick. Excited about the very real-looking ID Meg had created to go with his costume, Evan had made a point of showing it off to anyone with a moment to spend listening to his explanation of what it was for. Rick, in ragged cut-offs and a red bandana with a black patch over one eye, had greeted everyone with a fierce sounding "Arrrgggghhh" while brandishing his foil-covered cardboard sword. And of course, both boys had been filled with satisfaction over the heavy sacks of booty they'd hauled home from their night on the town.

But for Meg and Kip, the night of pranks and trick-or-treating had been a waking nightmare. Every knock at the door sent a totally unreasonable frisson of panic running up Meg's spine. Kip didn't seem distressed about the raps on the door or the giggling children who stood on the other side when the door got opened, but he followed Meg everywhere as if tethered by a very short leash. His nose nearly touched her thigh at every step. Meg had no idea why he was so nervous.

Maybe she should have let Ben stay home to man the door, and she should have accompanied Evan and Rick on their rounds.

But the unreasoning panic that greeted the idea when they'd discussed who went and who stayed had been hard to hide. Just the thought of working her way down dark streets with kids dressed up in ghoulish costumes leaping out of dark places without warning had brought on rivers of sweat and alarm. She'd elected to stay home and let Ben go out with the boys.

She'd lived through the evening, but sleep hadn't come easily and when it did, she'd been disturbed by hellish dreams.

Kids lurking behind trees intent on scaring their younger siblings had become kids lurking in alleys committed to tossing deadly things at unwary soldiers. Every scene of carnage Meg had witnessed in Iraq had been relived and quite a few more created by her fertile and frightened brain. She'd ended up getting out of bed and prowling the house before finally curling into the corner of the sofa with Kip sitting sentry at her side. Until Ben had come looking for her.

What'dya think, Mrs. Cameron?" Danny's question brought Meg back to the here and now in her Elf Workshop. Danny held up his sticky creation. "I think my mom is going to love it."

Meg shut off the disturbing memories and

admired Danny's efforts.

"I'm sure she will. Why don't you set it here to dry? You can go wash your hands, and by the time you get back it will be ready to wrap up. Okay?"

"Okay," Danny agreed. He carefully set his luminary at the back of the table where it couldn't fall off. Then, unexpectedly, he wrapped his arms about her middle and gave her a hug. "I love you, Mrs. Cameron." Then he was off running down the hall to the men's room to wash up.

Meg sank down onto a chair and surveyed the mess that needed cleaning up. Bits and pieces of construction paper in all hues littered the table and floor. The bag that had once bulged with tea lights was nearly empty, and only three of her mother's jars remained. Scissors and paste and crayons lay scattered across the child-sized tables that had been her Elf's Workshop.

Her mother had been an unexpected blessing. Mary Ellen had arrived sober and eager to help. And considering the popularity of the workshop, those extra hands had been a Godsend. Remy had come by to collect Mary Ellen a half hour earlier. They had a date, her mother had whispered, her eyes sparkling with excitement. Meg had hugged her mother and told her to have a good time. What a world of difference Remy had made in her mother's life this time around.

If only Mary Ellen had come to this junction in life when Bobby had begged her to get help, what a difference that would have made in Meg's life. But that was water over the dam. Meg wasn't going to waste energy wishing for things she couldn't change. She was just going to be thankful for any good going forward.

Lurking uncomfortably at the back of Meg's mind was the question, what if she hadn't been such a distraction the first time Remy came into Mary Ellen's life? Would her mother have faced her addiction and turned her life around fifteen years ago if CJ hadn't demanded that Remy leave after he'd groped Meg that night in the kitchen? Had Meg robbed her mother of all those years without ever knowing?

"Hey, Chuck. Didn't expect to see you here. Where have you been hiding?" Ben's voice came unexpectedly from the other side of the fabric-covered room dividers, jerking Meg out of her troubled thoughts.

"Didn't expect to be here," Chuck replied. "Anne insisted. She wanted an excuse to see you."

"Anne doesn't need an excuse to see me."

Ben's voice faded out as if he'd turned to face the other way, perhaps searching the hall for Anne.

Anne didn't need an excuse to see Ben? Hadn't Ben told her as recently as last week that he'd been avoiding Anne Royko? What was going on?

"She said you've been avoiding her," Chuck echoed Meg's thoughts.

Ben's voice was an undistinguishable mumble.

"I don't think she ever forgave herself for —" Chuck coughed. Ben must be thumping him on the back judging by the sounds. Meg didn't hear the rest of what Chuck said between clearing his throat and Ben's helpful whacks.

"Well, I forgave her. She did me a big favor . . ." Ben's voice faded again.

Danny returned, his hands still damp. "Can I wrap it now?"

Reluctantly, Meg turned to help the boy choose the paper he wanted and wrap the luminary for his mother. Danny chatted happily, but Meg's brain kept sorting through the odd bits of conversation she'd overheard, trying to make sense of it.

Anne Royko wanted an excuse to see Ben? And Ben said she didn't need an excuse. He'd also said he forgave the woman. But for what? What was going on between Anne Royko and Ben?

First she'd found out Ben had handed over her totes and the Elf Workshop project without apparently any hesitation. Then he hadn't asked for the totes back because he didn't want the woman in the house? Why? Meg could have sworn Ben had been on the level with her about the whole thing. She could have sworn he'd never been unfaithful to her either. Was there a side to Ben she had never seen?

"Thanks, Mrs. Cameron." Danny gave Meg another hug and then headed for the archway leading out of the workshop with his awkwardly wrapped bundle held tight in his arms.

Meg looked at her watch. Only a few minutes until the fair was set to wind down and clean up would begin. The likelihood of any more children showing up was slim, so Meg began to gather up the mess.

The luminaries had been a huge success. The children had been thrilled with the idea and had trooped through her workshop in droves, leaving a whirlwind of debris behind. Meg stepped out of the workshop area to grab a fresh trash can liner. Ben and Chuck were seated on one of the old pews that had been relegated to the hall when the new ones were installed inside the church a couple years back.

Ben lounged back against the wall with one foot balanced on his other knee. Chuck hunched over with his hands between his knees and his head down. Ben had one hand on his friend's shoulder and was talking, gesturing frequently with his free hand.

Forgetting where she'd been headed, Meg watched the earnest conversation. Were they still discussing Chuck's sister Anne? Or something else? With jerky haste, Chuck brought one hand up and dashed it across his face as if erasing tears.

Meg's heart suddenly hurt. It took something serious to make a man like Chuck Royko cry. Chuck had been a Special Forces soldier for almost fifteen years before leaving the Army the previous year due to repeated injuries. He was one of the toughest men Meg knew.

Ben dropped his foot to the floor and gripped his friend's shoulder more firmly. After another long comment punctuated with more hand gestures, Chuck looked up at Ben and smiled. Meg's heart relaxed. Chuck said something that made Ben laugh. Then the two men got to their feet and wandered off to the table that held what remained of the baked goods sale.

Meg remembered her mission and crossed the room to get the plastic bag she needed to finish cleaning up the craft mess in her workshop area. As she stowed scissors, crayons, and leftover construction paper in the bright blue tote, she kept replaying Chuck's angry gesture in her mind. Didn't seem likely it was woman trouble. He'd been as close to engaged as possible before his last deployment, and Georgia had been the first person he'd seen when he woke up at Walter Reed. Couldn't be his latest injury. He'd been home too long, and the last surgery had been more than a year earlier. And it probably wasn't Anne. Chuck was a caring brother, but his tone of voice as he'd told Ben why he was here carried more humorous resignation than distress.

"You about ready to head on home?" Ben stood, head bent beneath the arch to her workshop. He took another step inside and straightened. "I'll carry that out for you." He nodded at the now filled and closed tote.

"Drop this in the dumpster on your way by?" Meg handed him the bulging trash bag. "I've got to turn in the profits to Aunt Bea." She held up the large manila envelope that held the proceeds of the workshop.

Ben hefted the tote onto one shoulder and grabbed the trash bag in his free hand.

"Where are the boys?" Meg hadn't seen them all day. They had been Ben's responsibility.

"Mom took them home for a sleepover. She planned to stop at the house to grab their church clothes and said she'd see us at mass in the morning." Ben wagged his eyebrows at her. "A whole evening just for us."

Ideas for a night without kids flitted through Meg's head. But there had been some stiffness between her and Ben the last few days after her refusal to consider a second mortgage and then her blow up over the what-do-I-do-next discussion. And then there was the night she'd fallen asleep on Meredith's couch and didn't come home until two a.m.

Ben's teasing look faded, and he frowned. "It was okay that I let the boys go, wasn't it?"

Meg shook her head. "Don't mind me. I'm just hungry and tired, I guess. A night alone with my favorite guy sounds wonderful."

"We could start at Ethan's. I'm in a mood for barbeque and you wouldn't have to cook."

Meg agreed to ribs, and Ben ducked back under the arch and disappeared.

Meg delivered the money to Aunt Bea and headed out to meet Ben in the parking lot. Her tote had been stowed in the back of Ben's truck, but Ben wasn't in sight. Meg turned slowly on her heel, searching for him among the straggle of cars still parked in the lot. Then she spotted him, bent at the waist with his palms resting on the open window frame of a sleek blue BMW.

Seated in the driver's seat, Anne Royko had her head tipped back, looking up at Ben with heavy lidded eyes and a teasing smile. She said something, and Ben bent toward her, turning his head as if to hear better.

A festering little pool of anger bubbled up in Meg as she watched the tableau. It erupted when Anne stretched up and kissed Ben full on the mouth.

Ben jumped back as if stung, but Meg was already headed for the bright blue car with an angry swarm of bees buzzing in her head. Before she reached it, Anne gunned the engine and peeled out.

"What was that about?" Meg demanded, coming to a stop in front of Ben.

Ben glanced at the disappearing car, then down at Meg. "What was what about?"

"You know very well what."

Ben rubbed the back of his head, looking confused.

Anger roiled in Meg's belly. All the hunger she'd felt just a few minutes ago fled. Now she just felt sick to her stomach.

"What is going on between you and Anne?"

"Nothing's going on."

Meg glared at Ben, more angry than she ever remembered being.

"Then why were you kissing her?"

"I wasn't kissing her. She kissed me."

In spite of the truth to his words and his reaction at the time, anger and doubt still clawed at Meg's insides. The embarrassed flush coloring Ben's cheeks didn't help. "Why were you even talking to her?"

"She's Chuck's sister. Besides, since when is it a crime to talk to another woman?"

"Since I overheard you telling Chuck she didn't need an excuse to see you and that you forgave her already. What I want to know is what are you forgiving her for?"

"For dumping me back in high school."

Meg started to reply, then shut her mouth abruptly as his answer sank in.

Ben reached out and curled his fingers around the back of her neck. "When have I ever given you a reason to think I care about any woman except you?"

Meg pulled away from Ben's hand, but her anger was already leaching away. All the little instances she'd been cataloging in her mind began to sound trivial and stupid. Ben had never given her a reason to doubt his fidelity. Not really.

"Especially, Anne Royko." Ben snorted. He shoved his hands into his pockets as he gazed down at her. "Chuck says Anne's never forgiven herself for tossing me aside for that banker's son. And maybe that's true. But I doubt it. The only person Anne has ever really cared about is Anne. She seemed to think it would be fun to have a little fling with me while you were out of the picture. It's why she begged me for the totes, only I didn't get it at the time. Anyway, she didn't get what she wanted, and I have no idea what she's up to now."

This time when Ben reached for her, she let him pull her into his embrace. "The only woman I really want kissing me is you." He tipped her head back and lowered his mouth close enough for her to kiss if she chose to. "If you're wanting to kiss me, that is."

Meg closed the distance between their mouths and brushed her lips across his.

"That's all I get?" Ben ran his tongue along his upper lip.

"Oh, Ben. I'm sorry. I don't mean to be such a witch. I don't know what gets into me lately." Her eyes smarted with a sudden surge of tears.

Ben kissed her stinging eyes. Then her mouth. His kiss was so gentle, yet so thorough it left no doubt about his sincerity. And she couldn't stop the tears.

"I'm sorry," she said again when he finally lifted his head.

"Then maybe it's a good thing we've got all night to kiss and make up."

Ben stirred and reached out for Meg. When his hand found nothing, he rolled up onto one elbow and opened his eyes. He was alone. Should he go after her? Again? Or wait? What had disturbed her sleep this time? Not nightmares. At least it didn't seem likely since her nightmares usually woke him as well as her. Most times he woke before the terror brought her out of sleep. But not tonight.

The kissing and making-up had been pretty energetic. And totally satisfying. No reason why either of them should be awake at just past two in the morning. Ben flopped back onto the bed and stared at the ceiling as the events of the evening replayed in his head.

When they'd gotten to Ethan's BBQ, Meg had suggested they get their ribs to go. Since they had the house to themselves, they might as well get comfortable and enjoy their alone-time. So, with the savory scent of the barbequed ribs hurrying them along, they'd driven home, showered, and changed into gym shorts and T-shirts. He'd dropped an old movie into the DVD player while Meg spread a beach blanket on the floor. Then they'd sat with their backs against the couch eating ribs with sauce dripping down their chins and laughing over Cuba Gooding Jr.'s antics in *Jerry Maguire.*

As the credits rolled, the making-up had begun right there on the living room floor with Kip watching and the remnants of their barbequed ribs and coleslaw dinner pushed to the side.

Afterward, he'd carried her to bed, and they'd made love a second time. He'd felt so sated and relaxed it had occurred to him that they might sleep right through church if he didn't set the alarm. But he'd been too lethargic and contented to do even that.

With a grunt of resignation, Ben rolled off the bed and stood. He found his pajama bottoms hanging on the bathroom door and slipped into them, then padded barefoot down the hall after Meg.

He found her in the kitchen. Her back was

to him as she scrubbed at something in the sink.

"What's wrong?" He'd been asking that question a lot lately. Far too often.

She jerked around, her eyes wide.

"Sorry, I didn't mean to sneak up on you." Ben crossed the kitchen. He put his hands on her shoulders and bent to kiss her.

"I — I couldn't sleep, and I remembered we left all the dishes and leftovers out."

"There were leftovers?"

"Well, not really. Or not much. But if there was anything, I think Kip finished them off." Meg pointed her chin toward the little mat by the back door.

Kip sat up quickly. His eyes were alert and his ears pricked forward. He'd heard his name and was probably waiting for instructions.

"It's okay, Kip. You can go back to sleep."

"He never sleeps when I'm up at night," Meg said as she put a handful of silverware in the dishwasher.

"Watching your back," Ben told her. "He seems to have decided it's his job to watch out for you."

"I noticed."

"And that bothers you." His agreement was not meant to be a question. He'd been watching her and noticing her reactions to the dog. Her awkwardness had disturbed him at first. Then she'd told him about Scout, and he'd thought he understood it better, but he still hoped she'd get over it.

"It did. Before." Meg turned and leaned against the counter. There were circles beneath her eyes.

"Before what?" Ben thought she'd been sleeping better lately. But the dark circles seemed to argue otherwise.

"Before we came to an agreement."

Ben looked at the dog. Kip tipped his head as if he knew what they were talking about and he agreed. His intent gaze flitted from Meg to Ben and back.

"You and Kip came to an agreement?"

"Yeah." The corners of Meg's mouth turned up, but her eyes still looked tired and a little sad. "The day I stalked out of here and wouldn't talk to you. I went down to the old pier. Kip followed. He waited while I got the snit out of my system. Then we talked."

Meg shivered.

"You're cold." Ben reached out and pulled her to him. She rested her head against his chest and circled his waist with her arms. "What did you and Kip talk about?"

Meg lifted her shoulders and then dropped them again.

"And I bet he's not telling, either."

Meg chuckled at that, then lifted her face to look up at him. "He seemed as lost as I felt. Like he didn't know what he was supposed to be doing. I could so relate to that. I told him, maybe I could help him find a new purpose in life. Hah! Isn't that a joke? I can't even figure out what to do with my life."

To Ben's dismay, her eyes filled with tears. Again. Twice in one day. "You will. Just give it time."

Meg's words sounded eerily like Chuck's. Alarm caught Ben off guard. Chuck had been so despondent when they'd talked. So unlike himself. The Chuck that Ben knew, the one he'd grown up with, had always been so upbeat. Always with a plan. Yet here he was, almost a year out of the Army and still with no idea what he wanted to do with himself. And it was weighing on his mind, dragging him down into a pit of despair. *Please, God, don't let the same thing happen to Meg.*

Meg laid her head back against his chest and sighed. "I saw you talking to Chuck today. What was he so upset about?"

CHAPTER 18

The name stenciled on the door declared this to be the office of Captain Natalie Allan.

If it was up to Meg, she wouldn't be here, but Colonel Jenks had set up this appointment along with two others. He'd told her it was just part of the standard list of things that needed to be checked off. Meg had been in a war zone, and before the Marines could release her from active service, she needed to see the company shrink and get a physical exam.

Meg turned the handle and stepped into the waiting area. A fresh-faced private who looked like she belonged in middle school glanced up and smiled.

"You must be Lieutenant Cameron."

Meg handed over the sheaf of documents Jenks had given her.

"Have a seat, please. Captain Allan will be with you in a moment."

Doctor Allan, Meg thought grimly. Getting an unplanned physical didn't bother her, but she hadn't come to Lejeune today prepared to talk to a shrink. Considering how her life had been going lately, the idea of talking to someone had occurred to her. But not seriously. Things weren't that bad. The nightmares and flashbacks were getting better, and the whole my-life-is-going-nowhere bit didn't seem to be a Marine issue. But her CO hadn't given her any wiggle room, so here she was. She sat in one of the sturdy vinyl-covered olive-drab metal chairs that lined one wall and waited. Hopefully the chairs in the doctor's office would be more comfortable. Something told her this session was going to be uncomfortable enough without the aid of unforgiving military-issue chairs.

"Have you been there, Captain?" Meg dragged her gaze away from the framed documents on the wall and looked at the young-looking doctor.

Captain Allan shook her head.

Meg resented having to discuss whatever war-related issues she might have with anyone, never mind someone who couldn't possibly know what it had been like. But Captain Allan seemed like a caring, earnest person, so Meg was trying to cooperate.

"My past postings do not have any connection to the question I just asked."

Meg wanted to look away but didn't.

"The list of things you've described to me. The nightmares and the anger. Especially the feelings of loss and the grieving. Those are normal, and you appear to be dealing with them fairly well." Doctor Allan took a short breath and pressed her lips together.

"Actually, the feeling of being restless is pretty normal as well. You were in a situation where you were on hyperalert every minute of your day. Even when you were sleeping, some part of you stayed ready to respond at a moment's notice. You had tasks that kept you busy from waking to sleeping. Some of what you did was routine, but there was intensity to the routine. You were commanded to carry out certain tasks, and you followed those orders.

"Now you're home, and there's no CO ordering your day for you. The routine, intense or otherwise, that kept you busy and engaged was suddenly removed. There would be something wrong with you if you didn't feel a sense of loss and a level of restlessness."

She paused, probably to give Meg a chance to respond. But Meg didn't have anything to add.

"That brings us back to the question of what was important to you before you were deployed. In order for you to figure out where you fit in now that you're back home, you need to consider the activities that filled your days before you left."

"My youngest son wasn't in school yet."

"So, you were a stay-at-home mom."

Meg had never thought of herself as a stay-at-home mom, but actually, that's pretty much what she had been. Much of her time was spent helping Ben out in the kennels, but Evan had been with her. And before that, so had Rick. "I suppose that's true, except when I was at the base. But that was just a few days a month and two weeks every summer."

"The boys are both in school now?"

Meg nodded.

"What were your plans for when that happened? You must have had some idea. Some plans or hopes that you wanted to get into when the boys grew up."

Meg considered her answer carefully. "I always thought I wanted to go into law enforcement. But something inside me has changed. All the time I was on active duty and going to college that was my plan. But, now that I've had some experience as a military cop, I don't feel so drawn to a lifetime of being a cop anymore. I don't think I'd make a very good detective, and I can't see myself breaking up domestic spats and bar fights forever."

"There are many avenues in the field of law enforcement." Captain Allan folded her hands on her desk with a look that seemed to say she felt like she was finally getting somewhere.

"I enjoyed spending time helping Ben with the dogs," Meg blurted out without thinking.

Captain Allan sat back in her chair. "Ben is your husband."

Meg nodded.

"And his dogs are . . . ?"

"He raises and trains dogs for police work. When the boys were little and I wasn't at the base, I used to help out. The kennel is right next to the house, and the boys could go with me."

"And the death of the dog in your unit changed all that?"

Meg's eyes were suddenly, painfully moist. She did not want to cry. Not here. Not in front of this calm, confident young officer. An officer who outranked her, but seemed so much younger and so untouched. She closed her eyes and willed the tears away.

"Have you helped Ben with the dogs since you returned?"

Meg shook her head. Then she opened her eyes and took control of the discussion. "Ben's dogs are the whole reason I got close to Scout in the first place. Having him around made home seem less far away. He spent most of his time with his handler, of course, but I used to sneak him treats. I got Ben to send me some of the training treats we use that the dogs love. So Scout would always come by to see if I had anything for him. But then — then — If I'd only been more vigilant, I might have seen that detonation plate. I might have been able to stop him —" The words of self-accusation spilled out before she could stop them.

"Soldiers sometimes lose their lives doing their job." Captain Allan leaned forward, her expression more intense. "It's no different with military dogs. Sometimes they lose their lives doing what they were trained to do. You can't hold yourself responsible."

"I know." Meg's voice squeaked.

"And now you are avoiding your husband's dogs because you feel you let Scout down?"

Meg nodded. "But there's one dog that arrived the day after I got back. We're fostering him temporarily. Ben brought him into the house. It bothered me, but I didn't say anything. It's just that Kip looks so much like Scout. He's a police dog. His handler got killed, and they brought him to Ben because he kind of . . . do dogs go into depression like people?"

Captain Allan raised her eyebrows. "I'm not really qualified in the field of veterinary medicine, but I understand that dogs do grieve."

"Well, Kip wouldn't come out of his crate, and he wasn't eating, so they brought him to Ben. Ben has a way with dogs. He can get dogs to do just about anything. It's kind of amazing the things Ben can do with dogs. That's what was fun about working with him. Watching him work with the dogs, that is.

"Anyway, after the first day or so, Kip started following me everywhere. Ben and I sort of had an argument one day, and I just needed to get away to think for a bit. Kip followed me. I didn't want him to, but he came anyway. I'm sitting there on the end of the dock, and he's watching me. Then he came over and sat next to me. He just got — he got inside my head sort of. That doesn't make any sense, does it?"

"How have things been with you and Kip since that day?"

Answer a question with a question. So typical of a shrink. They want to make you think you are working things out by yourself. "Better."

"And with Ben?"

"What about with Ben?"

"You said the two of you had argued, and you walked out on him. Is that how you've been dealing with disagreements?"

"I don't know what you mean." Of course, she *did* know.

Captain Allan frowned.

"No, that's not how I deal with disagreements. Except that once. Ben and I don't argue a lot." *Ben doesn't argue a lot, but I've certainly done my share of provoking him.*

"Don't shut your husband out, Lieutenant. He's your other half. Your lifeline and support. He may not have experienced what war is like firsthand, but he cares about you more than anyone else does, and I'm willing to bet, worries about you more than anyone else. His job hasn't been easy either.

"The military is great at preparing men and women to go to war, but they don't do nearly enough to prepare soldiers to come home. Your husband, on the other hand, will probably do anything to help you find yourself again. Lean on him. Talk to him.

Let him help with this time of readjustment."

Meg flashed back to Ben pleading with her to let him help. The look of pain that crossed his face when he said he just hoped there would still be a place for him in her life when she figured out what she wanted. And his instant forgiveness for all her crap every time she said she was sorry.

Captain Allan spoke as though she knew Ben personally.

The doctor looked past Meg and then shook her head with a rueful expression on her pretty face. "Our time is up for today, but I think you've begun to find a few of the answers you need. At least there are things for you to think about and perhaps act on. Perhaps it's time you asked Ben what you can do to help out around the kennels again. You enjoyed it before, and I think you will again. Look at it as a way to honor Scout's sacrifice. And next time, perhaps we will talk about Captain Bissett."

The doctor stood. Clearly Meg was dismissed. She wanted to protest that John Bissett was not part of her problems, but she wasn't given the opportunity.

Captain Allan came around the corner of the desk and stuck out her hand. "It was nice to meet you. I know you don't think I understand what it's like, but I do honor your service and thank you for it."

Meg took the doctor's hand. She swallowed and then looked the doctor in the eye. "Thank you for your time." She did an about-face and left the doctor's office.

She passed the young private in the outer office without a word and let herself into the hall. The doctor assumed Meg would be back. But unless Colonel Jenks insisted or the captain refused to sign off on the paperwork, Meg had no intention of returning. She didn't want to talk about John Bissett. Her issues with him had nothing to do with leaving the Marine Corps. Hopefully she'd get her psych-eval box checked without another session with Captain Allan.

Striding quickly down the hall past the walk-in sick bay clinic, Meg almost didn't notice the dog sitting at the feet of the old man in the wheelchair. But it was hard to miss the bright orange vest the dog wore, and in spite of her urgent need to get out of the building, she paused and glanced back.

The old man's trembling hand rested on the dog's head. His broad smile made it clear he enjoyed the dog's presence. The middle-aged woman holding the end of the leash wore civilian attire with a visitor's ID pass dangling from a lanyard around her neck. She glanced briefly at Meg, then back to the golden retriever with the lolling tongue and liquid eyes. Meg read the bold patch stitched onto the dog's orange vest before she headed for the door.

Therapy Dog. What on earth is a Therapy Dog? Meg shoved the door open and stepped out into the warm North Carolina sunshine. She sucked in a huge breath of the fresh fall air. Was the atmosphere in that place always that oppressive, or was it just her? She unfolded her cap and set it on her head, squared her shoulders, then set off toward her car.

"Marissa."

Meg whirled on one heel.

John Bissett! As if the doctor's suggestion had conjured him up.

"Are you following me?"

Captain Bissett saluted. Belatedly Meg realized that she should have done so first. She returned his salute.

"Well, are you?"

"Am I what?" He frowned.

"Stalking me?"

Now he looked offended. And hurt.

"Sorry. I didn't mean that. I just didn't expect —" Meg swallowed the nervousness clogging her throat. "I thought you were —"

"Gone? I will be. Tomorrow. I'm just tying up a few loose ends."

"Where to, this time?"

"Afghanistan."

Meg felt herself blanching. She'd wanted him sent somewhere besides Lejeune, where there were too many opportunities for her to keep running into him, but not back to a war zone.

"Not to a hot spot, though," he said as if reading her mind. "Want to grab a cup of coffee and wish an old friend good luck?"

The man would be gone tomorrow. Out of her life forever. Maybe she owed him at least a cup of coffee. He'd been a good friend when she needed one. He'd almost been more than a friend, but that wasn't exactly his fault. She hesitated.

He started to reach out to touch her shoulder and then apparently thought better of it. "I'm sorry about what happened, Marissa. You were hurting, and I took advantage. I hope you can forgive me and forget it ever happened." His mouth quirked up on one side, and a look of doubt clouded his eyes.

She started to remind him no one called her Marissa, but John was taking all the blame for her shameless behavior. An officer and a gentleman to the core.

"Nothing happened," she muttered, not quite meeting his gaze.

He hesitated, his green eyes searching her face. "So? We good for one last cup of joe?"

"Sure." She owed him that much. They turned together and stepped off in the direction of the base café. "What do you know about therapy dogs?"

"Not much." John glanced at her. "But one did visit me in the hospital. He was making the rounds with his owner. Cheered the guys up no end to have a big goober of a lab come by. I only saw him the once, though."

"I just passed one in the hall." Meg jerked her head back in the direction of the building housing the sick bay and doctors' offices. "A nice old golden retriever. I didn't know they let dogs into those places."

They stepped up onto the curb, and John reached to open the door for her. "I saw service dogs in the hospital, too. They're a whole different thing though. They get special training and then get paired up with just one vet. They're allowed to go everywhere, like guide dogs for the blind."

"I met one a week or so ago," Meg admitted as she slid into a booth.

John sat across from her and signaled the waitress for two cups of coffee.

By the time the coffee arrived, Meg had explained about Ron and his dog Lola. By the time the coffee was drunk, and they were ready to leave, she'd told him all about Ben, the mortgage, and Ben's plans for a facility that trained more dogs like Lola. She'd even told him about Kip. She'd flushed with embarrassment when she recalled the scene following Scout's death, but John had acted as though he hadn't noticed. Meg had no idea why she'd just blurted all that stuff out. But John had let her do all the talking.

She should have been asking him more about where he was headed and what he'd be doing.

As they stood on the curb, preparing to go their separate ways, Meg got flustered all over again. Instinct urged her to give him a hug. It might be the last time she ever saw him. Training kicked in, and she saluted instead.

John returned the salute. "Take care of yourself, Marissa."

"Keep your head down, John."

He nodded and turned to leave. Meg watched him walk away and prayed he'd get through the coming deployment in one piece. And that life would be good to him. He deserved it.

CHAPTER 19

When Meg turned into her driveway a police cruiser sat parked next to Ben's truck with the back door open. Ben squatted on the ground next to the cruiser nose to nose with Kip. Both man and dog looked up as Meg's car approached.

She pulled up on the far side of Ben's truck and turned the engine off. Her heart thumped, and her chest felt uncomfortably tight. Until just a few days ago, anything that involved Kip had caused her heart to quail, but things had been different since their walk to the end of the dock and back. For weeks, she'd been waiting for the police officer who'd brought Kip to come and retrieve him. Now he was here, and she wasn't so sure she wanted the dog to go after all.

Sliding out of the car, Meg walked around the back of Ben's truck and approached the cruiser. Kip trembled, his ears angled back in an anxious posture and his tail tucked up so tight the tip of it touched his belly. Ben spoke to the dog in a low, calming tone. The same tone Ben used when he rubbed her back, soothing her after she woke from a nightmare. Meg stopped a few feet away, not wanting to intrude. Not sure she wanted to witness Kip's distress or the heartbreaking scene that might follow when the dog was ordered to get into the cruiser.

"He seemed fine a few minutes ago," the police officer observed, scratching his head. He glanced over at Meg, then back down to Ben, still squatting next to Kip.

"He's been fine around the house. Good with the family and all." Ben ruffled the fur at Kip's neck. "He seems to enjoy playing with the boys, too." Ben stood. He moved to Kip's side and placed one hand on the dog's head. "I took him to the beach last week and fired a few blank rounds to see how he'd react. It wasn't good. I thought maybe I'd just been a little hasty. Rushing things, you know? Considering his refusal to get into the cruiser, I'm thinking it might take a lot longer."

The officer grunted. Looked at the dog, then back to Ben. "I know it's an imposition —"

"Not at all," Ben cut him off. "He can stay

as long as he needs to." Abruptly Ben turned and noticed Meg, as if he hadn't realized she hadn't gone directly to the house from her car. "Unless . . . ?"

"Unless what?" Meg asked, closing the distance between them.

"Meg, this is Jerry Brady, Wilmington PD. Brady, my wife Meg."

The officer stuck out his hand, and Meg took it. "Nice to meet you." Meg tried to keep her voice neutral. She was so conflicted about what might or might not happen to Kip. And that conflict unsettled her.

"Same here, ma'am. You all have been very generous, and we appreciate it."

"Unless what?" Meg asked again, looking pointedly at her husband.

Ben looked oddly abashed. "I guess I should have consulted with you before offering to continue fostering Kip."

"You didn't consult me when he first got here. No reason you should now. But either way, I'm good with it. I'll let you guys decide what's best." She turned on her heel and headed for the house. For reasons she could not fathom, her eyes had suddenly filled with tears. And she didn't care to explain them to Ben, never mind cry in front of a perfect stranger.

Ben watched Meg stride across the dusty

driveway toward the house in shock. What shocked him most, he wasn't sure. Her accusation that he hadn't consulted her before taking Kip on, which he couldn't deny, or the tears he'd seen in her eyes just before she'd turned away.

He turned back to Officer Brady, not sure what he was supposed to do now. But Brady had already closed the back door of the cruiser and was sliding into the driver's seat.

"I'll give you a call next week," Brady said as he pulled his door shut.

Ben threaded his finger through Kip's collar. Not that he thought for a moment that the dog would bolt after a car he'd just shown quite clearly he had no interest in getting into, but habit died hard. Securing any animal when cars were moving just came as second nature.

Brady waved out the open window as he turned out of the driveway. The cruiser made the jog across Stewart Road and then went right onto Jolee Road and disappeared from sight. Ben glanced down at Kip, who now had his tongue lolling out of one side of his mouth. All shivering had ceased, and the dog's ears were erect and eager. Kip clearly related the sight of the police cruiser to the death of his handler, and it disturbed him. Unwillingly, Ben faced the fact that

Kip might never see a cruiser without trembling and would most likely never return to police work.

But right at the moment, that reality took second place to whatever was going on with Meg. The last few days or so, she'd seemed okay with Kip being around. So the tears now? Along with the accusation that he hadn't consulted her before agreeing to foster the dog in the first place. Confusion didn't begin to describe what was going on in Ben's head. Or the sudden pain in his heart.

Meg had been equally upset the day she summed up Ben's character as being defined by the dogs and his choice of career. He'd offered to give them up if it was what she wanted, but he hadn't believed for a minute that she would ask that of him. He'd been serious, but he hadn't thought that was really what was at the bottom of her despondency and distress.

Maybe it was time to talk about it?

Without Kip to influence her.

Ben headed for the kennel with Kip trotting obediently at his side. Columbo met them at the door, and both dogs checked each other out, sniffing with interest, but without animosity. Ben considered the option of putting Kip in one of the runs, but by then both dogs were seated at his feet, side by side, patiently waiting to see what happened next. He decided to leave Kip free.

He closed the door and headed to the house. A leaden sense of dread puddled in his gut, and he had to force himself to open the kitchen door and go inside.

Meg stood at the counter chopping vegetables. She didn't turn around when he entered.

"He staying?"

"You mean Kip?" Of course she meant Kip. Who else would she be talking about? "For now, but that can change. What do you want me to do?"

"I don't want you to do anything." She continued to slice carrots.

Ben feared for her fingers considering the aggressive way she chopped at the vegetables. He crossed the kitchen and reached around her, removed the knife from her hands, and set it on the cutting board.

Meg placed both hands on the counter but still didn't turn to face him.

"What's the matter, Meg?"

She shook her head.

"Something's bothering you, but I can't fix it if I don't know what it is."

A teardrop splashed onto the counter next

to her hand. Distress shot through Ben like a bullet. He wrapped his arms about his wife and began rocking her. With his head bent down beside hers, he just held her tightly. He had no idea what to say.

"Help! Daddy!" Evan barreled into the kitchen and grabbed a fold of Ben's pants.

Ben dropped his arms from Meg and squatted down in front of his agitated son. "What's up?"

"Rick cut himself. He's bleeding all over the place."

"Where is he?" Meg dropped the dish-towel she'd grabbed to dab her eyes with.

"In the bathroom. He tried to shave with Daddy's razor, and he's bleeding every-where." Evan's voice rose in intensity, half panic, half excitement.

Meg bolted for the hallway.

Ben followed, but Evan's grip on his pants slowed him down. Meg dashed through the bathroom door first.

"Rick?" Meg reached for her son.

"Mom." Rick sounded annoyed. "Evan, why did you have to go bringing Mom in here?"

"How bad is it?" Meg asked, grasping Rick's jaw.

Rick jerked out of reach. "Dad?"

Rick had his hands clutched over his

groin. Blood dribbled from a cut on his chin. Nowhere near as much blood as the excitement in Evan's voice had suggested. For a moment Ben felt like smiling, but he stifled it.

"Please, Mom. It's just a nick. I'm okay. Dad, tell her she can't come in here."

"What do you mean, I can't come in there? I'm your mother, and you're hurt."

"It's nothing."

"It's not nothing."

Meg grabbed a facecloth and began dabbing at the blood on Rick's chin.

"Mom! I haven't got any clothes on!" Rick was clearly more distressed about his mother seeing him naked than about the cut on his chin. "Dad?" Rick looked pleadingly toward Ben. "Can you please make her go away?"

"I'm your mother, Rick. I changed your diapers. You haven't got anything I haven't seen before." Meg went on mopping at the cut, which continued to dribble bright red drops of blood onto the tile floor.

"But I'm not a baby anymore," Rick protested. He backed away from his mother, his face pinched with embarrassment and his hands still clutching his private parts.

"I'll take care of it." Ben stepped between Rick and Meg. "Go finish fixing dinner, and we'll be out in a few minutes." He took the facecloth from her hand.

Meg looked confused. She peered past Ben and then angled her head up toward his. "But, I —"

Ben kissed her briefly on the mouth and turned her toward the door. "You too, you bloodthirsty little imp," Ben told Evan, who'd been hanging on every word with relish. Such high drama didn't happen every day, and he was clearly enjoying every emotion-packed moment.

Evan lifted his shoulders and dropped them with a huge aggrieved sigh. "Awright." He followed his mother from the blood-spattered bathroom.

Ben shut the door. Then turned back to his son.

"What possessed him?" Meg asked Ben as soon as he reappeared in the living room after putting the boys to bed. The subject of Rick's little fiasco in the bathroom had been taboo during supper. Ben had given her a stern frown when Rick slid into his seat at the supper table with an adhesive bandage covering the cut on his chin. Frustrated and feeling more left out than ever, Meg had fumed and stayed stubbornly silent through most of the meal. She hadn't even made a token protest when Rick asked Ben to tuck them in. If the boys didn't want her intruding into their privacy, she wasn't going to force herself on them.

Ben shrugged as he dropped onto the ottoman in front of her. "Not sure what put the idea into his head in the first place, but once there, he was convinced he was growing a mustache."

"No way!" Meg protested. He was only seven. Her baby was only seven. Years away from having to think of shaving.

Ben chuckled. "Not unless you count the peach fuzz he's had since he was born." Ben reached out to put his hands on her knees. He started to say something, but Meg cut him off.

"Did you punish him?"

"We talked."

"You talked." Meg's echo was heavy with sarcasm. That's all Ben ever did with the boys. Have a talk. He never meted out punishment.

"I think he scared himself more than he did us."

"So, what's up with all the squeamishness over me seeing him naked?" Meg hadn't meant to ask. She'd meant to keep her hurt feelings to herself, but the question slipped out anyway.

"He's growing up." Ben squeezed her knees and inched the ottoman closer.

"He's just a baby."

"It's a boy thing. If you'd had a father around when you were seven, would you have wanted him to see you in your birthday suit? I don't know. Maybe girls are different, but I think that's about when I started banishing my mom from the bathroom when I was getting into the shower."

For a moment, Meg was diverted by the image of Ben, small, blond, and embarrassed about being naked in his mother's presence. Ben was right. She'd never known who her father was so she didn't know if she would have been just as uptight about him hanging around while she was dressing. The first time she'd been faced with anything similar, she'd been terrified. But that had been Remy lounging on her bed when all she had on was a towel and she'd already begun to develop. Not the same thing at all.

"We need to talk about Kip."

Meg jerked back to the present. To the abrupt change of topic. "What about Kip?"

"You said I didn't ask your opinion about fostering him. And you were right. I thought maybe we should discuss it since it looks like it's gonna be more than just a few weeks."

"I said, whatever you decide is fine." Meg didn't want to have to make a decision. Her feelings about Kip were all over the map. One minute she wanted him gone. Another moment, she was thankful for his presence, silent and reassuring, especially in the dark of night when she wandered sleepless through the house.

When she'd rounded Ben's truck and seen Kip shaking like a leaf in front of the open cruiser door, she'd wanted to throw herself in the dirt and wrap her arms about him to reassure him that no one was going to force him into the car. He'd been there, solid and accepting when she had her little meltdown and soaked his fur with her tears. She'd wanted to be there for him in his terror.

But she'd stood back, barely looking at Kip as Ben introduced her to the police officer. Then she'd fled to the house barely able to see where she was going for the tears filling her eyes. How did she feel about Kip staying with them indefinitely?

"If he stays much longer, sleeping in the house, playing with the boys, and being around family, it could easily become permanent," Ben started to explain. "If he's never able to return to police work, that is. I'd say that requires a consensus. At least some discussion."

Until that very moment, she'd not even noticed that Kip had not come into the house with Ben earlier. "Where is he now?"

"He's out in the kennel."

"You put him in a crate? All by himself?" Meg's heart protested. Kip hadn't done anything to deserve isolation. "You banished him to the kennel?"

Ben wagged his head and grinned. "Not exactly banished. I did leave him in the kennel, but he's loose with Columbo for company."

Meg pushed Ben's hands off her knees and stood.

"Where are you going?" Ben shot to his feet.

"To get Kip."

"But we need to talk." Ben caught her hand. He was frowning now. Looking worried.

Meg pulled free. "We can talk later." She headed for the door, leaving Ben sitting on the ottoman by himself.

Captain Allan's advice to sit down and have a serious discussion with Ben about working with him again, working with the dogs again, taunted Meg all the way out to the kennel building. Ben had just given her the perfect opening to bring it up, but she'd deliberately avoided it. The jumble of mixed

267

signals her heart was sending out about Kip confused her. She didn't know how she felt about going out to work with the rest of the dogs yet.

Kip was one thing. She'd more or less come to terms with him being around. But that wasn't the same as spending every day training dogs who looked just like Scout. Dogs she knew would be going into harm's way once they left Ben's kennel. The idea of working with a dog, getting to know it and care about it, then hearing later that it had been shot terrified her. Could she bear such an ending? Again? Did she want to take that chance?

CHAPTER 20

"I got to thinking about our last conversation via Skype and wondered if you thought about it at all," Ben asked as Meg turned out the light and sat down on the edge of the bed. He reached for her, and she let him pull her down into his embrace. "So, did you?"

"We talked a bunch of times via Skype. I can't recall all the things we might have talked about." She snuggled into him and ran her hand over his abdomen. "I remember talking about whether men were beautiful or not."

Ben grunted. She'd gotten him so turned on in spite of the fact she was thousands of miles away. He'd been thankful the boys had not been present for that little Skype discussion. Meg slid her roaming hand a little lower. He was getting pretty turned on right now, but they needed to talk.

"Men are handsome," he offered his usual

rebuttal. He covered her hand with his own and stopped what she was doing with it. If he let her keep it up, they wouldn't talk. They'd make love. Then she'd fall asleep.

"But I was referring to the option of trying for baby number three." If she felt so left out and aimless, maybe a baby would help. A new baby would be totally dependent on her, and he remembered how wrapped up in the boys she had been when they were infants.

Ben had always wanted a big family. Like the one he'd grown up in. Meg had never seemed to have a strong opinion one way or another. Back then she'd been focused on the idea of a career in law enforcement. But now that she'd changed her mind and, in fact, had no idea what she wanted, maybe a baby would fill some unmet need she couldn't find the words to explain.

Uneasily, Ben realized Meg had gone very still. "You told me you wanted a little girl." He tried to get the discussion going again.

"I wanted a girl when I was pregnant with Evan."

"They say the third time's the charm."

"Maybe, but it's not a guarantee."

"Nothing in life is a guarantee, Meggie." Ben cupped his wife's chin and turned her face up toward his. He kissed her briefly on the mouth. She was so contrary lately, he was worried. She wouldn't talk about Kip, didn't want to discuss the dogs in general, but then turned around and insisted on bringing Kip into the house rather than leaving him with Columbo for the night. Now she seemed to be dancing all around the idea of getting pregnant again. "You want to tell me what's really bothering you?"

She rolled out of his embrace and folded her arms across her chest.

"I tried to tell you the other day, but you didn't get it." Her voice was sharp, the words like pellets thrown at him so hard they stung.

"I didn't get what?"

"That I don't know who I am anymore. I don't know what I want. How can I know if I want a baby if I don't even know who I am?"

"Then let's talk about what you do know." Ben felt desperate. He wanted to be there for her, but he didn't know where *there* was. He rolled up onto one elbow and cupped the side of her face with his hand. "I want to fix whatever's wrong."

She pulled away from his touch and rolled off the bed onto her feet. She grabbed her robe and wrapped it about her naked body. "You can't fix everything, Ben." She stalked across the room to the door and started down the hall.

Ben got to his feet, found his briefs, and pulled them on. Then he followed her.

She was standing at the big bay window in the living room, shoulders slumped, staring out into the night. He came up behind her and put his arms around her. "So, maybe I can't fix it, but I still want to help, Meggie. You just have to tell me what you need."

"I can't tell you what I don't know." Her voice sounded small.

Ben's heart jerked in pain. His own and hers. What had happened to the easy friendship they'd always known? She used to tell him everything. The good things and the bad. About her feelings, her fears, the things she hoped for and dreamed of. Everything. Everything except what Remy had done to her when she was just a kid, that is. That last thought zapped him like a Taser. Meg had never told him about Remy.

Had something happened to her that involved another man?

Had she been violated? That shocking possibility hit Ben like a sluice of ice water.

He thought back over the last three weeks of intense lovemaking. There had been a hint of desperation to it some of the time. A feeling of neediness. But then, he'd been pretty needy himself after a year apart. Surely a woman who'd been raped wouldn't behave that way. She would have flinched at his touch. Like she had back when they were first becoming intimate. Before Ben had found out about Remy and the trauma Meg had experienced. Meg had been just the opposite of traumatized since she got back from Iraq.

Another blast from the emotional Taser.

Was there someone else? Was she in love with this man John who she called out to in her nightmares? That would certainly explain why she couldn't tell Ben what she needed. A woman could hardly tell her husband that what she ached for was the love of another man. Not unless she was getting ready to end the marriage.

Ben's throat went tight, and he felt suddenly dizzy.

"Do you still love me?"

"Of course, I love you." Meg whirled out of his embrace and turned to face him. "I've always loved you. But I just need to be alone right now. Please, Ben. Just leave me alone for a little bit."

Ben dropped his hands to his sides. He wanted to haul her into his arms and hold her so tight neither of them would be able to breathe very well. But he'd promised to give her whatever she needed, and she'd asked him to leave her alone.

Without touching her anywhere else, he bent and kissed her on the forehead. "I love you, Meggie. And I'm a man of my word. I'm just praying this alone time you need so much is just temporary, because one thing I do know for certain is that I need you. I don't know how I'll live without you, if that's what you find you want."

He turned and walked back to their bedroom. He glanced back once. She was still watching him, so he blew her a kiss that she didn't return. Then he took himself to bed.

"You can't fix this for her, Ben. No matter how much you love her and no matter how hard you try, you can't fix it for her. She has to fix it for herself. And before that she has to want to fix it."

"But, Dad," Ben pleaded. "It's killing me. I've gotta be able to do something." He'd come to talk to his dad because he didn't know where else to turn. Cam had once been where Meg was right now. He'd been hurt and disillusioned by the reality of war. He'd lashed out and tried to push Ben's mother away. But here they were, still married and still in love all these years later.

Cam had to know what Meg needed. What Ben could do.

"I can't do nothing." His eyes stung. He turned away and gazed out over the Atlantic Ocean through the watery sheen. His whole life was falling apart, and there was nothing he could do to save it?

"I didn't say do nothing." Cam's voice was quietly reassuring. "There's a lot you can do. Some you can't, but more that you can." He came to stand beside Ben and rested his hands on the sturdy wooden railing. Ben could feel the heat of his father's body, as calming as his voice. Ben wanted to turn and feel himself folded into his father's embrace. To have someone bigger and wiser than he was take charge and fix the ache in his heart. But he wasn't five years old anymore, and this wasn't a broken toy.

"The number one thing you need to do is to understand that what Meg is going through is not something you are responsible for. Don't take it personally when she lashes out or withdraws into some personal little hell. The second most important thing is to just keep on loving her. Be there for her no matter how hard she makes it for you at the moment. And make sure she knows you are there for her, no matter what.

"Stick up for the boys if you need to, but

be gentle about it. Most of all don't be afraid to show her you are hurting too. She loves you. She's just too caught up in her own world of hurt right now to see what she's doing to you, so you need to tell her. Help her see that she's got to make the first move before things can get better."

His father pushed himself away from the railing. "Let's go for a walk. I want to tell you about a young man I once knew. I'll just let your mom know where we're going."

Ben took his time driving home, thinking about the things his dad had revealed about himself, about his marriage, and how close he'd come to making sure Ben never happened at all.

His father had always seemed so solid. So reliable and so grounded. Ben couldn't recall a single time his father had raised his voice, even when Ben or one of his siblings deserved a thorough scolding. The only time he'd ever seen his father cry was the day his baby brother had fallen out of a tree, and Cam had rushed to the lifeless little body, begging Jake to be okay. They'd all cried that day. Tears of relief when Jake finally regained consciousness. Tears of release after hours of anguished waiting and praying around a bed that was way too big for the little body laying so still and lifeless in the middle of it. Those tears Ben understood.

But the picture of a tormented young man on the verge of suicide was so at odds with everything Ben thought he knew about his father that Ben hadn't been able to find any words in response. He could no more picture his dad throwing his treasured worry stone away in a rage than he could imagine Cam shouting at the love of his life, telling her she'd be better off without him. And nothing Ben's mother had done had been able to fix Cam's broken soul until Cam himself realized what he'd nearly thrown away and sought the help he needed.

Cam had pulled the little stone from his pocket and studied it for a bit before he'd embarked on the unpleasant story of his younger self. That smooth little stone had lived in his father's pocket for as long as Ben could remember. He had played with it as a child. He recalled the warmth it retained whenever he'd fished it out of his father's pocket to look at. But he'd never known the whole story until tonight.

If Ben had found a similar stone on the beach he'd have taken it home to Meg, but he hadn't. Besides, that was his father's thing. Meg deserved her own talisman.

Last night had been Ben's dark night of the soul. It wasn't going to be easy, but now he knew where he would find the strength to get through the difficult days ahead. Cam didn't believe for a minute that Meg had fallen out of love with Ben or into love with another man. Or that she might have been unfaithful. It was not unheard of. Deployment was hell on relationships. Soldiers all too frequently received Dear John letters from home and just as frequently found solace in the arms of someone closer to hand when life was hanging by a thread. But his father said he'd bet the farm that was not what was bothering Meg.

He'd done his best to describe the intense closeness that soldiers felt for each other. It was a bond like no other. The ultimate adversity of war and imminent death fused those bonds so strongly that men would run into certain death to save a buddy. It was unlikely that Meg would not have felt that way about the men and women she served with, but that would not have taken the place of the love she had for Ben.

His father had sounded so certain and his explanation so convincing, Ben felt better already. He hadn't shared his doubts about keeping the kennels with his father. The idea of letting them go was a kind of last resort thing and only if Meg gave him some indication that she wanted him to. But it was still on the table. The most important thing in his life was Meg. So long as she was his, he could deal with anything else.

Maybe he'd try teaching. If it hadn't been for the dream of training dogs, he'd have been a middle school history teacher. Until Ben's junior year in high school, he'd hated history. Then he'd ended up in Jack Bowman's American History class. Bowman had made history come alive. His methods were totally different from any teacher Ben had ever had before or since, but they had been very effective in lighting a fire under reluctant students of history. Ben knew he could be the same kind of teacher and perhaps make the same kind of difference in other young people's lives. If he had to give up the kennels, he'd be a teacher. Just so long as he still had Meg in his life.

CHAPTER 21

Meg sat on the top step planning what she would say to Ben. She heard the phone ring, but she didn't want to answer it. Now that she had made up her mind to follow Dr. Allan's advice and share everything that had been eating at her with Ben, she didn't want to be distracted by someone soliciting a donation or wanting to offer her a deal on her credit card rates. If it was important, they'd call back. Or Ben would pick up the call out in his office and deal with it.

The phone stopped ringing, and Meg went back to thinking through what she would tell Ben. Where to start? She should tell him about John.

John hadn't leapt immediately to her mind when Ben asked her if she still loved him. In fact, she hadn't been thinking about John at all until after Ben had gone and left her to the solitude she'd begged him for. Much later it had occurred to her that if she could have doubts about Ben and Anne Royko, Ben might be just as uncertain about her.

Meg couldn't deny the bond she shared with John Bissett. But it was mostly about being battle buddies. It was the same powerful bond that held them all together: Meredith, the only other woman in her unit, Sgt. Keek Miller, Pudge, and Glen the Joker who were always on the convoy runs with her. Doc Manoli and even Father McAlpin, the chaplain, were part of that tight little band of brothers and sisters.

What Ben would have a hard time with was what had almost happened in the wake of Scout's death. What for far too many shocking, heart-pounding minutes, she had wanted to happen. That she *had* wanted it was going to hurt Ben the most.

Whatever doubts haunted Ben's soul, two things that he'd said haunted Meg. *Do you still love me?* And *I just hope that when you figure out what you want, there's still a place for me.* She did still love Ben. She would always love him. And if he wasn't a part of her life, there would be nothing left to hold her together. But he seemed to doubt both. She had to open up and tell him so. Which meant trying harder to explain the source of her melancholy and digging into feelings she didn't want to face. And owning up to guilt that shamed her.

Meg stood up and wiped her sweaty palms on her thighs. Ben was her personal lifeline. Just as Captain Allan had suggested. But as the doctor pointed out, Meg had to reach out and grab that lifeline. Ben couldn't grab it for her.

She went down the stairs and started across the gravel driveway. Her heart pounded, and her chest felt constricted. But she was going to ask for Ben's help. There was no need for this anxiousness. Ben loved her. He was her rock. Her steps quickened.

When she opened the door to the kennel, Columbo didn't greet her, which was odd. He was a self-appointed doorman for the place. Both guard and greeter.

"Ben?" Meg's voice echoed in the quiet cavernous building. All the dogs were outdoors. Perhaps that's where Ben was. Meg hesitated. She'd forgotten Mike would be out here, too.

Then she squared her shoulders. *Suck it up, Marine. Oorah!*

She strode down the walkway between the training area and the runs to the door leading to the outside training yard. She blinked in the bright glare of sunlight and then brought her hand up to shield her eyes.

Two dogs sat at attention in front of Mike

in the middle of the yard. The rest of the dogs were in their runs. All except for Columbo. Meg opened the gate and headed toward Mike and the dogs. She was a little surprised to find that she didn't feel that gut-tightening awfulness that had filled her the last time she'd been out here.

Mike looked up as Meg approached.

"Where's Ben?"

Mike nodded back in the direction of the kennel building. "In his office, last time I saw him, ma'am."

She'd known Mike for years, but she guessed the formality was due to her being the boss's wife now that Mike worked for them. "Thanks." She turned and headed back to the building.

It was still just as silent and still. And again, Columbo did not greet her. She retraced her path between the training area and the runs, back to the far end of the building where Ben's office was located.

Her steps quickened almost to a run as she reached his door, but she stopped dead when she looked in.

Ben held the phone in one hand, but not up to his ear. His face was ashen. Columbo sat in front of him whining softly in his throat.

"Ben?" Meg stepped into the room and

crossed it in three strides. "What's wrong?"

Now she was the one asking *what's wrong.* Something was horribly wrong for Ben to look like that. If her heart had felt constricted before, now it felt like it had stopped beating. "Ben."

She squatted next to the dog and pulled Ben's chair around so she could see into his face. She removed the phone from his grasp and set it back into its cradle.

"Chuck's dead," Ben said with an anguished sob. His eyes were awash with tears. "He killed himself."

Meg stopped breathing for several heartpounding moments. *Chuck committed suicide?* The reality hit her like a freight train. Soldier suicides were becoming all too common, but Chuck? *Oh, God, not Chuck!*

Meg fell onto her knees and snaked her arms about Ben's waist. He buried his face in her neck and clung to her, his chest heaving.

"I just talked to him. Just two days ago," Ben moaned. "Why didn't he tell me things were so bad?"

"Maybe he didn't know," Meg said, trying to soothe her husband.

"He was laughing," Ben protested.

"Maybe it was an accident?"

Ben shook his head. "He put a gun in his

mouth, Meg. Hardly an accident."

"Oh, Ben. I'm so sorry. Oh, my God, I'm so, so sorry."

Ben stood, and she stood with him, unwilling to let him leave her embrace. He held her, resting his chin on the top of her head. His entire body shuddered. Meg hugged him tighter. She hadn't realized she was crying until she felt his shirt growing damp beneath her face. She leaned back and looked up. Tears ran down Ben's cheeks as well, dribbling past his chin and into the collar of his shirt.

"I have to go over there," he whispered brokenly.

"I'll go with you." She tried to wipe his face with the palms of her hands, gave up, and grabbed the hem of her T-shirt.

"The boys?" Ben stepped back and finished the job of drying his face with his shirtsleeve.

"Mike will watch for them. I'll call and get your mom to come over. Or Kate. Do you want me to call Will?"

"That was Will who called me."

"I'll just be a minute, then." With a purpose and something that she knew how to organize, Meg sprang into action. She hurried out to ask Mike to watch for the boys to get off the bus and keep an eye on them until some family member could arrive to take over. Then she went back to the house to call for back up.

Neither Ben's sister Kate nor Sandy Cameron answered the phone, so Meg called her brother instead. The boys loved having Stu over to babysit. Probably because he let them watch things on TV that Ben and Meg never would have allowed. And he tended to haul them down to Ethan's for ribs rather than cook anything himself. But the boys loved ribs as much as they loved Stu. Better yet, Stu would probably be here before the bus dropped them off, and he'd keep them so entertained that they wouldn't think to ask questions about where their parents were or why.

"We should stop at Winn-Dixie," Meg said as Ben pulled out onto Stewart Road. "I'll get cold cuts and rolls and bread and stuff. Soda and tea and beer too. There's bound to be a lot of people, and Mrs. Royko won't be in any state to figure out what to feed everyone. Better if there's stuff there that anyone can put out when they need to."

Ben looked across the truck's cab at her, his eyes still bleak. "Do women always think of these things? Or just you?"

"We all do," Meg muttered absently. Her mind was still compiling a list of things she should get. "Stop at Ralph's. I can grab some of those New York bagels everyone loves, too."

When they arrived at the stately southern home that had been in the Royko family for three generations, Meg was proved right. Ben hadn't considered the number of people likely to drop everything and be here within hours of the news.

Cars lined both sides of the long curving driveway and were parked in either direction along the side of the road. Considering the sheer number of grocery bags they had in the bed of the truck, Ben was glad there was still one space left in the driveway across the street. Another of Ben's high school friends had grown up here, and he was sure the Quinns wouldn't object to him using their driveway.

What am I going to say to Mr. and Mrs. Royko? Or Anne and Donald? What could anyone say?

Ben swallowed hard, blinked back another onslaught of tears, and climbed out of the truck. He gathered up most of the bags of groceries his wife had bought and let Meg grab the bagels and two jugs of sweet tea. He'd come back for the camping chest filled with ice, soda, and beer.

They crossed the street in silence. He glanced at Meg, trying to discover if she was as shocked and distressed as he was. Words didn't begin to describe all the emotions churning in his gut. He just prayed that Meg would not freak out. Chuck had seen action in places too much like where Meg had been. Ben couldn't begin to guess what kind of nightmares might be awakened for Meg.

Because of all the groceries, they left the front walk and detoured around the back to deliver them straight to the kitchen.

The door opened as if someone had been watching for them, and almost immediately, they were engulfed in Aunt Bea's motherly embrace. She hugged them both, an arm about each of their necks. Her eyes were red, but she was all bustling business.

"Bring those things right here." She stepped aside and indicated a folding table that had been set up inside the screened-in porch. Ben should have guessed Aunt Bea would be over here organizing things. The Quinns and the Roykos had been neighbors since they'd been newlywed couples, long before Chuck was born. Bea was Chuck's godmother, too. No wonder her eyes were red-rimmed.

Beatrice Quinn ushered Ben and Meg

through the kitchen and into the parlor where there was barely even standing room. Charles Royko stepped forward first and drew Ben into a hug. His eyes were as red as Aunt Bea's, but at the moment, he was dry-eyed.

"I'm so sorry." Ben managed to get the words out with difficulty. Charles passed him along to his wife Jeannie and turned to hug Meg.

"Mrs. R." Ben pulled the diminutive, gray-haired woman into his embrace. This time his voice did fail him, so he just stood there rocking her for the longest time, wishing he was anywhere else.

Someone tapped him on the shoulder. With a murmur of regret, he turned away from Chuck's mother and looked into the face of his mirror image. Will's eyes were full of shock and disbelief. Without a word, the brothers embraced, hugging each other hard, patting each other on the back, unwilling to let go.

Unwilling until, with a wail of despair, Anne threw herself at the twins. Will stepped back, and Anne flung her arms about Ben's neck and wept noisily into his shirt. "Why didn't he — tell us — something was — wrong?" Anne pleaded between hiccoughs. Anne was a self-centered woman, but she and Chuck had been close. Ben understood her anguish. He shared it.

Chuck had told Ben things weren't good. Yet somehow, Ben hadn't read between the lines. Hadn't heard the utter despair that must have led to this final, irrevocable act of a desperate man.

Ben let Anne weep without offering any answers to her question. Guilt ate at him. He should have known. Should have seen how bad things were.

Later that evening, after tucking the boys into bed, Meg found Ben sitting on the porch with a half-drunk bottle of beer in his hand. The cardboard carrier sat beside his chair; only two bottles still had caps on them. Ben was not a drinker. Meg was alarmed.

Suddenly, the shoe was on the other foot. For the last month, she'd been the one prowling the house at night, trying to avoid sleep and outrun memories she didn't dare face. And it had been Ben coming to find her and offer solace and understanding.

She didn't know what else to say that she hadn't already said at least three or four times since Ben had gotten that heartbreaking call earlier that afternoon.

Chuck had been Ben's best friend since

grade school. Ben, Will, and Chuck had called themselves the Three Musketeers and shared everything, from trouble to triumph. They'd been on the same teams in school and got into the same scrapes out of school. They'd hunted together, both birds and girls. They'd gone off to college together, too and been inseparable until graduation and adulthood arrived and different choices of career sent them in different directions. But they'd stayed close. Chuck had been an usher at their wedding.

Losing Chuck would have hit Ben hard anyway. Losing him in such a horrible way was shattering.

Not wanting to sit in the other chair, too far away to even reach for his hand, Meg sat down in Ben's lap and wrapped one arm about his shoulders. She took the nearly empty beer from his hand and dropped it into the carton with the other empties. Then she snuggled in with her head on Ben's shoulder and took his hand in her free one.

"I wish I was smart and knew all the right words to say."

"Nothing much anyone can say," Ben murmured.

Ben was done with tears, but the misery in his voice tore at her heart.

"I just wish he'd told me how bad things

were. I mean, *really* how bad. Why didn't he ask for help?"

"Maybe he didn't know what to ask for." Meg thought about her own aimless confusion over the last few weeks. Not that she'd ever considered taking her own life. Or even come close. Her gut had twisted with indecision, and at times it felt like she was coming out of her skin, but she had never been desperate enough to end her life.

But frustration and lack of purpose took their toll on anyone. Especially someone who had been so intensely involved as Chuck had been. Then there were the nightmares that no soldier ever fully escaped. A Special Forces guy for most of his career until injuries got him medically discharged, Chuck's nightmares must have been a thousand times worse than hers. He'd seen so much more and been further into the depths of hell than she ever had.

How had Chuck managed to avoid the mandates for discharge that sent her to see Doctor Allan? Or maybe he had seen an Army shrink but had skated by not talking about the things that haunted his nights and stalked his days.

"Maybe he thought it made him less of a man if he admitted he was in trouble." Meg tucked Ben's arm about her waist and pressed her hand to his chest where she could feel his heart beating steadily beneath his clean white T-shirt.

"But he was kidding around about that plate in his head last time we talked. He told me he was talking to aliens and that the plate was really a receiver some Army intelligence people had invented. I thought he was joking."

"He probably was. Joking, I mean. Not talking to aliens. It's easier to joke about the really bad things than to admit they really get to you."

"But he could have told me anything. I'd never think less of him. He should have known that." Ben pleaded for understanding.

Meg suddenly remembered seeing Chuck swiping at his eyes when he and Ben had been talking while she cleaned up her workshop. "Why was he crying that day at the fair?"

"A buddy he served with got killed in a car wreck," Ben answered after a pause. "He was upset because he didn't find out until too late to go to the guy's funeral. He felt like he let his fellow soldier down."

"Yeah, well. He would." Meg pulled away to look into Ben's face. "If something like that happened to Keek, or Pudge or Meredith, or the Joker — and I failed to show up to honor their memory, I'd have been just as distressed. I'd have felt like I let them down."

"But he didn't hear about it in time. How is that his fault?"

"Depends. Could be the family kept it small and didn't tell many people. But what if Chuck didn't pick his phone up for three days? And what if someone had been trying to reach him? He'd blame himself for that."

She sat up and put her hands on either side of Ben's face. "You didn't let Chuck down, Ben. He let himself down. He let his family down, too. He was in a lot of pain, but he didn't reach out for help. You can't help someone who doesn't want to be helped."

"What about you?"

"What about me?" Did Ben think she was suicidal?

"I keep asking you what's wrong, but you won't tell me anything."

"That's different." She'd been on the verge of telling him when this all happened. But right now he didn't need more pain and more problems. She'd let him get through Chuck's funeral before she dumped her load of guilt and anxiety on him.

"How is it so diff—"

Meg stopped his words with her mouth. His lips felt stiff and unresponsive, but she deepened the kiss. He tasted of beer and smelled of shampoo and the mountain-fresh scent of his just-washed T-shirt. When he finally gave in and responded, his mouth was hungry and demanding. Meg melted into him, taking the harsh assault eagerly. They both needed to banish the unspeakable and find release.

"Take me to bed, Ben."

"Mmmm," he mumbled, his mouth never fully leaving hers. His hands were already under her pajama top, his calloused palms cool and rough as they closed around her breasts.

"Now," she gasped, as excitement raced through her. They couldn't make love on the front porch. Even if it was completely dark outside and there was rarely traffic at this time of night. "Ben?"

Ben stood in a rush, carrying her with him. She wrapped her legs around his waist as he strode through the door and shut it behind them with his heel.

The lovemaking was fast and furious. Without foreplay or words. When Ben finally flung himself onto his back, spent and breathing hard, there were tears running down his cheeks again.

CHAPTER 22

The morning following Chuck's death dawned clear and warm. A perfect day for all the Veterans Day festivities the people of Tide's Way had planned in spite of the sudden, stricken sadness his act had visited on the small community. School was out, and most folk had the day off. The boys begged to go to the town parade.

The last place Ben wanted to be was at a parade honoring soldiers. Captain Charles Royko Jr. should have been marching with the rest of the veterans from the local VFW. He should have been saluting when the rifles were fired at the cemetery and applauding the various speakers. But he'd chosen not to be there in the most final way he could.

Ben went anyway.

He was more worried about Meg than he wanted to admit. Chuck's suicide created a whole new and far sharper focus on Meg's erratic behavior since she'd returned from Iraq. She wasn't exactly moody, but she tended to pull into herself far more often than he remembered. Actually, he didn't recall her ever being so self-contained and contemplative except for the first few days after her first overseas deployment. Although that one had been far briefer and not into a war zone.

Meg had declined to participate in the parade when first approached by the commander of the local VFW. Ben remembered the day the man had come to talk to her about it and her vague explanation of why she wouldn't be going. It hadn't mattered so much to him, so he hadn't pressed her for more.

But this morning she'd showed up in the kitchen an hour before the parade was to start decked out in her class A uniform looking even more remote than usual. She'd left ahead of Ben and the boys to leave herself enough time to find out where she needed to be. She had not offered any explanation for her change of plan.

So, here he was, standing in the midst of the cheering crowd, trying not to be crushed by the festive atmosphere. Trying not to think about Chuck. Trying not to worry about Meg.

Evan had wormed his way to the front of the crowd dragging Ben with him so as not to miss a single thing. Evan had a small American flag which he waved with vigor as the high school band approached. Rick, older and more aware of the events of the day before, had been more subdued. But he'd still been excited to be marching with his Cub Scout pack, decked out in his freshly ironed uniform with his Progress Toward Ranks patch dangling from his right pocket button.

It was small as parades go, but Tide's Way was small. Patriotic to the core, but small. Flags flew on more than half the lawns in town, and there was a higher than average percentage of citizens who'd served at one time or another. Today every single flag was at half-staff, and Ben wondered how many people had raised their flags on this particular Veterans Day with the holiday in mind and how many had lowered the colors to mark Chuck's passing.

Evan yanked on his jeans. Caught unaware, with his thoughts far away, Ben was jerked back to the here and now.

"There's Mom!" Evan jumped up and down and waved his little flag even harder. "Mom!" he shouted over the noise of the crowd and the lingering sound of drums.

"Mommy."

Behind the row of military flags, Meg turned and smiled at them, then waved briefly at her son before facing forward again. She was trim and sharp. The best looking Marine *ever* in Ben's opinion. But Chuck had looked sharp in his uniform, too. Outside, all squared away and looking as formidable as any soldier who had ever worn a Special Forces beret. But inside, crushed by the things he'd seen and done.

Did those same self-destructive seeds lurk in Meg? Was the strangeness he'd felt in the last weeks a part of that pit of despair that had claimed Chuck? The concern Ben had been feeling for weeks intensified. Chuck had been hiding the worst of his depression so well that even those who knew him best had not seen his suicide coming. Was it possible Meg could be doing the same thing? Hiding it even from the man who loved her the most?

Ben hadn't exaggerated when he told Meg she *was* his life. She had no idea how hellish the last year had been for him. Or how afraid he'd been that she might be wounded. Or worse. But the relief he'd felt watching her walk toward him the day she'd returned had been eroded with worry every day since.

How many times had he asked her what

was wrong, only to be sidetracked by sex or told that she needed time to sort things out? But she hadn't sorted it out or confided in him.

Just be there for her and let her know you are hurting too. That had been his father's advice. But it was easier said than done. Last night was a perfect example of how effectively she'd managed to avoid discussion of any issues she might have.

He watched the back of Meg's head until it disappeared from sight.

The week passed in a blur. Classmates Ben hadn't seen in years began arriving from all over the country. They stopped by the house alone or in groups. Will seemed to be there any time he was not on duty or sleeping. They talked about the good old days. Remembered Chuck from high school and before. They talked about the pranks the Three Musketeers had pulled. Almost no one mentioned the many citations and awards Chuck had earned as a soldier.

It was a struggle to stay dry-eyed through the funeral. Ben had been asked to give the eulogy, and it was one of the hardest things he'd ever done in his life. But it was the only thing he had left that he could do for the friend he felt he'd failed.

The gathering back at the Royko home after the burial was even harder. Ben sensed that Meg was struggling with something, and he desperately wanted to be with her. He wanted to be alone with her and beg her to tell him everything. Instead, it seemed that Anne Royko had decided Ben was the support she needed to get through it all. She clung to him at every possible moment, until, in spite of his sincere sympathy for her loss, he wanted to tell her to get lost and leave him the hell alone. He'd never been so angry with a woman in his life. And since it seemed so inappropriate, he was disgusted with himself for feeling that way.

Meg stood on the far side of the room chatting with two of Chuck's fellow soldiers. She glanced up, and Ben caught her gaze. Wordlessly, he pleaded with her to come to his rescue. But it wasn't Meg who saved him from saying something he shouldn't.

Two women, well-dressed and vaguely familiar, approached and pulled Anne into their embrace. Anne let go of Ben with reluctance and turned to her friends from the city. Ben beat a hasty and totally undignified retreat.

It didn't seem right to leave so soon, but he desperately wanted to gather his family up and take them home. He found Mrs.

Royko and gave her a hug. He made her promise to call him if there was anything he could do. He edged into the group where Meg was still chatting with the two soldiers and tapped her on the shoulder, then jerked his head in the direction of the door. Now he just needed to say goodbye to Mr. Royko and Donald, if he could find them, and round up Evan and Rick.

All of the people he sought were out in the backyard.

By the time he'd finished his goodbyes and had his sons corralled, Meg appeared.

She didn't question the early departure, but she did give him a hug before leading the way around the house and down the drive to her car.

They were halfway home before Evan spoke up. "Is it wrong if I laughed at something?"

Meg was driving and kept her eyes on the road, but Ben turned in his seat and looked at his son. "Of course, it's not wrong."

"Kevin said we shouldn't be laughing because his uncle was dead. But it was funny, Daddy. Cooper put Mrs. Royko's little kitten on top of the dog's head, and the dog was trying to lick it."

"Well, I don't think Kevin's the authority here. God made people to enjoy life and gave them things to laugh about. Besides, Uncle Chuck would have been laughing too."

"Kevin said Uncle Chuck wasn't really my uncle either. Rick said so, too." Evan frowned at his brother. "But he is. Right, Daddy?"

"He was an honorary uncle. He was your godfather, and he loved you. And he loved to laugh."

"See? I told you." Evan turned to stick his tongue out at Rick.

Meg looked at Ben and rolled her eyes. Suddenly Ben felt like laughing too. He'd been too solemn all week. Too burdened with all the ways he might have failed as a friend. And grieving because he'd never be able to put them right. And Evan, with five-year-old logic, zoomed right in on one of the important things in life. To enjoy every moment that one was given because no one ever knew how many moments they were going to get.

"Do you miss it?"

"Miss what?" Meg looked at her husband, completely confused about his meaning.

"Being over there."

"Being over where? At the Roykos'? Hardly!"

Meg had been more than ready to leave the reception at the Royko home. Watching Anne cling to Ben had been bad enough. Watching Ben let her cling had been worse. She had wanted to march over and peel the woman off her husband and tell her to find someone else to weep all over. But that would have created a scene to end all scenes.

Ben didn't need her irrational jealously. He didn't need her making scenes. He was grieving his friend, and that was enough to cope with.

"I didn't mean the Roykos'," Ben said softly. He wasn't looking at her. He was watching the boys playing about in the small waves lapping at the shore and managing to get their jeans wet in spite of the chilly ocean water and Meg's admonitions to the contrary.

Meg didn't say anything.

"I meant Iraq."

Meg shook her head, then because he still wasn't looking at her, she said, "No. I don't miss Iraq."

She began gathering up the remains of their picnic supper and stowed them in the cooler.

Ben's hand closed around her wrist with surprising force. "Stop shutting me out."

Meg let go of the potato chip bag and sat

304

back on her heels. Ben let go of her wrist. "I'm not shutting you out."

Ben closed his eyes for a moment and then opened them again. His jaw tightened, and a pulse jumped in his temple. He was clearly upset, but she wasn't sure why.

"So, if you don't miss Iraq, what are you missing?"

Meg stared at Ben, not sure where to begin. Not prepared to begin a difficult discussion with her sons playing close by.

"Chuck said he missed it. He said that he wished he could go back. Is that what you really want? To go back to the war?"

There was no missing the pain in Ben's question.

"I don't wish I could go back," she assured him. "Of that I am very sure."

He pulled his knees to his chest, laced his fingers together, and hugged his legs. He studied her face.

"Some guys *do* miss the action," Meg admitted. "A lot of guys. Maybe Chuck did, too. It's hard to explain if you haven't been there." Meg sat back down and scooted closer to Ben's side. She glanced toward the water where the boys were getting increasingly wet but were still cavorting safely in shallow water.

"You miss missiles screaming into your

little outpost in the night. You miss getting woken up a dozen times. Sleep is fitful enough without all the noise. You miss the constant threat of explosive devices erupting under the vehicles or worse, under your feet. Guys that are really out there miss the hellish nightmare even more, but you miss it all in a good way. It just takes a while to become comfortable with being safe again. That's why I'm jumpy. It's why that stack of books falling off the counter had me in a cold sweat the other day. It's why I bolt out of bed when something wakes me up unexpectedly. So, I miss it, but I don't. I'm not sure if I'm making any sense."

Ben unlaced his fingers where they were wrapped about his knees and reached over to gather her hand into his. "I get that part. But Chuck said he missed his *life* there, and now I'm afraid that's what you were trying to tell me when you said that you didn't feel like you fit in here at home anymore."

Meg shook her head once, then stopped. "Well, maybe a little," she admitted. "There's a camaraderie that's hard to describe. The band of brothers thing. It goes deep. It becomes part of who you are. It's why soldiers will jump on grenades to save their buddies' lives. It's why some soldiers expose themselves to enemy fire to drag a downed comrade to safety or administer first aid. Then you come home, and it's gone. That closeness is gone. And you feel a little lost. I think that's what Chuck might have been trying to explain. It's why so many men go back in again even after getting out. They try civilian life, and it doesn't work. They feel like they'll never fit in. Like no one will ever understand. And they want that other thing back. That place where they felt like they made a difference. But Chuck couldn't go back because of his injuries."

"But you're not injured. You could go back." Ben's hand gripped hers until her fingers hurt, as if by holding on tight enough he could keep her from wanting to go back. His thumb drew frantic little circles on the back of her hand.

"I've already submitted all the paperwork to resign my commission."

Ben's thumb ceased circling, but the tightness of his grip didn't lessen. "Are you sure that's what you want?"

"I'm —" Meg tried to return the pressure of his grip. "I'm sure."

He relaxed, but not completely. "You won't miss it? The camaraderie, I mean?"

Meg started to shrug but stopped herself. "I'll — yes, I'll miss it. But not enough."

"Not enough for what?"

Shrieks of laughter erupted from the water's edge. Evan was now completely soaked, and his brother was not far from it. They were scooping handfuls of water and flinging them at each other.

"We'll have to go home soon, or they'll be freezing." Meg started to get up.

Ben didn't let go of her hand. "Not enough for what?"

"Not enough to go back," Meg said, leaning toward him. "Not enough to leave my boys motherless." She kissed him. "Or you a widower."

CHAPTER 23

Will Cameron walked into the kitchen without knocking. "Hey, Kip. How're they hanging?" Rick bounded in behind him, the shirt of his scout uniform half out of his trousers and his hair full of leaves. "Hit the shower, young man," Will called after Rick as he skipped through the kitchen and down the hall.

Ben snorted and turned back to the pizza dough he was rolling out. "Some watch dog you are, Kip. You didn't even growl to announce we had company."

"He knows me. I'm not company." Will squatted to the dog's level and scratched behind his ears. "Right, Kip? I told Rick to leave his muddy shoes on the porch. Yeah, you like that, don'tcha, big guy?" Will finished giving Kip a thorough scratch and stood.

"You're staying for pizza night, right?" Ben slopped sauce over the last of the dough, then started in with the cheese.

"Have I ever declined a meal I didn't have to cook for myself?" Will shucked his own not-so-muddy boots and parked them beside the door.

"You need to find yourself a wife and settle down." Ben tore off the top of a package of pepperoni slices and winked at his twin.

Will glanced around the kitchen, then looked back toward Ben. "You have one, but you're still cooking."

"It's my pizza night. My choice."

"Where is Meg?"

"Out with the girls. Margie picked her up to go to a baby shower for Jenny Crawford out at that fancy new place by the bridge." With the last of the pepperoni arranged to his satisfaction, Ben opened the oven and slid the pans onto the racks.

"That's Beau's wife, isn't it?"

"You know any other Jenny Crawfords?"

"No. But I didn't know Beau was going to be a daddy finally. I'll have to rag on him a little next time I run into him."

"Your day will come, and you know what they say about who laughs last." Ben set the timer and began collecting napkins, plates, and glasses to put on the table. "Grab a couple beers," he told Will as he headed into the dining room.

Will collected two bottles from the fridge and popped the caps off, then followed Ben. "How are you doing?"

Ben glanced up from setting the table. He didn't pretend not to know what Will referred to with the sudden change of subject. "I was going to ask you the same thing."

"Okay, I guess. It's still a shock. I still have a hard time believing he did it."

Ben sat down and reached to take one of the bottles from Will's hand. "I still can't help feeling guilty I didn't suspect he was in trouble."

"Makes two of us," Will agreed, taking a chair across from Ben. "I've been busy lately. But not so busy that I couldn't have made time to check on him."

"I wish . . ." Ben began, then hesitated. He hadn't told Will about Meg and the dog issue.

"You wish what?" Will folded his arms on the table edge and leaned closer.

"If we were already training dogs for vets here, Chuck might have agreed to participate."

Will shrugged. "Might have. Might not have. You can't fix what you don't know."

"But I might have made a point of asking. Which means, I'd have paid more attention to just how desperate he must have been. He might have agreed just to help me get the program off the ground even if he didn't think it would make any difference." He might have been a skeptic like Meg. But even so —

"How's Meg handling it?"

"Are you reading my mind?"

"Not so good, huh?" Will took a swallow of beer and set the bottle carefully back into the wet ring it had made on the polished wooden surface.

"I'm scared, Will. She won't talk about any of it. At least not about herself."

"Did she talk about Chuck?"

"We took the boys to the beach for a picnic after we got back from the funeral. I was wallowing in guilt and feeling bad for myself. I think she thought the picnic would take my mind off it, but it didn't. We talked some, and she tried to explain why some guys wish they could go back into the fighting. But when I asked her what she felt, she shut off like someone pinched a hose."

"She's not getting deployed again right away, is she?"

"She's getting out. And she says she's okay with that. But she's not. She just says she doesn't want to make me a widower and the boys motherless, but she won't say what she really feels about getting out.

"The dogs bother her, too. She told me she felt guilty about one of the bomb dogs getting blown to kingdom come, but even then she didn't tell me all of it. She hasn't been out to help in the kennels since she got back, and Kip gave her the creeps when he first came."

"But you said she was over that. I thought she was good with Kip now."

The dog heard his name and got up from the hall doorway and came to stand by Ben's chair. He patted the dog's head then began to scratch his favorite place at the base of his ears. Kip leaned into him, enjoying the attention.

"She says she feels useless. Like I don't need her anymore." The all-too-familiar feeling of despair began to ease into Ben's chest.

Will snorted. "Hah! I need to take that woman out for a drink some night and fill her in on just what a big basket case you were while she was gone. Not to say you're less of a man or anything, but when she's not around, you're just not yourself. She needs to know that."

"That's not it. Or not all of it. She doesn't know what she wants to do with herself."

"I thought she was going to apply for the

police force."

Ben shook his head. "I thought so too. It's all she ever talked about. Being like Bobby. Like you, even. But apparently her stint as a military MP changed her mind. So, now she just feels like she has nothing. Which is kind of how Chuck described what he was feeling. Like he had nothing."

"Which explains why you are worried. But Meg's not like that."

"I didn't think Chuck was like that either."

"Meg has you and the boys. Like she said, she doesn't want you to be a widower. She'd never —"

"Is the pizza ready yet?" Rick bounded into the dining room. His hair was damply plastered to his head, but he was clean and apparently starved.

"Did you put your dirty clothes in the hamper?" Ben got up to check the pizza.

"Yup." Rick followed him back to the kitchen.

"Go collect your brother and we can eat."

Rick bolted back down the hallway, calling out Evan's name.

"And remind him to wash his hands," Ben called after Rick.

He slid the pizza from the oven, tested it, and dropped the pans on the granite counters.

"She'd never do that to the boys either," Will said in a quietly confident voice.

Ben wanted to be comforted by his twin's assurances. But he'd seen the ravaged faces of Mr. and Mrs. Royko and Anne and Donald. Surely Chuck must have considered how they would feel if he was gone. But he'd been too miserable to let that stop him.

"She just wouldn't." Will grabbed Ben's shoulder and squeezed hard.

"That's what Dad said." Ben rummaged through the utensil drawer and found the pizza wheel. "After he told me how close he came to ending it all and leaving Mom behind."

Will's jaw dropped, and his eyes went round. "You're kidding. Right?"

Ben shook his head and started running the pizza wheel through the steaming pies.

"Now you've got *me* worried," Will said, his voice fading away to a whisper as Rick and Evan scampered through the kitchen and into their seats at the dining room table.

"I think Jenny was surprised, don't you?" Meg waited beside the car for Margie to unlock the doors.

Margie dug into her purse for her car keys. "I felt bad at first, that it was so soon after — after Chuck — but then I thought, maybe it was good for everyone to have something to feel good about. Baby showers are always fun. And Jenny was so cute about it." The locks clicked. Margie reached in back to toss her purse onto the rear seat.

"I expected to see Georgia," Meg said as she slid into the passenger seat of Margie's sporty little Ford Focus and buckled her seat belt. "I would have thought she'd come with her Aunt Abby since Abby Frank doesn't drive."

"Georgia hasn't been at work since it happened. She's not handling it very well." Margie put the car in gear and headed toward the road.

"I thought they broke up. Months ago."

"Chuck broke it off. Georgia's still in love with him. *Was* still in love with him."

"I never did learn why Chuck broke it off. Ben never said. When I left, I kind of expected her to be wearing a wedding ring by the time I got back. They'd been engaged forever."

Margie shook her head. "Maybe Ben didn't know. Georgia didn't even tell me much, and you know how tight men are about talking things out. It happened right after Chuck got out of rehab. He was having a hard time with headaches and nightmares. Instead of coming home to Georgia's apartment, he went home to his folks' house and set up camp in the room over their garage."

Meg didn't have to work hard to imagine what it must have been like for Chuck. Still seriously handicapped by his wounds, maybe even wishing he hadn't survived. And if the nightmares and flashbacks were bad enough, he might have been worried that he would do something to hurt Georgia by mistake.

"Georgia went over there as soon as he got back, but he told her he didn't want to see her anymore. Just like that." Margie sounded as if she was still put out with the man in spite of what had happened since. "When he first got brought home from Germany, she took a leave from work and spent about every waking minute up at the hospital in Maryland where he was being treated. She thought he'd be coming home to her apartment. She was devastated when he told her it was over. It's going to take her a long time to get over him."

Meg stared out the side window, watching the houses go by as Margie talked. A lot of engagements didn't survive the separation of deployments or the realities of serious injuries. A lot of marriages didn't. But Chuck and Georgia had been together a long time. It wouldn't have mattered how disfigured or impaired Chuck had been; Georgia would have stuck by him.

"I hope you're not giving that sweet man of yours a lot of grief."

Margie's question caught Meg like a slap on the back of the head from a spiteful drill sergeant.

"You aren't, are you?" Margie prompted.

Meg fidgeted with the purse in her lap.

"Are you?" Margie's inquiry was more pointed this time.

"Maybe," Meg answered reluctantly. Was she giving Ben grief? Did not telling him everything give him grief? She'd meant to protect him. But now that she thought about it, Chuck might well have broken off the engagement to protect Georgia, and in doing so he'd hurt her far worse than having stuck by him through rehab, temper tantrums, nightmares, and sulks had.

"What exactly does *maybe* mean?"

Margie pulled into the parking lot in front of Ethan's Ribs. This late at night the dining room was closed and most of the building dark. Just a couple cars, probably Ethan or one of his crew still cleaning up before heading home.

"Well, I didn't tell him our marriage is over, if that's what you're thinking."

"But things aren't good between you?" Margie turned the engine off, and the car went silent.

"They're good. Okay, anyway."

"And you're still sleeping together?"

Meg nodded. Sex was the one thing they hadn't had a problem with. In fact, the sex was great. It was just everything else.

"So, if it's not sex, then what is it that's just okay?" Margie was persistent, and she read between the lines. They'd known each other far too long. "This doesn't have anything to do with Remy McAllister, does it?"

Meg shook her head. "No. I think I've made my peace with him. Or at least, I've forgiven him and moved on. And he's been good for my mom. She's been sober for almost a month. She goes to AA twice a week. And I think she really loves him."

"Glad to hear it. I saw her a couple weeks ago. She had lunch with a lady I didn't recognize. But I didn't wait on them, so I didn't realize how much had changed."

"It was probably her AA sponsor. I forget her name, but I've met her. She's nice. Amy something, I think."

"So, it's not Remy," Margie said, getting back to her subject, "and it's not your mother's drinking. And it's not sex. What *is* wrong?"

The lights went out in Ethan's. Two dark figures made their way from the rear of the building to the two cars parked in the far corner of the lot. Meg watched the head-lights come on and wondered if Ethan, or his partner Michael, would come over to check out the car loitering in their lot. No one did. Both cars pulled out and headed in the opposite direction. Meg turned back to Margie, still waiting doggedly for Meg to answer.

"It's hard to explain."

"Try me."

"I'm not the same person who left here a year ago."

"Is anyone ever the same after they've been in a place like that?"

"Ben thought so."

"I don't think that's true. Ben's far too intelligent to think that kind of experience would leave you untouched. I think it's more like he was just relieved to have you back and didn't stop to wonder how those changes might get in the way of your rela-tionship. Of the relationship you had before you left, anyway. He loves you, Meg. You know that. And he always will."

"Ben's not the one who's got the issues. It's me. I don't want the same things I wanted before. I don't think the same as I did before. I don't even know if I feel the same."

Margie opened her mouth to say something and then shut it. The dead quiet of the night hung between them. "You still love him, don't you?"

"I do." Meg blinked hard to stop the tears that wanted to burst forth.

"Then it's just a communication problem. You just need to sit the man down and explain what's going on in your head. And your heart. And then you need to listen to what he's feeling and thinking."

A hiccoughing chuckle burbled its way up Meg's windpipe. "You'd make a good shrink."

"Yeah, well. Waitresses and bartenders get a lot of on-the-job training." She restarted her engine, and the headlights flicked on again. "Maybe what you guys need is a weekend away. Just the two of you."

"Maybe."

Maybe what Meg needed was to just lay it all out there. Her wavering emotions about Ben's service dog project. Her suspicion that she might have gotten pregnant the night of Chuck's death. Her shame over what had happened with John. Her growing reliance on and love for Kip. Everything.

She didn't doubt for a minute that Ben loved her and would hear her out. He'd still love her even if he knew it all. He'd be hurt, but what if she'd hurt him more by not telling him everything? People were always more afraid of the things they didn't know than those they did. Ben knew things weren't right, and he wanted to help.

Too many times Ben had asked her *what's wrong*? And too many times, she'd said *nothing*. Dr. Allan and Margie were right.

Ben deserved her trust.

CHAPTER 24

Meg checked the little cooler packed with chicken sandwiches, grapes, cookies, and chips. She added a bottle of wine, two plastic glasses, and a handful of napkins. She set the cooler by the door and sank down onto one of the stools to wait for Ben to come in from the kennels.

Kip whined and nudged her hand. She patted his head. Then she slid off the stool and knelt in front of him. He licked her chin and whined again.

"Thanks for the encouragement, Kip." She buried her face in his fur. Why had it taken her so long to understand and accept the comfort this dog offered with such unstinting love? Why had she been so bull-headedly blind to the possibilities of the program Ben wanted to start? "Time for me to swallow my pride and admit I might have been wrong. Right, Kip?"

Kip nuzzled her cheek but said nothing.

The sound of Ben's boots coming up the porch steps made the dog jump to his feet. Meg stood as well and waited.

Ben opened the door and stepped in. He hung the leash he was carrying on the hooks beside the door. He began to unlace his boots, then stopped and looked up at Meg. He glanced around the kitchen, then back at her with a frown on his face. "What's up?"

"I packed us a lunch to take to the beach." Meg tried to stay calm in spite of the thudding of her heart.

"Beautiful evening for it." Ben bent and began retying his boot.

"Don't you want to change? Maybe put on a pair of flip-flops?"

"A shower wouldn't hurt either. Do I have time? Where are the boys?"

"Rick is at his friend Sam's, and Evan went to my brother's house for the night. It's just us."

A slow smile spread across Ben's face. "Sweet. I'll hurry."

Meg waited, anxiously reciting the things she needed to tell Ben. She'd considered the weekend away that Margie had suggested, but that would have taken too much planning and too much time. Now that she'd decided to spill her guts, she wanted to get it done before she lost her nerve and went back to avoiding the difficult subjects. It was Friday. The boys were gone for the whole night. They had as long as it took. And if there were going to be any fireworks, they had plenty of privacy for it.

Ben returned to the kitchen sooner than Meg expected. His hair was still wet, and he wore his favorite cargo shorts and a frayed and faded Tar Heels T-shirt.

"Any specific beach?" he asked as he grabbed his own jacket and hers off the hooks.

Meg shrugged, then, "Our special beach?"

"Like that, is it?" Ben grinned and opened the door. He grabbed the cooler and stepped out onto the porch.

Kip watched them intently, his gaze bouncing from Meg to Ben and back.

Ben glanced at the dog, then at Meg. "Should we take him or leave him?"

"Take him." Meg could use all the encouragement she could get. This shouldn't be so hard. Ben was Ben. He loved her, and he wanted to help. He wanted to understand. But in spite of the fact that she had been sharing her problems with him since she was sixteen years old, and in spite of the fact that he'd always been there for her, she still felt breathless and a little afraid.

She felt like she guessed it might feel on a

first date with someone you really wanted to impress. Except her first date, if you didn't count her senior prom, had been with Ben. And by the time he'd taken her out on a real date, they'd known each other for more than four years. So she didn't really know what a first date felt like.

She just felt breathless and worried and eager all at the same time.

They didn't talk as Ben drove his truck toward the beach. He turned the radio on and found a song they both liked then just paid attention to the road with his fingers drumming lightly on the steering wheel.

The memory of a long-ago night, the first time Ben had brought her to this beach, came to her. She'd been just as nervous, but for a totally different reason. That night it had been Clay Aiken singing "This is the Night" on the radio in Ben's refurbished Mustang, and how appropriate had that been. Tuning out the words currently playing on Ben's truck radio, Meg let the lyrics to Aiken's song drift through her head. *Don't wait. The moment can vanish so fast.* She had already waited far too many moments. This was the night to bare her soul and let Ben in.

Her heart raced a little as her anxiety built. Ben pulled into the tiny lot behind the dunes. In spite of the nice night, theirs was the only vehicle in sight. Ben slid from the truck and walked around to the back of the truck. Meg hung back for a moment. Then she drew in a big breath and let out a long sigh, grabbed the blanket, and got out. *Showtime! Oorah!*

Two paths led off between the dunes. To the left, the sun was just setting, leaving a bright orange and pink sky as a backdrop. To the right, a half-moon had already risen against the pale gray-blue of the eastern sky.

Ben opened the rear gate and signaled for Kip to jump down. Then he grabbed the cooler and hurried to catch up to Meg who was headed toward the path to the ocean beach. Briefly, she let her hand touch the top of the anchor that guarded the path before striding on.

Ben tapped the top of the anchor, too, in case it was a good luck thing. His first thought when she'd suggested this picnic and he'd found out the boys were elsewhere, was that this was a date. They'd had so few opportunities as a couple lately, he'd been touched. And a little excited. But she'd been totally mute the entire drive out here, and worry had replaced anticipation.

The more he thought about it, the more

he became convinced that there was something much more sinister about this tête-à-tête. As he followed her through the dunes, his gut began to clench with apprehension. His chest felt tight, and he had to suck in a deep breath to banish the uncomfortable feeling.

The path broadened and then ended, and the soft expanse of pale gray sand spread in all directions. Dusk created long shadows behind every small hillock of sand and painted the hard damp sand at the water's edge with a shimmer of orange. Waves broke and ran up the beach in the endless rote that Ben usually found relaxing. But tonight he was anything but relaxed.

Meg spread their blanket well above the incoming tide and began unpacking their picnic dinner.

"We should have brought the camp light," Ben said as he dropped to his knees at the edge of the blanket. "It'll be too dark to see what we're eating before we're done."

"I thought of that, but I decided I liked candles better." Meg reached back into the cooler and brought out four short, fat candles. She pressed them into the sand along the top edge of the blanket, then reached back into the cooler and produced a lighter.

Nothing could have been more romantic. Ben wished he could surrender to the serenity of their surroundings and banish the anxiety churning in his gut. But Meg was far too solemn. Even when she was intent on creating romance, she usually had a teasing grin on her face. Tonight was leading to something far more portentous.

Kip nosed along the edge of the dunes checking out all the interesting scents. Meg took a bite of her sandwich and set it back onto the wrapper it had come from. As hungry as he'd been half an hour ago, Ben didn't feel like eating now, but he forced himself to pop a few grapes into his mouth.

"We should come here more often like this." Ben grabbed a few potato chips. "Just the two of us."

"Mmmm," Meg murmured, gazing off toward the ever-darkening horizon above the sea.

"Is something wrong, Meg?" Might as well get it out in the open if he could.

"Not wrong, exactly." Meg glanced at Ben, then back toward the ocean.

"Then what?" His heart was not behaving the way it was supposed to.

Meg re-wrapped her partly-eaten sandwich and dropped it back into the cooler. Apparently neither of them felt much like eating. Ben helped her collect the uneaten picnic. Then they sat, close enough to touch, but not touching. The candles flickered as darkness fell. Kip came back from his foray and settled at the foot of the blanket, his head up, alert and watchful.

"What's wrong, Meggie?" Ben reached out and took her hand in his.

"Remember the first time we ever made love?"

Not the subject Ben had expected. "How could I forget? The back seat of that damned Mustang. What was I thinking?" He tried for humor, desperate to banish the dread creeping up his spine.

"You always promised me you'd wait for me to be ready for sex, but I didn't really believe you."

"You didn't trust me?" *Where is she going with this?*

"I trusted you. At least about most things. But you were all grown up when we first met, and I was just a kid. You were so beautiful I just knew there were tons of girls who'd have jumped into bed with you in a heartbeat if you'd hit on them."

"Men aren't beau—" Ben cut off his standard comeback. "I didn't want tons of girls. I wanted you. I was willing to wait." His chest felt so tight breathing hurt.

"You were the same age as CJ, and I know he'd hooked up with half a dozen girls before he married Sarah. He talked about it when he didn't think I was paying attention. Him and Stu. Stu played around before he was even out of high school. I wanted to believe you were saving yourself for me, but it just didn't seem like you could. I mean, most guys don't wait until they're nearly twenty-five."

"I'm not most guys."

"I know." Meg's voice came out barely more than a squeak. As if her breathing hurt as much as his.

"Meggie?" Ben cupped her chin with his free hand and turned her face toward his. His heart was flat out racing as he tried to figure out what was going on in her head.

"We promised there would never be anyone but each other. Ever." Tears brimmed in her eyes, but she was fighting them. His Meg, still trying to be tough. No matter what kind of pain was going on inside her. "Ever," she repeated, her voice catching.

"And there never has been."

She shook her head.

"I don't know what you think went on between me and Anne Royko, but I can assure you there was never anything like that. She hit on me, but, Meg, I promise you, I never strayed. I never wanted to."

"I know that. And I know all the crap she's been up to while I was away was about what she wanted. I know you wouldn't ever cheat on me."

"Then what's the problem?"

A tear dribbled down her cheek, and he wiped it away with his thumb.

"Why are you asking about the first time we made love and about me waiting for you to grow up? Why are you crying?"

"I'm not crying."

"Yes, you are."

Meg shook her head hard as if she could stop the flow just by denying it.

Ben spread his legs and tugged her over until she was sitting between them, her own legs stretched out inside his. He tipped her back to rest against his chest and wrapped his arms around her. "Tell me what's wrong, Meg. Whatever it is has been wrong since you got home. I kept thinking you'd tell me when you were ready to talk about it, but I think the time is now."

Meg trailed her fingers through the sand beside Ben's leg. Then she dusted the sand off and let her palm settle on his thigh. Her other hand crept up and settled on his forearm where it rested across her chest.

"I'm waiting," Ben reminded her. He

tightened his arms about her.

"It's not about you. It's about me."

Ben's heart lurched to a painful stop in his chest. Then it shuddered just as painfully into an uneasy rhythm. He sucked air into his constricted lungs and forced his mind to stop jumping to conclusions.

"What about you?" He forced himself to breathe evenly. "What about you?" he repeated softly.

Please, God, don't let her tell me she's fallen in love with another man. This John she mutters about in her sleep. Please, God, I can take anything. But not that.

"It's about me and John."

This time his heart really did stop. Ben was sure of it. But he refused to let go of Meg. He couldn't bear to look into her face right now. He was glad her head was resting against his chest and she was facing the other way. He didn't want to see what was in her eyes. Not if she was going to break his heart.

Maybe he shouldn't have demanded she tell him. He could have gone on forever without ever knowing and pretending everything was fine. He could have gone on believing John was just her friend and nothing more. And he would still have had her in his life. And in his bed. But he'd pushed, and now the truth was coming whether he wanted it or not.

Meg tipped her head back and looked up at him. He kissed her on the forehead. "What about you and John?"

Meg grabbed his wrists and pulled his arms apart, freeing herself, then scrambled onto her knees facing him.

Moonlight and the flickering of the candles played across her face. He couldn't make out her expression, but the fact that she no longer wanted him to hold her seemed to tell him everything. His heart cracked and shattered. Strange that he couldn't hear the broken shards falling, but only the soft chuckle of waves breaking on the sand.

"It's not what you think." Meg sat back on her heels.

His head throbbed. His heart had gone AWOL. Ben tried to reach for her hand, but she pulled it back into her lap and wrung her hands together nervously.

What am I going to tell the boys? Or my parents? How am I going to go on living without her?

"I only told you the half of it when you asked me about John that first day."

That much he'd known for weeks. But he hadn't wanted to know what was coming.

334

"You mean, about being friends? About becoming friends after his father died?"

She nodded.

"What else is there that you need to tell me now? That you maybe should have told me back then?" It amazed him that he could speak so calmly with so much havoc going on inside him.

Meg stared at her hands as she twisted her wedding ring around and around on her finger.

"Were you — are you and John —" Ben swallowed hard. "Are you in love with him? Is that what you're trying to tell me?"

Meg's head jerked up, and her eyes went wide. The expression of shock on her face was plain even in the flickering light of the candles she'd set out. She shook her head vehemently. "Noooo . . ."

"No?" Suddenly breathing seemed a little easier. "You're not in love with him?"

"I care about him. I care about him a lot, but not like that. I don't love him. Not any more than the rest of the men and women I served with." The words tumbled out, almost running over themselves. She leaned toward him and repeated herself. "I never loved John. Not like I love you."

Ben swallowed again, hardly believing he was going to ask her this, but knowing he wouldn't ever be at peace again until he knew the truth.

"Did you sleep with him?"

Again she shook her head as if an angry swarm of bees were attacking her.

"Then what?" He was completely confused now. It was about John and about Meg, but they weren't lovers, and she'd not cheated on him. So, what was it? What could possibly have her tied up in knots like this?

"I wanted to." Meg's voice was so tiny and brittle Ben could barely hear her.

"You wanted to what?"

"I wanted him to make love to me."

That stopped Ben's recovery in its tracks. "You wanted him to make love to you, but he wouldn't?" Adultery was an offense punishable by court martial. That much Ben knew. Perhaps this Captain Bissett cared more about his career than about Meg.

Ben tried to picture Meg propositioning the man and being turned down. Tried to understand why she might even do such a thing.

But Meg was still shaking her head.

Ben swallowed hard and tried to erase all the questions careening about his brain.

"Then suppose you start at the beginning, because I don't understand what you're trying to tell me."

Meg sat motionless for several interminable minutes. Ben could swear he could hear his heart beating out the seconds. Then she squared her shoulders. She glanced at Kip, then brought her gaze back to meet his.

"We were just friends. That's all we ever were. That's all we are now, or maybe not even that anymore." Meg took another deep breath.

Kip glanced at Ben, then Meg, and then back toward the darkness of the beach, keeping watch.

"When Scout was killed, I was convinced it was my fault."

"You told me that before, but —"

Meg leaned toward him and pressed a finger over his lips.

"I know it's not. It was never really my fault. But at the time I felt like it was. I'd been trained to expect booby traps and buried IEDs. It was my job to spot likely places and guide convoys around them."

"But it was Scout's job, too," Ben jumped in to remind her. "That's what he'd been trained to do. That's why —"

"I know," Meg cut him off. "And he found that bomb, and he alerted to it like he was trained to. What he didn't know — what I didn't see in time — was the detonator that had been fashioned of two bare wires between a folded square of metal. It was buried a few feet away from the bomb. Scout sat on it."

Ben wanted to drag her back into his arms and cradle her like a baby. He could only begin to imagine how horrifying such an experience must have been to watch. His own mind scuttled away from the image of a dog getting blown to pieces. But she'd come to love that dog. How all this related to John, Ben had no idea, but that Meg had suffered was all that mattered. He reached for her, but she put her hand against his chest and held him away.

"Don't! Don't stop me. I have to get it all said, or I might never find the courage again." She took another deep breath and hurried on.

"Afterward, when I was blaming myself and carrying on like a raw recruit, John tried to comfort me. He tried to tell me all the same things you've been saying. All I wanted to do was forget everything I'd just seen. I didn't care how, but I wanted to just forget about everything. John was there, and you weren't. He was holding me. And —"

Meg looked up at Ben then, and her gaze locked with his.

"At some point I realized that John was

aroused. Like very aroused. I knew when he was going to kiss me. I could see it in his eyes, and I didn't stop him. I even thought about you, but I didn't stop him.

"I kept telling myself I should get out of there and run back to my billet. But I didn't. I just let it happen. Then I was kissing him back. I don't know why. I never thought about him that way before, and I don't understand why I felt that way then, but I wanted him to go on kissing me, and I wanted him to do a lot more than just kiss me."

She stopped speaking as abruptly as she'd begun and looked away finally. Ben waited, and when she didn't go on he took her now unresisting hands in his.

"Who put a stop to it?" he asked as gently as his ragged breathing would let him.

Meg stared out over the dark sand, then back to Ben. "Me." Her voice was small and tight.

Ben felt a huge load lift off his chest. They had a lot to talk about maybe and some trust issues to mend. But, she wasn't leaving him. She hadn't stopped loving him, and her feelings toward this other man had not ended in betrayal. He wouldn't let this come between them now — or ever.

It might have been helpful if he could have

talked to his brother, or even his father, but that wasn't going to happen before this conversation was over. Ben had never been in such a situation. He didn't have a clue if the urge for sex was a normal reaction to a scene of such carnage and death. Maybe it was. Maybe Meg didn't understand her reactions any better than he did. But her desire and her reaction to this other man's behavior were clearly eating her up even though she had not given in to it.

Her oft muttered, *I can't do this, John,* suddenly made sense. Perhaps this Captain Bissett would have taken advantage of her had she been willing. She'd said he was aroused. And he had initiated the kiss. But maybe not. Either way, the bottom line was Meg had said *no.* She had kept her promise to Ben in spite of temptation. In spite of needing comfort in a situation Ben would never experience.

He pulled her all the way into his lap this time. She balked briefly, but he was bigger and more determined.

He cleared his throat, which thankfully no longer felt like a knife was slitting it open, and hugged her tight. "Being tempted and giving in to temptation are not the same thing, Meg."

She huddled against him, her arms

wrapped tightly around her own body. He wanted them around him, but he could be patient. He could wait forever if he had to. Now that he knew the whole truth of the matter.

He had to find a way to put her guilt into perspective. To ease the self-reproach that had been sitting like a ticking bomb between them for far too long. Their faith was central in their relationship and their lives. Maybe that was the path toward forgiving herself.

"Think of it like this." He pressed his cheek to the top of her head. "When Jesus went out into the desert and fasted for forty days, the devil came to him urging him to turn the stones into bread to ease his hunger. After all those days of not eating, Jesus had to be starving. He had to feel an enormous desire to give in to the temptation and put an end to the pain in his belly. But he didn't. He told the devil to be gone."

"Jesus was God," Meg argued.

"Jesus was a man. He felt all the same things you and I do."

"But wanting sex isn't the same as needing to eat."

"You're missing the point, Meg. Hunger and lust are two of the most powerful human urges. Christ would have felt just as tempted to satisfy his hunger as you were to give in to desire. The sin isn't in being tempted. It's in giving way to the temptation. It's in letting your physical needs become stronger than your faith."

"You make me sound like a saint. But I'm not."

"You were tempted. But you didn't sin. You were in pain, and you wanted comfort. But you told the devil no. You've done nothing to feel guilty about."

"I feel like I betrayed you." Meg unfolded and looked up at him.

"I don't feel betrayed."

"Not even now that you know everything?"

"Especially now that I know everything."

Tears pooled in Meg's eyes, and her chin quivered. "I don't deserve you." Her tears glistened in the candlelight, then slowly overflowed and ran down her cheeks. Ben kissed her cheeks, then her eyes, tasting salt and thankfulness.

"And one other thing." He tried to make his voice stern. His heart soared like a homing pigeon being given the command to fly home. "Don't ever, ever be afraid to tell me anything again." He brought his mouth to hers. "Promise me," he whispered against her lips. "Promise me," he repeated.

"I promise," Meg answered before wrapping her arms about his body so tightly that he almost couldn't breathe.

Ben let himself fall backwards, taking Meg with him. He nestled her into the crook of his arm and gazed up at the rising moon. He felt like the luckiest man in creation right at the moment.

"Were you ever tempted?" Meg broke into the quiet murmur of the sea.

"All the time," Ben answered.

"I mean, were you ever tempted to cheat on me?"

He rolled onto his side and gazed down at her. "Never."

When they returned to the house, Ben went into the living room to light a fire in the fireplace. Meg fed Kip and then detoured into the bedroom to don a pair of ruffled shorty pajamas that were girlish, rather than sexy. She was in the mood for sex, but there was still a lot of stuff she hadn't confessed yet. And she'd promised herself tonight was the night to tell Ben everything.

"I thought maybe we'd have that wine we didn't end up drinking at the beach." Ben sat cross-legged on a quilt in front of the crackling fire. He held up the bottle, then, without waiting for her to respond, half-filled two wine glasses he'd chosen over the plastic ones she'd packed in the cooler.

She joined him and accepted the glass he offered her. Kip hovered in the doorway as if not sure of his welcome. Meg patted the corner of the quilt. Kip came over and sat down. She put a hand out to ruffle his fur, then turned to Ben.

"Is he ever going back to police work?"

"I don't think so." Ben reached across her to give the dog's ear a scratch. "I asked Officer Brady if the family of the fallen handler wanted to adopt him as a pet."

Meg's heart froze. For weeks she'd wanted the dog gone. Now she wanted him to stay. For the rest of his life. "And?"

"They didn't. Brady asked if I could look around for an appropriate family."

"So —" Meg paused, then, before Ben could reply, she hurried on. "We can adopt him. I want to adopt him. Can we?" She stared down at her wineglass, turning the stem between her fingers.

"You aren't trying to replace Scout, are you?" Ben tipped his head to the side so he could look into her eyes. "Because that wouldn't be fair to Kip."

"I know that." Meg returned Ben's intent gaze. "But I had an idea. About what his next job could be. Him and me together, I mean."

"Kip might be a good candidate for a service dog. I was thinking that if I . . . if we . . ." Ben floundered and didn't finish his thought.

"I know what you were thinking. You thought if you did start up a training program for service dogs Kip would be one of your first rescues. And I wanted to talk about that, too, but first. Ben —" She grabbed his free hand. "Maybe I'm your first soldier. I think Kip and I were meant to be together."

Ben returned the pressure of her hand. The look on his face said all she needed to know. She set her glass down carefully, then stretched up onto her knees and wrapped her arms about his neck. "Thank you."

Ben's glass clicked softly against the surface of the nearby coffee table. Then his arms were around her, drawing her into his lap. "Welcome home, soldier."

EPILOGUE

April — five months later.

Meg stepped off the porch and stopped to admire the azaleas rioting in full bloom along the side of the house. The tulips were up, too, nodding in the breeze, and the dogwood along the drive had already begun to spread carpets of white petals beneath them. Everything was blooming.

Including herself. She caressed her growing belly with one hand, marveling at how good she felt now that the morning sickness had passed. Life was definitely good.

"Come, Kip," she said, tapping her thigh. They set off across the drive, circled past the big kennel building, and then stepped onto the newly installed flagstone walkway that led to Ben's new venture.

At first glance, the brand new Charles Royko, K-9s for Heroes facility that Jake had overseen construction of looked as if it had been there for years. Jake had taken pains to create a retreat for the veterans who would be coming to be paired with their service dogs. Designed along the same lines as Ben and Meg's house, but set far enough back for privacy and quiet, it was a haven that blended into the peaceful surroundings. All three buildings on the property were sided with gray cedar shakes and had dark green roofs, but like the house, the new building had a porch that wrapped around three sides with a view of the marsh and the waterway beyond it.

Meg paused to admire the effect of Ben's vision and Jake's expertise. The Cameron men were a remarkable group, all very different, but talented and good at what they had chosen to do with their lives. And unstinting in their passion and support.

During those first troubled weeks when Meg had struggled to fit in after returning from her year in Iraq, Ben's love and understanding had given her the strength to own up to her issues and deal with them. He hadn't tried to tell her what he thought she should do, but instead, had listened to the ramblings of her confused and guilt-ridden mind, letting her work through all of it at her own speed.

She'd been back to visit Captain Allan a few times before her final discharge, but mostly it had been Ben who had been the rock she'd needed to hang onto while she sorted out her life. Being out of the Marines had been a frightening prospect at first. Being a Marine had defined most of her adult life, and she'd been terrified that she wouldn't know who she was if she ceased to be one.

As she admired the new building and all it stood for, Meg remembered, as she had so many times since he'd said the words, Ben's declaration that she was what defined who Ben Cameron was. That and his love for her and their boys. In the months since then, she'd discovered just how true those words had been. His words had also given her the courage to discover who Meg Cameron — wife and mother — was. And it felt pretty darned satisfying.

She resumed her walk toward the building and ran a hand over her belly again. In just a few more months there would be two little girls joining the family that defined who she was. Twins ran in Ben's family. Ben was a twin. But somehow the idea that she might become the mother of twins hadn't occurred to her when Ben said he wanted a daughter. He was beside himself pleased that there were going to be two.

Tears prickled behind her eyes as she

climbed the new stairs and crossed the porch. The dogs were important, but it was love and family that defined who Ben was, and now she knew to the depths of her soul, that was what defined her as well. The soldiers she was helping mattered very much to her, but Ben was where her heart lived.

Jake finished tying a big yellow ribbon around the upright post of the railing.

"Nice touch," Ron Davis said, viewing the result. He absently combed his fingers through the fur on Lola's head. He nodded his head approvingly. "I like it."

"You like what?" Ben asked, coming up behind his newest employee.

Ron gestured to the ribbon.

"It was your idea," Ben reminded him.

"I didn't think you'd take me seriously."

Jake came down the last three stairs and joined them. "How long until they get here, do you think?"

Ben consulted his watch. "Ten minutes, maybe."

"Where's Meg?" Ron asked.

"Bustling around inside putting books out where they might get picked up and read and making sure everything is just right."

"How is the therapy dog program going?"

Jake asked.

A warm, happy glow settled in Ben's gut. He'd known Meg would find her way eventually, but that she would find it helping other soldiers heal amazed him. She'd put her personal nightmares aside and traveled three days a week to Lejeune to take on the nightmares of men recovering from all kinds of wounds, both physical and emotional.

There were nights when he held her while she wept. Not for herself but for the men she and Kip visited. The strength she'd found to cope on a daily basis with their nightmares and the hell each wounded soldier was living through humbled him. He'd always thought he was the strong, patient type, but Meg outclassed him by a mile.

"It's going well. Really well," Ben answered Jake's question.

"She's an amazing woman," Ron said.

Jake nodded. "She was instrumental in getting this place pulled together so quickly. I just got the building up. She did everything else."

His brother was right. While Jake labored to get the construction completed, and Ben worked with the dogs that were now ready to be paired with their individual soldiers, Meg had overseen everything else: the decorating, the furnishings, the hiring of a cook and housekeeper, provisioning the pantry, shopping for linens, and even the making of the beds until ten p.m. last night.

She might have had her doubts about the program originally, but once she decided it was a project worth pursuing, she gave her all. Along with the trips to Lejeune, teaching Rick to hunt, taking Evan to soccer, and being the best wife a man could have, Ben called her super woman. His super woman. His heart swelled in thanksgiving for all the blessings in his life. But most of all, for Meg.

"I think I hear the cavalry arriving." Ron pointed down the drive.

Ben's mother's big van turned off Stewart Road, followed by Will's Jeep. They disappeared behind the kennel, and the sounds of their engines died.

"I'm just in time." Meg dashed out of the house and hurried down the stairs to Ben's side. Kip followed her. He stopped to sniff Lola on his way by, but she ignored him. She was working; Kip wasn't. But after being snubbed, he came to sit on Meg's left side. All of them turned to face the tight knot of men moving uncertainly up the walkway.

As they neared the foot of the stairs, Meg stepped forward, her hand extended to the first man in the group. "Welcome home, soldier. I'm Meg, and I'm so glad you're here."

RECIPE

BEN'S FAVORITE APPLE-CHOCOLATE CHIP COFFEE CAKE, FROM THE KITCHEN OF SANDY CAMERON.

Set oven at 350 degrees then grease and flour Bundt pan

Peel, core and slice apples to measure 3 cups.

Mix together:

2 cups flour
1 tsp cinnamon
1 tsp baking soda
1 cup sugar

Add and mix well:

3/4 cup vegetable oil
2 eggs
2 tsp vanilla

Finally, fold in:

3 cups sliced apples
1/2 cup chocolate chips
1/2 cup walnuts or pecans chopped

Sprinkle surface with 2-3 Tbsp. of sugar and bake at 350 degrees for 1 hour. Cool on rack 10-15 minutes before removing from pan.

ACKNOWLEDGEMENTS

Writing may look like a one-man job — there is only one name on the cover of the book. But it isn't so. From my high school English teacher, Fred Keyes, to my newest critique partner and everyone in between, I owe a huge debt for helping me to become the writer I am today.

I'd like to thank my editor, Deborah Smith whose encouragement and support made this book possible, and Debra Dixon who always comes up with incredible covers.

A big thank you to Lilly Gayle who is my authority on anything North Carolina, from diction and idiom to what's on the table or growing in the garden.

John McHale retired now from both the US Marine Corps and the Army Reserves is my go-to guy for anything Marines — but please don't hold him responsible for mistakes that are solely my own. My other military buddy, Col. Douglas Curtis Ret. US Army is also a great resource for information and ideas.

Sheri Martinez and Lola — thank you Sheri for your service to our country and for all the good work you are doing with K-9s for Warriors, and to Lola for watching your back.

My critique partners, Nancy Quatrano who helped me keep my conflict true and cheered me when I got it right. And Betty Johnston who read my work with her heart.

And as always, my biggest cheerleaders, my kids: Alex, Lori, Rebecca, Bobbi, Noel and Jeff, Nick, and Joe.

ABOUT THE AUTHOR

Skye Taylor

I have been a member of Romance Writers of America since 1995 and of the Ancient City chapter in St. Augustine, Florida, for the last five years, where I have served as secretary, conference chair and treasurer. I am also a member of Florida Writers Association. My publishing credits to date include several non-fiction essays about life as a Peace Corps Volunteer, one mainstream political intrigue, *Whatever It Takes,* and book one of the Tide's Way series, *Falling for Zoe.*